STALKING the DRAGON

ALSO AVAILABLE BY MIKE RESNICK

STALKING the DRAGON

A FABLE of TONIGHT

A John Justin Mallory Mystery

MIKE RESNICK

an imprint of **Prometheus Books**
Amherst, NY

Published 2009 by Pyr®, an imprint of Prometheus Books

Inquiries should be addressed to
Pyr
59 John Glenn Drive
Amherst, New York 14228–2119
VOICE: 716–691–0133, ext. 210
FAX: 716–691–0137
WWW.PYRSF.COM

13 12 11 10 09   6 5 4 3 2

Library of Congress Cataloging-in-Publication Data

Resnick, Michael D.
    Stalking the dragon : a fable of tonight : a John Justin Mallory mystery / Mike Resnick.
        p. cm.
    ISBN 978–1–59102–745–4 (pbk. : alk. paper)
    1. Private investigators—Fiction. 2. Dragons—Fiction. 3. Manhattan (New York, N.Y.)—Fiction. I. Title.

PS3568.E698S724 2009
813'.54—dc22

                                                                          2009017862

Printed in the United States on acid-free paper

To Carol, as always,

and to John Justin Mallory's lovely ladyfriends at Pyr:

Grace M. Conti-Zilsberger
Jacqueline Cooke
Amy Greenan
Chris Kramer
Jill Maxick
Lynette Nisbet
Lynn Pasquale
Nicole Sommer-Lecht

"All right, go ahead, berate me," sniffed Periwinkle. "Pretend I'm just an *object*, that I don't have feelings and dreams and sexual needs like anyone else."

"If you've got 'em, they're like *nobody* else," said Mallory. "Now are you going to show me my image, or do I have to go next door to Madame Magenta's?"

"The tarot reader?" said Periwinkle. "Watch out for her, John Justin. She's out for you."

"And which of her four hundred pounds do you think is going to catch me first?" replied Mallory sardonically.

"Well, let me see . . ." said Periwinkle. "She tilts to the left, but she scratches with her right hand, and—"

"*Goddammit!*" bellowed Mallory.

"All right, all right," said the mirror petulantly as it finally displayed his image. "I was just trying to answer your question."

"Shut up," said Mallory.

"You tell him, John Justin!" said Felina, leaping lightly to the floor and approaching him. "Next thing you know he'll be asking you to skritch his back. That's *my* job."

"Scratching the mirror's back?"

"*Skritching*," she corrected him. "And no, it's not my job to skritch the mirror's back. It's my job to have my back skritched by you."

She sidled up to him, turned her back, and rubbed it up and down against his hip.

"Later," said Mallory, pulling out a comb that was missing three teeth and starting to run it through his hair.

"How much later?" persisted Felina.

"Seventeen years," said Mallory.

"Is that more or less than an hour?" asked the cat-girl.

"Yes," said Mallory.

"What's this all about anyway?" asked Periwinkle. "I can't remember the last time you combed your hair. And isn't that a new shirt you're wearing— or at least a clean one?"

"I just got it back from Chen Li Kugleman's Laundry, Chop Suey, and

CHAPTER 1

5:21 PM–5:48 PM, Valentine's Day

John Justin Mallory stood before the mirror, hands on hips, an a
expression on his face.

"Do you mind?" he said irritably.

"Do I mind playing an endless series of Bettie Page movies for yo
I could be showing you Shakespeare?" replied Periwinkle, his magic
"Of course I mind, and let me add how thoughtful it is of you to ment

Bettie Page's image was instantly replaced by Laurence Olivier I
up a pair of test tubes in a laboratory.

"What the hell is *that*?" demanded Mallory.

"A chemistry problem," answered Periwinkle. "Tube B or not Ti
The mirror laughed so uproariously that it almost fell off its hook on t

"You're not even smiling. You have no sense of humor whatsoeve
Justin." A tragic sigh. "All right; here's *Hamlet*."

"I didn't laugh when you showed me *Abbott and Costello Meet i*
either," said Mallory. "May I just have my image, please?"

"Why?" asked Periwinkle. "You haven't shaved in three days an
late on your haircut. You're going to walk into the barber shop and th
if you want them to take five months off the top." The mirror paused t
fully. "Let me guess: You blew your haircut money betting on Flyaway

"His money probably crawled away on its belly," said a voice from
refrigerator in the next room. "Even then, Flyaway couldn't have caugl

Mallory turned to glare at the owner of the voice, who was hu
shape and feline in almost all other aspects.

"When I want your opinion," he said, "rest assured I'll ask for it

"That's what Flyaway does," replied Felina from atop the refri
"He rests assured."

"Go kill a mouse or something," growled Mallory. He turned bac
mirror. "And you—let's have my image, and be quick about it."

Bagel Shop." Mallory grimaced. "I guess it had been there seven months. He wanted to charge me rent."

"What's the occasion?"

"This is February 14," said Mallory. "Does that mean anything to you?"

"It means if yesterday wasn't February 13, we've got a hell of a class-action lawsuit against the calendar company," replied the mirror.

"It's Valentine's Day."

"And you have a hot date, and you're watching Bettie Page take off her clothes to get in the mood?" said Periwinkle. "*Now* it all makes sense."

Mallory stared at the mirror, ignoring the image of the middle-aged detective that was staring back at him. "You have an exceptionally vile mind, you know that?"

"Hey, my last two owners never asked for Bettie Page movies," said Periwinkle.

"They were a corrupt magician and an incompetent military officer," noted Mallory.

"True, they did ask for films of teenaged girls with barnyard animals," continued the mirror, "but they never asked for Bettie Page, and they never hung me where I was surrounded by peeling paint."

"Well, that makes it all okay, then."

"You're not skritching, John Justin," purred Felina.

"The seventeen years aren't up," said Mallory, adjusting his tie in the mirror.

"Oh," said Felina. She fell silent for a few seconds. Then: "Are they up yet?"

"I'll let you know."

"That's very thoughtful of you, John Justin," she said. Then: "Now?"

Mallory sighed and began scratching between her shoulder blades.

"I had no idea seventeen years was such a long time," said Felina, wriggling in pleasure. Suddenly she hissed.

"What's the problem?" asked Mallory.

"You're scratching," she said. "I want you to skritch."

"Old war wound," said Mallory. "All I can do with that hand is scratch."

"You didn't have it yesterday," said Felina accusingly. "When did you get it?"

"Eighteen years ago," said Mallory.

The answer seemed to satisfy her, and she went back to purring contentedly.

"So who are you dating?" asked Periwinkle. "The usual?"

"The usual?" asked Mallory, puzzled.

"Some bimbo whose bustline equals her IQ."

"I haven't had a date in the two years I've been in this Manhattan," said Mallory.

"Then I wish you all the luck in the world," said Periwinkle. "Get her drunk. Take her back to your apartment. Score early and often."

"Are you quite through?" asked Mallory.

"For the moment," said the mirror. "But you still haven't told me who you're taking out for dinner."

"Winnifred Carruthers."

"The fat broad?" said Periwinkle, shocked, as Felina burst into giggles.

"The *stocky* br—" Mallory cut himself short. "The stocky woman."

"She's got to have twenty years and thirty pounds on you, John Justin," said Periwinkle. "Surely you can do better than that!"

"She's my friend—*and* my partner," said Mallory. "And the only person in this Manhattan who's never deserted me."

"I keep *meaning* to desert you, John Justin, really I do," said Felina apologetically. "But I always forget."

"Thanks for the thought," said Mallory.

"Well, the fat broad may be your partner," said Felina, "but I'm your . . ." She paused, frowning. "What am I, John Justin?"

"The office cat."

"She may be your partner, but I'm the office cat," said Felina. "If you're going to take her out to dinner, you have to take me as well."

"Lay off," said Mallory. "She has no one else. If I don't take her out, who will?"

"*I* will," said Felina. "Does she like mice?"

"Shut up, both of you," said Mallory. "It's Valentine's Day, and I'm taking my partner out to dinner."

"Why bother?" asked Felina. "We could eat her right here."

"You're all heart, Felina," said Mallory.

"Am I really?" she said happily.

"Well, all appetite, anyway." He fiddled with his tie. "I wish I knew how to tie a Windsor knot."

"They don't go well with forty-dollar suits," said Periwinkle. "Especially *old* forty-dollar suits."

Suddenly the office door opened.

"Put on your makeup and loosen your girdle," said Mallory, putting the finishing touches on his tie. "I'm taking you out to dinner."

"I call that downright generous of you," said a deep masculine voice, "considering that we haven't even been introduced yet."

Mallory turned and found himself facing a huge man dressed all in buckskins. He stood almost seven feet tall, and his head was every bit as broad as his shoulders. He had large dark eyes, a pushed-in nose, a pointed chin, and a goatee, but his most unique feature was the two horns growing out of the sides of his head.

"Well," said the man, staring at Mallory's dilapidated desk and the photos of the Playmates, Joe DiMaggio, Seattle Slew, and the 1966 Green Bay Packers hanging on the wall behind it, "it sure *looks* like a detective's office. Except for *that*," he added, gesturing to the other desk, with its pens and pencils neatly laid out next to the small vase filled with flowers. "Where do you keep your arsenal?"

"Who the hell are you?" said Mallory, staring at him.

"Name's Brody," said the man, extending a huge hand, which Mallory took. "Buffalo Bill Brody. Ever hear of me?"

"I can't say that I have."

"Damn! Don't you read the papers?" said Brody.

"Not when I can help it."

"He reads the *Racing Form*," added Periwinkle, "but after all these years he still doesn't know how to correctly interpret it."

"Well, I'm in town for the big show," said Brody.

"Some Broadway opening?" asked Mallory.

"Eastminster, Mr. Mallory," said Brody. "Eastminster." Mallory looked confused. "Biggest show in the country, maybe the world. I got me a dragon farm out in New Mexico. Show my dragons all over the Southwest. But until this year, I never had a reason to come to Eastminster. Now I do. According to all the papers, I've got the favorite."

"Okay, you've got the favorite," said Mallory.

"Except that I *don't* have her."

"You want to explain that to me?"

"She's been kidnapped, Mr. Mallory," said Brody. "Or dragonnapped, or whatever the hell the word is. I need you to find her."

"Are you sure you need a detective?" said Mallory. "I mean, how the hell hard can it be to hide a dragon in Manhattan? It's kind of like hiding a T. Rex, isn't it?"

"Not all dragons are huge," replied Brody. "As it happens, Fluffy is eleven inches at the shoulder."

"They call that a miniature?" asked Mallory, remembering poodles back in *his* Manhattan.

Brody shook his head. "Miniatures are twelve to eighteen inches. Fluffy is a toy dragon."

"Well, let me revise my initial statement. It will be impossible to spot an eleven-inch anything in Manhattan if someone wants to hide it. There's not much you can do until you get a phone call demanding ransom."

"Damn it, man!" bellowed Brody. "She's due in the ring at four o'clock tomorrow afternoon! She wasn't kidnapped for ransom! She was kidnapped because some rival knows that's the only way he can win the show."

"How much is the show worth to the winner?" asked Mallory.

"A ten-cent piece of ribbon and a trophy that can't be melted down for a hundred dollars."

"Then I don't understand."

"I'm a *sportsman*!" said Brody. "I've spent my whole life trying to come up with something good enough to win Eastminster, and I'm not going to take this lying down!"

"When did she turn up missing?" asked Mallory.

"About three hours ago."

"Where did you last see her?"

"She was in her pen in my hotel suite, with a couple of tarantulas I brought along to keep her company," said Brody. He smiled. "She just loves those spiders." A brief pause. "I went down to the restaurant for lunch, and when I got back the spiders were still there, but she was gone."

"What's she worth on the open market?" asked Mallory.

"Nothing."

Mallory frowned. "The potential Best in Show winner is worth nothing? That doesn't sound right, Mr. Brody."

"Call me Bill."

"Whatever I call you, it doesn't sound right."

"She's worth a quick hundred thousand or more to *me*," he said. "Between the price her offspring will bring if she wins, and the reflected glory on the ranch and the breeding program, she'll be worth at least that much after tomorrow. But she's not worth anything to anyone else. She's the most easily identifiable show dragon in the country, maybe the world. Put her in the ring, or let a knowledgeable visitor see her on your farm, and she'll be identified in two seconds and you'll be up on felony charges."

"Have you got any photos of her?" asked Mallory. "Not that I can tell one toy dragon from another."

Brody reached into his pocket and pulled out some snapshots of a scaly dragon that seemed to be all edges and angles.

"*Fluffy?*" repeated Mallory. "It looks like anyone who runs a hand over her will come away needing stitches."

"She's sweet and lovable," said Brody. Then: "Well, except when she gets mad. I can loan you my kennel manager. He knows her inside out. I'll send him here if you take the case."

"Maybe we'd better discuss our fee first."

"*Our?*" repeated Brody, glaring at Felina. "Do you mean that cat-thing is the famous Colonel Winnifred Carruthers?"

"No, Colonel Carruthers is out of the office right now. Our standard rate is—"

"Don't bother me with details," said Brody. "I'll pay you a thousand dollars right now, and there's a five-thousand-dollar bonus if you return her to me by ring time."

Mallory swallowed hard. "I think I can speak for my partner when I say that we find the terms acceptable."

Brody reached into a pocket, pulled out a wad of bills that Mallory decided could choke a full-sized dragon, or at least a gorgon, and peeled off ten hundreds.

"I'll draw up a contract," said the detective.

"Not necessary," said Brody. "Just find her."

He turned and walked to the door.

"Where can I contact you?" asked Mallory.

"I'll be at my hotel, just in case there *is* a ransom demand."

"That's what I meant," said Mallory. "What hotel are you at?"

"The Plantagenet Arms," said Brody. "Stupid name for a hotel. What'll they call the next one—the Tudor Legs?"

"Wouldn't surprise me at all," said Mallory. "There are one or two things I have to do first, and then I'll be stopping by."

"Why? I want you out searching for Fluffy."

"She was stolen from your room," explained Mallory. "It's a logical place to look for clues."

Brody shrugged. "If you think it'll help . . ."

"It couldn't hurt."

A tear rolled down Brody's cheek. "I want my sweet little fire-breather back, Mr. Mallory."

"We'll do our best."

For a moment Mallory thought the huge man was going to start crying in earnest. Instead, Brody stifled a sob and left the office.

"What did you think?" asked Mallory.

"The man clearly has an unhealthy relationship with his dragon," replied Periwinkle. "By next month you'll be asking for movies of them together."

"What *useful* did you think?" said Mallory wearily.

"I think he looks silly in buckskins."

Mallory turned to Felina. "I don't suppose there's much sense asking you for an opinion."

"Sure there is, John Justin," she said.

"Okay, I'm asking."

"What's an opinion?"

"Forget it."

"I can't until you tell me what it is."

"It's just like a Turkish cigarette, only different," said Mallory.

Felina smiled. "Good. *Now* I can forget it."

"Forget what?" asked Winnifred Carruthers, entering the office and kicking off her galoshes.

"I don't remember," said Felina.

"It's starting to snow out, John Justin," said Winnifred, hanging up her overcoat. "I thought maybe I'd make a pot of tea to warm me up before I walk the rest of the way to my apartment."

"You're not going to your apartment," said Mallory.

"I'm not?"

"No. I'd planned to take you out for dinner, but we just picked up a job."

"What kind?"

He told her about Brody and showed her the wad of hundreds. "We got about twenty-two hours to find the dragon if we want that bonus."

"The case is solved," announced Winnifred. "Do we have to return Fluffy to get the bonus, or merely tell this Brody where she is?"

"He's paying us to bring her back to him."

"Then the case is solved and there's no bonus."

"I don't suppose you'd care to explain that?" asked Mallory.

"Don't you read anything but the *Racing Form*, John Justin?" said Winnifred.

"He reads all those men's magazines he has hidden in the bottom drawer of his desk," offered Periwinkle helpfully. "Well, he looks at the pictures, anyway."

"If everyone's through dumping on me, perhaps my partner can tell me how we solved the case and lost our bonus less than five minutes after I accepted the damned job?"

"Fluffy is the favorite for Eastminster," began Winnifred.

"I know that."

"Can you guess who owns the second choice?"

There was a momentary silence.

"Please don't tell me what I know you're going to tell me," said Mallory.

Winnifred smiled grimly. "You guessed."

"Well," said Mallory, "I suppose the next step is to see if he's really got the dragon."

"He's the most powerful demon on the East Coast," said Winnifred. "Are you sure you wouldn't rather just return our retainer?"

"We'd be setting an unacceptable precedent," replied Mallory.

"But you're talking about the *Grundy*!"

"He and I are old friends."

"You're mortal enemies," Winnifred corrected him.

"That too," admitted Mallory. "You're *sure* he has the second choice?"

"A chimera, yes," said Winnifred. "It won here last year, before the dragon had begun showing."

"Well, I might as well get it over with," said Mallory, picking up the phone. "You want to leave?"

"No," said Winnifred. "We're partners. I won't desert you, John Justin."

"*I'd* like to leave," offered Periwinkle.

"You're part of the furnishings," said Mallory. He turned to Felina. "How about you? Everyone else has voiced an opinion."

"Will he tear you limb from limb, pluck your eyes out, cut off your head, and make a stylish jacket out of your skin?" she asked.

Mallory shrugged. "He might."

"Then I'll stay."

"I knew I could count on you," said the detective dryly.

Mallory dialed G-R-U-N-D-Y and waited for the demon to appear. Nothing happened.

He hung up, picked up the receiver, and dialed again. There was still no response.

"That's odd," he said, frowning. "That's always brought him before."

"Maybe he's guilty and doesn't want you to know it," suggested Periwinkle.

"You don't understand him," answered Mallory. "He revels in being guilty. He should be here right now, bragging about how he kidnapped Fluffy without a single person spotting him."

"Then why isn't he?" asked the mirror.

Mallory shrugged. "Beats the hell out of me."

"Does this mean he's *not* going to tear you apart and pluck out your eyes, John Justin?" asked Felina, disappointment writ large on her feline face.

"It's a possibility," said Mallory.

"I never get to have any fun," complained the cat-girl.

Mallory walked over to the coat rack and donned his trenchcoat and battered fedora. "Maybe you can have some yet," he said.

"Where are you going, John Justin?" asked Winnifred.

"To the Grundy's castle," replied Mallory. "I want to take a look around there."

"I'm coming with you," said Winnifred.

Mallory shook his head. "Someone's got to stay here in case Brody calls to tell us he's received a ransom demand or sends his kennel manager by. I'll take Felina. It's getting dark out, and she can spot his henchmen—well, hench*things*—better than I can."

"I hate it when you deal with him," said Winnifred.

"He's a demon of his word," answered Mallory. "That's better than I can say for most of the men I know." He turned to Felina. "Come on."

"First skritch my back, then feed me three parakeets, a swordfish, and a hippopotamus, and then maybe I'll go."

"I guess I'm going alone," said Mallory.

"One parakeet and a triple whaleburger with cheese?"

"Good-bye," said Mallory, opening the door and bracing himself for what was coming next.

Ninety pounds of fur and sinew flew through the air and landed on his back. "I've reconsidered, John Justin!" purred Felina. "You can't survive without me!"

"You leap onto my back too many more times and I don't know if I can survive *with* you," grated Mallory, waiting for her to jump lightly to the floor.

They walked out the door, caught a northbound buggy pulled by a rhinoceros, tipped the gremlin driver when he let them off at Central Park, and then Mallory turned north. The trees had lost their leaves and the barren branches stretched out toward the darkened sky like skeletal fingers.

"This way about five hundred yards or so," he said. "I think."

Felina smiled. "There are fish up ahead."

"He's got a moat surrounding his castle," said Mallory.

"*Big* fish," said Felina.

Mallory kept walking.

"*Really* big fish."

Suddenly the still night air was split by a hideous roar.

"And *loud*," said Felina.

"Fish don't roar," said Mallory.

Felina merely looked at him and smiled an inscrutable catlike smile.

A flock of harpies flew overhead. One swooped down toward Mallory. "*Go back!*" she crooned. "*Escape while you can!*"

Felina leaped up, claws extended, but couldn't reach the harpy.

"His theatrical effects haven't improved much," noted Mallory.

They continued walking, and suddenly the Grundy's huge Gothic castle loomed before them, illuminated by torches.

"Well, that's one way to save on your electric bill," remarked Mallory.

There was another roar.

"I *like* fish," said Felina hungrily.

Mallory watched as a six-ton creature broke through the surface of the moat.

"I think they like you even more," he said.

Another even larger monster surfaced and stared at them.

"I want *that* one," said Felina, pointing toward it.

"Darn!" said Mallory. "I left my fishing rod at home."

"Just reach in and pull him out," said Felina.

"Now why didn't *I* think of that?" replied Mallory sardonically.

The creature roared again, staring straight at Mallory.

"Well?" said Felina impatiently.

"Maybe later."

"I'll starve to death!"

"That's too bad," said Mallory. "I guess I'd better cancel that carton of catnip I ordered."

"Well, maybe not *quite* to death," she amended.

"I can't tell you how relieved I am," said Mallory, staring at the drawbridge that crossed the moat.

"Are you going to stand here all night, John Justin?" asked the cat-girl.

"Just casing the joint. Do you see anyone or anything on the other side?"

She peered into the dark and shook her head.

"Something's wrong," said Mallory. "This place is *always* protected."

"Oh, I didn't say there wasn't anyone there," said Felina.

"Yes you did."

"I said I couldn't *see* them, and I can't." She sniffed the air. "But I can *smell* them."

"How many and what kind?"

She sniffed again. "A thing, and another thing, and then another thing, and . . ."

"Thanks a heap," said Mallory. He walked to the foot of the bridge. "Let me know if any of those things are sneaking up on me."

"Yes, John Justin."

"Yes, you'll let me know, or yes, they're sneaking up?"

"Yes, I'll let you know," said Felina.

"Thanks."

"And yes, they're sneaking up."

Suddenly a leprechaun carrying a small spear raced across the drawbridge with a savage war cry.

Mallory stood watching him for a moment, then turned to Felina. "If he gets within five feet of me, he's yours."

"Hey, Mac, I'd watch that if I were you," said the leprechaun, skidding to a stop ten feet away. "Slavery went out with the Seventh Amendment." He frowned. "Or was it the Fourteenth Commandment?"

"It's okay," said Mallory to the little leprechaun. "She's not going to own you. She's going to kill you."

"She is?" said the leprechaun, his eyes widening. "But that's ridiculous! What did I ever do to her?"

"She's my bodyguard."

"But she's a female!"

"You noticed."

"That's what we get for ever letting them read and write. Have her kill, clean, and cook one of the moat monsters while you and I relax and discuss the errors of giving them the vote. Louie, this could be the beginning of a beautiful friendship."

"I'm not your friend," noted Mallory. "In case it's slipped your mind, you were just threatening me with your spear."

"That was *business*," said the leprechaun with a shrug. "I'll tell you what: Let's go over to the Emerald Isle Pub and cement our camaraderie with a couple of pints. Your treat."

"Some other time," said Mallory. "Right now I have to see the Grundy."

"Say not so, my dear friend. If you try, I'll just have to run you through."

"Felina, take his spear away and throw it in the moat," said Mallory.

The cat-girl grabbed the spear out of the leprechaun's hands.

"You're destroying a beautiful friendship!" whined the leprechaun.

Felina hurled the spear at a moat monster, which opened its mouth and swallowed it whole.

"Now look what you've done!" whined the leprechaun. "I just know that's going to come out of my pay!" He glowered at Mallory. "You're going to be sorry for this, fella. My companions are waiting for you on the other side of the bridge, and they're going to tear you to pieces."

"Right!" yelled a high-pitched voice from across the bridge. "You cross this bridge and you're a dead man. We'll tear you limb from limb. There won't be enough of you left to bury. We'll pull your guts out and stomp on them. We'll play marbles with your eyeballs. We'll use your ears for ashtrays. We'll—" There was a retching sound. "I think I'm going to be sick!"

"Why does he do it?" murmured Mallory, shaking his head in wonderment.

"Do what, Dead Man?" asked the leprechaun.

"He's the most powerful demon on the East Coast," said Mallory. "He just walks past things and they die. So why does he hire a bunch of incompetents to guard his castle?"

"It's not enough that you fed my livelihood to the moat monster?" complained the leprechaun. "Now you have to insult me too?"

"Enough talk," said Mallory. "I'm here on a job, and it's time I started doing it. Is your boss at home?"

"I'll never tell!"

"Felina?"

The cat-girl, an evil grin on her face, stretched her hand out in front of the leprechaun's nose. One by one, each finger sprouted a razor-sharp two-inch claw.

"Second floor, west wing, third bedroom on the left!" said the leprechaun, just before he ran off through Central Park.

"Come on," said Mallory, heading off across the drawbridge.

"Who goes there?" demanded the same high voice he had heard before.

"Me," said Mallory.

"Advance and be recognized, Me," said the voice.

Mallory walked to the end of the bridge and found himself confronting a troll, an elf, and a goblin.

"That's far enough," said the elf in its high-pitched voice.

"Tell your boss that his greatest enemy is here to pay him a visit," said Mallory.

"You're the cook at Ming Toy Epstein's Kosher Pizzeria?" said the elf. "The poor demon was sick for days."

"His *other* greatest enemy," said Mallory.

"Can't be," said the elf confidently. "John Justin Mallory is a tough dude. He wouldn't walk around unarmed in the middle of the night."

Mallory jerked a thumb in Felina's direction. "*She's* my weapon."

"My word!" said the elf, staring at her. "Is she loaded?"

"I'm starting to lose my patience," said Mallory. "You know you're not going to keep me out, and I know you're not going to keep me out, so why not just stand aside?"

"Right," said the elf, pointing to the goblin. "*He's* going to keep you out."

The goblin walked over and whispered something in the elf's ear.

"Right now?" demanded the elf.

The goblin nodded.

"Well, all I can say is that it's damnably awkward," said the elf. He sighed and turned back to Mallory. "Can we postpone your duel to the death for a couple of minutes?"

"No," said Mallory.

"All right, then." The elf turned to the troll. "Take him apart, Herm!"

Herm the troll approached, spear at the ready, and Felina positioned herself between him and Mallory.

"Hold everything!" yelled Herm. "Fins! Fingers! Time-out!"

"What's the matter?" demanded the elf.

"Trolls are afraid of cat-people," whined Herm. "I thought everyone knew that."

"So rise above it," said the elf.

"It's in my contract," insisted Herm. "I don't have to fight cat-people."

"I'll get you a commendation, and recommend that we pay you double time for killing her."

Herm shook his head. "Ain't gonna do it. Can't make me do it."

"It's just a cat-person, for goodness' sake!" yelled the elf.

"That's it for you, Charlie!" said Herm. "I'm reporting you to the shop steward tomorrow morning."

"Oh, don't be such a baby!" yelled Charlie.

"And now you're insulting me. Oh, this is going to cost you, Charlie!"

The troll turned and walked off into the darkness.

"Well, I guess it's just you and me," said Mallory.

"The hell it is!" snapped Charlie. "I'm not a combatant, I'm a supervisor! You'll have to come back in the morning when I have a new crew to defend the castle."

"I haven't got till morning. I'm going in now."

"I can facilitate things!" said Charlie quickly. "Give me half an hour to assemble a team of cutthroats and mad dog killers!"

"Nope," said Mallory. "Now are you going to step aside, or do we have this battle to the death that you were so hot to promote a minute ago?"

"I have a better idea," said the elf. "Let's cut a deck of cards. If you're high, you can go in. If not, you jump into the moat and let the monsters eat you."

"Afraid not, Charlie," said Mallory.

"You wouldn't hit a guy with glasses, would you?" said the elf desperately.

"You're not wearing glasses."

"I misplaced them!" said Charlie. "But I know right where they are! If you'll wait here five minutes, I can be back with them."

"No."

"Where's your sense of fair play?" whined Charlie.

"I left it in my other suit," said Mallory. "Now step aside."

He took a step forward, and the elf leaped out of his way, then gave vent to a hideous scream.

"Now look what you made me do!" wailed the elf. "I just stepped in something, and this was my best pair of boots!"

"It was in the line of duty," said Mallory. "Write a request for reimbursement."

The little elf's face brightened noticeably. "Hey, you're all right, Mallory! I don't suppose you'd like to share a couple of pints at the Emerald Isle Pub and cement a growing mutual admiration."

"Not right now," said Mallory, approaching the gate leading to the castle's interior with Felina right behind him. "I have business inside."

"I'll be waiting for you," promised Charlie. "Always provided the Grundy doesn't tear off your head and spit down your neck and pull out your liver and . . ." Another retching sound. "I'm going to be sick again!"

Mallory and Felina entered the castle.

"Keep an eye out for guards and traps," said the detective.

"It doesn't come out," replied Felina.

"Okay, keep an eye in for them."

"Yes, John Justin."

"You know the Grundy's scent. Is he close by?"

She sniffed the air, nodded, and pointed straight ahead.

"Not up the stairs?" asked Mallory.

She pointed straight ahead again.

"Okay, let's go take a look."

He began walking forward, passing through rooms filled with musty, uncomfortable-looking Victorian furniture, all possessed of uninviting hard angles, and finally came to a small atrium.

"You're *sure?*" asked Mallory.

Felina smiled and pointed . . . and suddenly Mallory saw a flash of movement out of the corner of his eye. He turned to look and saw a tall being, a few inches over six feet, with two prominent horns protruding from his hairless head. His eyes were a burning yellow, his nose sharp and aquiline, his teeth white and gleaming, his skin a bright red. Usually he dressed in crushed velvet and satins, but this time he wore a perfectly tailored tuxedo. The ruffled shirt hid the two mystic rubies that Mallory knew were suspended around his neck on a golden chain.

His back was to Mallory, and he had a chimera on a leash. The creature—thirty inches at the shoulder, with the front legs of a lion, the torso of a goat, and the tail of a snake, bright red, and snorting smoke—struck a pose, and he reached into a pocket and tossed it a writing, snarling *thing*, which the chimera caught and swallowed in a single motion.

"Good evening, Mallory," said the Grundy, still with his back to the detective. "I expected you, of course."

"Is that why you sent the second string out to guard the bridge?"

The Grundy turned and smiled. "They are there only to detain visitors long enough for me to decide what to do with them."

Felina eyed the chimera hungrily, and the Grundy pointed at a spot just in front of her feet. A bolt of lightning shot out from his finger and melted the floor inches from where she stood.

"Tell your pet that *my* pet is not to be touched."

"I think she gets the picture," said Mallory. He looked around. "So where are you hiding him? Or is it her, or perhaps it?"

"I beg your pardon?"

"Fluffy. Brody's dragon."

"I didn't steal her."

"Stealing her would make you the favorite to win Eastminster," said Mallory. "It wouldn't run contrary to your ethical precepts, either. Why don't you make my job easy and just return her to me and we'll forget it ever happened?"

"I have never lied to you, John Justin Mallory," said the Grundy. "I am not lying now."

"But you knew I was coming here."

"I am the most logical suspect," agreed the Grundy.

"Okay, if you didn't steal her, who did?"

"I don't know."

"Oh, come on!" snapped Mallory. "You're the Grundy! Nothing goes on in New York that you don't know about!"

"I have been preoccupied working with Carmelita," said the demon.

"Carmelita?" repeated Mallory.

"The most perfect chimera ever hatched," said the Grundy, indicating the creature at the other end of the leash. "She is the defending champion of Eastminster, and I have every intention of winning again tomorrow."

"And stealing Fluffy makes it that much easier."

"I did *not* steal her," repeated the Grundy. "It's against my principles."

"You kill tens of thousands of people, you wreak havoc whenever you can, and you tell me that stealing a dragon is against your principles?" said Mallory.

"My *sporting* principles," the Grundy continued. "Winning Eastminster without defeating Brody's dragon would be a hollow victory. I want that dragon there in the ring! I intend to beat it fair and square."

Mallory stared at him for a long minute. "All right," he said at last. "You're a lot of things I don't like, but a liar isn't one of them."

"Let me go a step further to prove my sincerity," said the Grundy. "Whatever Brody's paying you to find his ugly little dragon, I'll double it."

"For the same job?"

"That's right."

"There's a four-thousand-dollar bonus if I get the dragon to the ring on time," said Mallory.

"I'll make it ten thousand," said the Grundy.

"You got yourself a deal," said Mallory. He paused. "It's amazing how often I wind up working for you, considering that you're Evil Incarnate and I'm a semi-moral man."

"I am neither good nor evil," said the Grundy. "I am simply a balance point between worlds. I have explained it to you many times."

"I understand the explanation," replied Mallory. "I'm still waiting for you to do your first good deed, or to see your first spontaneous act of generosity."

"On some other world," said the Grundy. "This one needs precisely what I bring it."

"Okay, so much for Philosophy 101," said Mallory. "Why don't you make my job really easy now that you've hired me, and tell me where the damned dragon is?"

"I don't know."

"You could find it in five minutes with your powers."

"Less," said the Grundy.

"Well?"

"I have to work with Carmelita," said the Grundy. He stared critically down at the chimera, who was growling softly. "She still has a tendency to toe out with her left forefoot, and she's occasionally too slow dousing her flame when the judge examines her teeth."

"Five minutes," repeated Mallory.

"That would certainly be a good deed," said the Grundy. "But I am a demon: my nature precludes me from helping you, much as I would like to bring this to an immediate resolution. I am willing to pay you, but you will have to earn your money on your own, John Justin Mallory."

He turned his back and began working with the chimera again, and finally Mallory walked back out of the castle, followed by Felina, who had been remarkably quiet since the Grundy had melted the floor around her.

"All went well, I hope?" said a voice, and Mallory found himself facing Charlie the elf.

"Could have been worse," said the detective.

"Good. Let's have a drink and discuss it. You buy the first four rounds."

"No, thanks," said Mallory.

"Boy, you're not very grateful that I let you live, are you?" complained Charlie.

"I've got work to do," said Mallory without slowing down. "Besides, your boss wants you in the atrium."

The little elf's face brightened noticeably. "He does?"

"Absolutely."

"What for?" asked Charlie. "I'll bet it's a promotion."

"He says Carmelita is hungry," said Mallory, starting across the bridge.

He looked back when he and Felina and reached the other side. Charlie was rooted to the spot, and was shaking so noticeably that Mallory could see it in the moonlight from eighty feet away.

"How did it go?" asked Winnifred as Mallory and Felina entered the office.

"He drives me crazy," complained the detective. "He could pinpoint the thief and the damned dragon in twenty seconds if he wanted to."

"He didn't steal Fluffy himself?"

Mallory shook his head. "He *wants* us to find her." He grimaced. "He's a *sportsman*. He wants the world to know his chimera is the better specimen."

"Then why—?"

"Who the hell knows?" muttered Mallory. "For a being who revels in being Evil Incarnate, that son of a bitch has more ethical baggage than a professor of philosophy."

"You're *sure* he wasn't responsible for this?" persisted Winnifred.

"I'm sure," said Mallory. "He's a lot of things good and bad, mostly bad—but he's not a liar."

"All right," she said. "There's been no message from Brody, no demand for ransom."

"Did his kennel manager show up or contact you?"

"No," replied Winnifred. "I suppose our next step is to inspect the premises and see if the thief left any clues."

"Your next step is to feed the office cat," said Felina.

"What about the hot dog I bought you at Greasy Gus's on the way back?" asked Mallory.

"That was then, this is now," said Felina.

"*Then* was about two minutes ago," noted the detective.

"That long?" said Felina, emitting a small, ladylike burp. "No wonder I'm starving!"

There was a knock at the door.

"Come in," said Winnifred.

The door slowly opened to reveal an undernourished green-skinned gremlin. "Mr. Mallory?" he asked hesitantly. "And Colonel Carruthers?"

"Yes," said Winnifred. "And you are?"

"Jeeves," said the gremlin.

"We didn't order a butler," said Mallory.

"You misunderstand," said Jeeves.

"It's possible," agreed Mallory. "I do that a lot these days. Why don't you enlighten me?"

"I am Fluffy's personal kennel attendant," said the gremlin. "I work for Mr. Brody."

"That's right," said Winnifred. "He *did* mention that he'd be sending you over. I thought you were the manager, though."

"I was, until Fluffy was stolen," said Jeeves. "I am at your service. Anything you need to know about dragons in general or Fluffy in particular, all you have to do is ask. My orders," he added apologetically, "are to stay with you until the case is solved and Fluffy has been found."

"Have you eaten?" asked Felina. "Maybe we should all go out for a meal and discuss strategy."

"Who can think of food at a time like this?" replied the gremlin.

Felina promptly turned her back and busied herself licking a perfectly clean forearm.

"What can I help you with first?" asked Jeeves. "Her diet? Her personal habits? Her endearing little quirks?"

"I think the first thing we need to do is inspect the crime scene, so to speak," said Winnifred.

"Whatever you say," said Jeeves. "Follow me, please."

Mallory turned to Felina. "Come on."

"I'm busy ignoring all of you," she replied.

"Ignore us later. Right now I need you to tell me if you can identify any scents at Brody's hotel."

"Oh, all right," she said, walking to the door. "I'm especially good on filet mignon medium rare, pheasant under glass, and lobster thermidor."

"I'm sure you are," said Mallory, "but I think there's very little likelihood that Fluffy was kidnapped by a lobster or a pheasant."

"Be quiet, John Justin," said the cat-girl. "I don't smell as well when I'm depressed."

"Don't feed me straight lines like that," said Mallory, following Winnifred and Felina out the door.

The four of them began walking to the Plantagenet Arms. After they'd gone three blocks, a goblin stepped out from between two buildings, blocking their way.

"Happy Valentine's Day!" he said, throwing a handful of confetti into the air. "Huzzah!"

"What are you selling?" asked Mallory wearily.

"Selling?" repeated the goblin. "I'm not selling. I'm celebrating."

"Fine. Happy Valentine's Day. Now please move out of the way."

"You can celebrate too, friend," continued the goblin. "Don't you want to give a heart-shaped gift to one of these two lovely ladies, or perhaps both of them if you're planning on losing the ugly little green wart during the night?"

"Go away," said Mallory.

"Just listen a minute!" said the goblin. "This is a legitimate business proposition. We can eliminate the middleman! I have in my possession not merely heart-shaped cards and gifts, but actual hearts. In fact, for the next three minutes I'm running a special on one that belonged to a little old lady who only got excited when praising the Lord in church on Sunday mornings."

"Felina," said Mallory. "If he's still talking in twenty seconds, he's all yours."

"How about Phar Cry, the greatest racehorse in the world?" said the goblin. "My friend Iggy is the night watchman at Jamaica. We could go over there and pick it up right now, if you don't mind a little blood and suffering."

"Okay," said Mallory to Felina. "Kill him."

"Hey," said the goblin, backing away. "I'm just doing my job. Have a heart." Suddenly he smiled. "Hey, that's a great line! Have a heart!"

He turned and raced off down an alley, screaming "Have a heart!" Felina tried to follow him, but Mallory grabbed her wrist.

"Stay with us," he said. "It's a depressing thought, but we might need you."

They continued their journey to the Plantagenet Arms. Along the way they passed a seemingly endless string of posters, some for the upcoming fight between Kid Testosterone and Brutus the Butcher, some for the new musical *My Fair Ladle (A Girl I Used to Spoon With)*, and quite a few advertising the Eastminster show. Carmelita, the defending champion, was prominently displayed in most of the Eastminster posters. Felina got too close to one of them, and suddenly Carmelita's image turned and snarled, and a flame shot out of her nostrils, barely missing the cat-girl. Felina hissed and displayed her claws, but the chimera was back in her original pose.

"Her day is past," said Jeeves contemptuously as he stared at the image. "She doesn't belong in the same ring with Fluffy."

"I wouldn't get into the ring with either of them unless I was up to date on my fire insurance," said Mallory.

"This is not a laughing matter, Mr. Mallory," said Jeeves. "Fluffy is the end result of thirty-seven generations of carefully planned breeding."

"It's my nature to be sardonic," replied Mallory. "I'm the result of even more generations of totally unplanned breeding."

The gremlin glared at him for a moment, then turned and continued walking. A few minutes later they reached the Plantagenet Arms, and passed through the lobby until they came to a huge bank of elevators. Jeeves walked past the first eleven and stopped in front of one labeled Express.

The four of them entered, and the elevator shot up to the fifty-fourth floor penthouse, where the doors slid open and they stepped out into the large living room of Brody's suite.

"Nice," commented Mallory, surveying the leather chairs and couches, a suit of armor, and half a dozen large gilt-framed prints, each of which showed British monarchs doing kingly things.

"Nice?" said Brody, walking in from another room. "Do you know what this place costs per day?"

"Probably about six years' rent on my office," answered Mallory.

"I doubt it," said Brody. "You're not in a high-rent district."

"I stand corrected. By the way, this is my partner, Colonel Winnifred Carruthers. Winnifred, this is our client, Buffalo Bill Brody."

Winnifred stepped forward and shook Brody's hand vigorously. "Pleased to meet you," she said.

"Can you show us exactly where you kept Fluffy?"

"She had run of the place when Jeeves or I were here," said Brody, "but he was out inspecting the grooming area over at Madison Round Garden and I was having lunch in the restaurant downstairs, so she was confined to her pen."

"May we see it, please?" asked Winnifred.

He nodded. "In the bedroom here," he said, turning and reentering the room he had come out of.

Mallory walked into the bedroom and uttered a low whistle. "I've seen smaller basketball courts," he remarked.

"Right there," said Brody, pointing to an enclosure that was perhaps four feet on a side.

"Asbestos?" asked Winnifred.

"Of course," replied Brody.

"There's no top," said Mallory. "What stopped her from jumping out— or flying out, for that matter?"

"She can only fly for perhaps ten or twelve feet, no more," said Jeeves. "And what stopped her is that her food was in the pen."

"Smart dragon," commented Felina approvingly.

"As for jumping," continued the gremlin, "dragons are not known for their jumping ability."

"The top of the enclosure is perhaps thirty inches," noted Winnifred. "Almost anyone could have reached over and picked her up."

Mallory turned to Jeeves. "Would she let a stranger do that?"

"Yes," said Jeeves. "She is a show dragon."

"Okay, she's a show dragon. So what?"

"You don't understand," continued the gremlin. "From earliest infancy she has been taught to accept being handled by anyone who approaches her, since one of them may be the judge, and you can't have a show dragon shrink away from being examined. It displays cowardice, and that counts heavily against a dragon in competition."

"So she'd follow anyone who took her out of her pen?" continued Mallory.

"She wouldn't necessarily *follow* them, but she would certainly allow herself to be carried," said Jeeves. "After all, we carry her from the grooming area to the ring so that her feet don't get dirty and no one inadvertently steps on her, so she's quite used to it."

"Felina?" said Mallory. "Go over to the pen and tell me what scents you can pick up."

The cat-girl approached the asbestos enclosure and inhaled deeply.

"I smell him"—she indicated Jeeves—"and him"—Brody—"and two tarantulas, and a dragon."

"Nothing else?"

She shook her head.

"You're sure?"

She sniffed again.

"Just the alligator," she said.

"What alligator?"

"The dead one."

Mallory frowned. "You say there was a dead alligator here?"

She nodded. "Yes. Absolutely. Positively. For sure. I think."

"Are you seriously trying to tell me Fluffy was kidnapped by a dead alligator?" demanded Mallory.

"No."

"No, she *wasn't* kidnapped by a dead alligator?"

"No, I wasn't seriously trying to tell you," answered Felina.

"You're driving me crazy," said Mallory. "Was she or wasn't she?"

"Excuse me, John Justin," said Winnifred. "May I try?"

"Please do," said Mallory.

"Felina, was this a freshly killed alligator?"

The cat-girl shook her head.

"If it was a whole dead alligator, or merely a pair of alligator shoes, could you tell the difference?"

"Not without seeing it," answered Felina.

Winnifred turned to Mallory. "There you are, John Justin. The thief was wearing alligator shoes."

"Maybe," said Felina. "He could have been wearing alligator underwear or alligator earmuffs."

"We'll take that under advisement," said Mallory. He turned to Brody and Jeeves. "What do dragons eat?"

"Oh, any number of things," said Jeeves. "Fish, birds, knights . . ."

"Tarantulas?" asked Winnifred.

"They were her *friends!*" said the gremlin, outraged.

"So where are they?"

"When it was clear she'd been stolen, *I* ate them," said Jeeves.

"Fluffy doesn't eat any of those things," added Brody. "She's my favorite, and I spoil her terribly. Her diet consists exclusively of chocolate marshmallow cookies."

"Very special ones," added Jeeves.

"Special how?" asked Mallory.

"They had to be shaped like little elephants."

"You're kidding, right?"

"I never kid about my precious little fire-breather," said Brody.

"Okay, she eats elephant-shaped chocolate marshmallow cookies," said Mallory. "If the thief doesn't know that, what else will she eat?"

"Absolutely nothing," said Brody. "But the thief *does* know it."

"What have you been holding back?" demanded the detective.

"There was a box of cookies on the dresser there," said Brody, indicating a nearby chest of drawers. "It was almost empty, but there were a few left. It's gone now."

"So whoever took her *does* know what she eats."

"Yes."

"But he's almost out of cookies, and elephant-shaped chocolate marshmallow cookies must be hard to find. If he gives her a lion-shaped one, or a rhino-shaped one, are you sure she'd refuse it?"

"Absolutely."

"Then our next stop is to find out who sells them," said Mallory. Another grimace. "You know, this really isn't the kind of trail I expected to find myself following when I became a private eye."

"What do we do now?" asked Jeeves.

"We go to the one place in town where I'll get the answer I need," said Mallory. "I am not looking forward to this."

"Dangerous?" asked Jeeves apprehensively.

"You have two guesses left," said Mallory.

"There's no reason for both of us to go there," remarked Mallory as they left the Plantagenet Arms. "It makes more sense for me to do it. It's right around the corner from my apartment."

"I agree," said Winnifred. "I'll start checking with the SPCA, and some of the local veterinarians, just in case Fluffy managed to escape."

Mallory looked unenthused. "That's a hell of a long shot," he said.

"I know," she said. "But I have to do *something* until we can come up with some leads."

"There's got to be something more productive." Mallory turned to the gremlin. "Jeeves, is there a local organization for toy dragon breeders and exhibitors?"

"Yes," answered Jeeves. "The Greater Manhattan Miniature and Toy Dragon Club. Their corporate offices are in a beautiful old brownstone on West 34th Street."

"Give Winnifred the address."

Jeeves pulled a notebook out of his pocket, scribbled something, tore off the page he'd written on, and handed it to her.

"Have them pass the word about Fluffy," Mallory told her. "No reason why we shouldn't get all the dragon breeders in the area working for us. They've got to have a certain amount of pride. Just explain that if Fluffy doesn't make it into the ring, Eastminster will probably be won by a chimera instead of a dragon."

"Good thinking, John Justin," said Winnifred, walking off. "I'm on my way." Suddenly she stopped and turned to him. "When and where do we meet up?"

"I don't know," replied Mallory. He lowered his head in thought for a moment. "I know there are dog ponds in the city. Jeeves, are they any dragon ponds?"

"Just one," said the gremlin. "It's at the north end of Central Park."

"Ten thirty?" said Mallory to Winnifred.

She nodded. "I'll find it." Then she was walking away.

"Okay," said Mallory. "Let's go." He looked around. "Where's Felina?"

"Right here," said the cat-girl, emerging from a shadowy area between two buildings.

"What the hell were you doing there?"

"There was this cute, adorable little mouse," she said. "He had soft brown eyes, and he looked so lonely that I went over to keep him company." Another ladylike burp. "He's not lonely anymore."

"I'm sure he appreciated it," said Mallory dryly.

"You'd think he would," she agreed, rubbing her stomach. "But he complained all the way down. Very crude language, too." She frowned. "What's worse than an ungrateful mouse?"

"Let me take a shot in the dark," said Mallory. "An ungrateful mouse with ketchup and mustard?"

Felina yowled with amusement. "That's a very funny answer, John Justin."

"Thanks."

"But you left out onions."

"Mea culpa."

"No, Bermuda."

"I stand corrected," said Mallory.

"So where are we going?" asked Jeeves.

"To someone who might be able to help us, once we plow through the usual bullshit."

"I don't understand," said the gremlin.

"You will," said Mallory. "It's in the next block."

They continued walking, and finally stopped in front of a large grocery store with a blinking neon sign proclaiming that it was Seymour Noodnik's Emporium.

"This is it?" asked Jeeves.

"That's right," replied Mallory. He turned to Felina. "You leave the fish alone."

"Why would I bother a fish?" she asked with an innocent feline smile.

"Beats the hell out of me," answered Mallory as the three of them entered the store. It was filled with the normal staples, plus signs offering specials on candied dragonflies' wings, chocolate-covered gorgon claws, toasted gryphon tails, and Texas Mediumhorn flank steaks. "But next time I won't pull you back out."

"Mallory, my friend!" cried a voice.

Mallory cast a sideways glance at Jeeves. "Here it comes," he said softly.

"Got a special on blue jay teeth," said Noodnik, approaching the detective's party wearing a blood-drenched apron over his clothes.

"Let me guess," said Mallory, staring at the bloodstains. "You pulled them all out with a pliers."

"That's my boy Mallory. Always good for a laugh." Noodnik paused. "No, I used an electric hedge trimmer. Works faster."

"I didn't know there was that much blood in a blue jay," remarked Mallory.

"More than a turnip, less than a buffalo," said Noodnik. "Speaking of buffalo, want to buy a filet of eight-legged buffalo?"

"There aren't any eight-legged buffalo."

"Well, not for the last twenty minutes or so," agreed Noodnik. "You here on a case?"

"In a way."

"Got a lot of lewd women in it?"

"Nope."

"Got *any* lewd women in it?" persisted Noodnik.

"Seems unlikely," replied Mallory.

"Damn!" said Noodnik. "Here I was hoping you'd brighten my day."

"You've already tortured a blue jay and a buffalo," said Mallory. "How much brighter can it get?"

"You got a point," agreed Noodnik. "Okay, down to business. What do you need to know? I can charge you five dollars an answer, or you can buy two ounces of powdered unicorn horn for the whole thing. Great aphrodisiac."

"It is?" asked Jeeves, suddenly interested.

"Well, not if you're a unicorn," qualified Noodnik.

"Seymour, no deals, no bargains," said Mallory. "Just answer my questions, or I'll go across street to Honest Sam the Greengrocer's."

"You'd do that to your oldest, closest friend?" demanded Noodnik.

"Of course not," said Mallory. "But I'd do it to you."

"All right," growled Noodnik. "What do you want to know? And by the way, where's your cat-thing?"

Mallory realized that Felina was no longer standing next to him and quickly looked around, but he couldn't spot her. He suddenly became aware of a commotion at the back of the store. He walked toward the crowd that had gathered and soon saw Felina perched on the top shelf at the end of an aisle, a bag of catnip clutched to her bosom.

"Come on, lady," said a store attendant. "You have to pay for it first!"

She hissed at him and began opening the bag. The attendant picked up a broom and started threatening her with the handle.

"Not smart," muttered Mallory under his breath.

An instant later the broom was in Felina's hands, and she was swatting the attendant to the cheers of the shoppers.

"All right, that's enough," said Mallory, stepping forward. "You," he said to the attendant, "go take a ten-minute break."

The attendant looked at Noodnik, who nodded his approval, and then he made a beeline for the front door.

"And *you*," said Mallory, "hand me the broom and come down right now."

"Maybe I will and maybe I won't," said Felina.

"Fine. Maybe I'll feed you again someday and maybe I won't."

She immediately hurled herself into the air, did a triple somersault, and landed right next to the detective.

"I forgive you, John Justin," she said, purring and rubbing her hip against his.

"I can't tell you how relieved I am," grated Mallory.

"You're paying for Sheldon's break time," said Noodnik, approaching them.

"Right," said Mallory. "Fate forefend that you should reward him for risking life and limb on behalf of your store."

"I'm glad we see eye-to-eye on that," said Noodnik. "As long as we're back here, can I sell you an apron? Only seventy-three dollars."

"For an apron?" said Mallory. "What the hell's it made of?"

"Unborn denim."

"I'll pass on that."

"Okay, how about a pair of size fourteen triple-A galoshes with your name inscribed on them?"

"My name?"

"Well, if your friends call you Universal."

"How about just answering my questions?"

"We'll get to that, but my function is to sell you."

"We'll get to it now, or I'm going to get my answers from Honest Sam."

"You really know how to hurt a guy," complained Noodnik.

"Of course I do. I'm a trained detective. Now are you ready to answer?"

"All right," said Noodnik. "But I'm writing you into the will in the morning."

"*Into* the will?"

"So I can write you out of it in the afternoon."

"Fine," said Mallory. "Do you have any elephant-shaped chocolate marsh-mallow cookies?"

"No."

"Do you know who does?"

"No. Now ask your questions."

"I just did."

"That was *it*?" said Noodnik. "This whole case hinges on chocolate marshmallow cookies?"

"Elephant-shaped ones."

"You'll have to give me a little time to see who makes them and who sells them."

"How much time?"

Noodnik shrugged. "I dunno. Maybe a couple of hours."

"I'll check back with you then," said Mallory, turning and walking toward the door as Felina and Jeeves fell into step behind him.

"You *sure* this hasn't got anything to do with lewd women?" Noodnik called after him in plaintive tones.

"I'm sure."

"No one's ever going to write your adventures up in a book," predicted Noodnik.

As they reached the street, Mallory turned to Jeeves.

"Your boss keeps referring to Fluffy as a fire-breather," he said. "Is she?"

"All dragons are."

"There's no sense just standing around while we're waiting for Noodnik to do his homework or for Winnifred to hunt up some leads," said Mallory. "Where would you take a stolen fire-breather where she couldn't burn her surroundings down?"

Suddenly Jeeves smiled. "I know just the place."

The gremlin led Mallory and Felina to the riverfront, then summoned a small launch.

"A *boat?*" exclaimed Mallory. "Where the hell are we going?"

"The one place a dragon can't do any harm," answered Jeeves. "I should have thought of it immediately. Most of the major dragon farms are there."

"Are *where?*"

"Why, Fire Island, of course," replied the gremlin.

They boarded the launch and it soon headed off toward their destination. Felina leaned over the water and stared at it, motionless. After perhaps a minute her hand darted out and came away with a small, squirming fish.

"I hope you're not going to eat that thing raw," said Mallory.

"Certainly not," said Felina.

"Good."

"I'm going to play with it first."

"Not on this boat, you aren't," said Mallory.

"You never let me have any fun," she complained.

"Our definitions of fun vary considerably."

"Not everyone likes movies of naked women," said Felina.

"Shut up and toss it back," said Mallory.

"Oh, all right," she said, quickly biting off the head and tossing the rest of the fish into the water.

Jeeves uttered a plaintive whimper.

"It's just a fish," said Mallory.

"It wasn't the fish," responded the gremlin uneasily.

"You look like if you hadn't started the day green, you'd be turning green right about now," remarked Mallory.

"I get seasick."

"In a launch on a river?"

Jeeves seemed about to answer him. Then a look of panic crossed his face and he raced to the side of the boat and leaned out over the water.

"Don't worry about it," said Mallory to the gremlin's heaving torso. "We'll talk later."

The launch stopped at a dock a moment later, and the three passengers got out and were soon on dry land.

The first thing Mallory became aware of was the acrid scent of smoke that seemed somehow organic. The second thing was the earsplitting roars. The third was the shadow of a huge dragon flying directly overhead.

"I think they've got an escapee," he said.

"No, it's just a training exercise," replied Jeeves. "See? He's wearing a bridle, and there's a troll on his back."

The dragon did a sudden loop-the-loop.

"He's going to lose his rider," said Mallory.

"That's why they use trolls instead of anyone important," said Jeeves.

"Like gremlins?" suggested Mallory.

"Precisely," said Jeeves as the troll slipped off and began his long descent, screaming all the way until he hit the water. He surfaced a minute later, cursing a blue streak.

"You're the one who knows Fire Island," said Mallory. "Where would you suggest we start looking for Fluffy?"

"She's so small and delicate we could look for months and never find her," answered Jeeves. "I think we should question some likely suspects. After all, you're a detective. That's what you do for a living."

"If all the dragons are as big as the one I just saw and the ones I can hear, there *aren't* any likely suspects," said Mallory. "Any one of these creatures could step on Fluffy, or inhale her, and never know it."

"Dragons come in all sizes," noted Jeeves. "You'll seek out those people with facilities to keep toys and miniatures."

"And where will I find them?"

Jeeves shrugged. "Somewhere on the island."

"Are you always this helpful?" asked Mallory sardonically.

Felina sniffed the air. "*I* can lead you to a toy dragon, John Justin," she said.

"Fine," said Mallory. "Let's go."

"For three canaries, a spotted owl, and a dolphin."

"One glass of milk, next time we pass a place that serves it."

"Okay, one glass of milk," she said. "And a moose."

"Don't push your luck."

"A baby moose?"

"Forget it," said Mallory, heading off to the island's interior.

Ninety pounds of feminine fur and sinew hurled itself onto the detective's back, sending him sprawling.

"I forgive you, John Justin!" purred Felina.

"Why am *I* so blessed?" muttered Mallory as he painfully picked himself up and began dusting himself off.

"That way," said Felina, pointing down a winding dirt road.

Mallory headed off in the direction indicated, following by his two companions. The roars became louder, and he decided it was getting warmer. Suddenly they came upon a farm in which half a dozen dragons, each the size of a T. Rex, were frolicking in a pasture, playfully shooting streams of fire at one another.

"Can I help you?" asked a gray-haired man, walking over to them.

"I'm looking for a dragon," said Mallory.

"You just found a whole batch of 'em, mister."

"A particular dragon," said the detective.

"Well, these here youngsters ain't so particular," allowed the man. "They'll eat damned near anything."

"I need a toy dragon."

"Can't help you out. I just specialize in the big fellers."

One of the dragons suddenly became aware of Mallory's group and trotted over to get a closer look.

"Is he dangerous?" asked Mallory.

"I suppose it depends on whether or not you're fireproof," said the old man. He turned to the dragon. "C'mere and say hello."

The dragon reached the fence and stretched his neck out over it.

"Let him smell the back of your hand," said the old man.

Mallory held his hand out. The dragon took a deep sniff, and it was all the detective could do to keep his entire arm from being inhaled.

"Now you and Cuddles are friends," said the old man.

"Cuddles?" repeated Mallory disbelievingly.

"Yeah," said the old man admiringly. "Ain't he a sweetie?"

"I have to admit it's not the first word that would have come to mind," said Mallory.

"Well, he's an adolescent now, but when he matures . . ."

"You mean he's going to get *bigger?*"

"Sure."

"Where the hell do you show him? I don't think they could get him into Madison Round Garden, even through the truck entrance."

"Not all dragons are for show," explained the old man. "Some are bred for hunting, some for sport like knight baiting. Cuddles here was bred to fight off any jet plane attacks over Manhattan, the Bronx, and Lower South Brooklyn."

"Sounds like a no-win situation to me," remarked Mallory. "He may be awesome flesh and blood, but he's still just flesh and blood against a jet fighter plane."

The old man smile. "He can melt a jet at two hundred yards."

"And they can shoot him at, what, two miles?" said Mallory.

"Part of his training program here is to learn evasive maneuvering."

"Isn't that his pilot's function?"

"They have a way of losing pilots," said the old man, rubbing the dragon's nose.

"I noticed," said Mallory dryly.

There was a sudden roar, and a sheet of flame shot out, singeing the dragon's hindquarters. It squealed in surprise while Mallory dove to the ground, then gingerly stuck his head up and looked around.

"What the hell was that?" he said.

"Oh, just Cutie-Pie," said the old man, indicating another huge dragon. "She saw me petting Cuddles, and she's jealous."

Mallory got to his feet. "Well, it's obvious the dragon I'm looking for isn't here. Is there a facility on the island that specializes in toy dragons?"

"Just down the road a stretch," said the old man. "Maybe half a mile, keep to your left when it forks, and look for the asbestos-lined doghouses."

"Thanks," said Mallory. Suddenly he saw a flash of white in the distance. "What's that?" he asked.

"The guy in the white lab coat? He's from the DDI."

"The DDI?" repeated Mallory.

"The Dragon Dietary Institute. He's testing some cockamamie theory that their diet gives them heartburn and that their flame is proof of it."

"What do these big dragons eat?"

"Anything smaller than themselves," replied the old man.

"With that broad a diet, it sounds like he's got a tough theory to prove."

"Still, it keeps him employed. I know writers and actors who'd kill for a steady paycheck."

"You can add detectives to the list," said Mallory, heading off toward the toy dragon farm. He turned to Jeeves as they walked. "If she's here, are you sure you'll be able to spot her?"

"She is the most recognizable toy dragon in history," the gremlin assured him.

Mallory looked ahead and saw the top of a farmhouse. "That must be it."

"I suppose so," said Jeeves.

Mallory grimaced. "We'll go through the motions, but I'll give plenty of ten-to-one that we're not going to find her here. This whole thing *feels* wrong."

"What do you mean?"

"If I were stealing the most valuable and recognizable dragon in the world, the last place I'd take her is to an island where everyone breeds dragons and can be expected to know who she is."

"But they're uniquely equipped to keep her here," noted Jeeves.

"They're not going to *keep* her anywhere," replied Mallory.

"I don't understand."

"She was kidnapped for one of two reasons: ransom or to set it up for some other animal to win the show tomorrow. She's been gone four hours, she's due in the ring tomorrow afternoon, and there hasn't been a ransom demand. Unless your boss gets a phone call soon, we have to assume she was kidnapped solely to keep her out of the show. If she's *that* recognizable, the thief can't pass her off as his own. There's a very easy way to make sure she misses the show and is never identified."

"Hold your tongue!" cried the gremlin. "I won't hear such talk!"

"Your devotion is admirable," said Mallory. "But it doesn't change the logic of the situation."

"Fluffy's alive!" snapped Jeeves. "I can feel it!"

"I'll keep looking for her right up until ring time, but I thought you ought to understand what the odds are."

"Speaking of odd . . ." said Feline, pointing up the road.

Fifty yards ahead of them six men, each with a toy dragon on a leash, paraded around in a large circle, while a seventh man, clearly acting as the judge, gave them a string of commands.

"A handling class for youngsters," remarked Jeeves knowingly.

"How can you tell they're youngsters from this distance?" asked Mallory.

"Because they need a handling class," answered the gremlin.

"Trot, dammit, don't fly!" yelled the judge as two of the dragons spread their wings and flew out to the ends of their leashes.

"All right, line 'em up and pose 'em," said the judge, and the six dragons were maneuvered into a single straight row.

The judge walked up and down the line making comments. "Left fore-foot's toeing out . . . Watch those wings . . . Moving his bowels—that's going to cost you points . . . I don't care if she *is* in heat, he's supposed to look at *me*, not *her* . . ."

Finally the judge leaned over to more closely inspect each dragon. The first wagged its scaly tail and jumped into his arms, the second backed away squealing in terror, the third was sound asleep, the fourth and fifth were in flagrante delicto. He came to the sixth, then yelped and jumped back.

"Shooting fire at the judge is a disqualification!" he screamed, rubbing his singed chin.

"You can't disqualify us," protested the handler. "This is just a class, not a show."

The judge put two fingers in his mouth and whistled, and a moment later four burly kennel attendants approached him. "I want that dragon de-flamed and neutered," he ordered.

"You can't do that!" yelled the handler.

The judge pointed to the handler. "Neuter *him* as well!"

The handler picked the dragon up in his arms and aimed him at the four approaching men. "Now!" he hissed, and a sheet of flame spurted out of the dragon's mouth.

"Don't just stand there!" demanded the judge as the attendants drew back. "Get them!"

"Maybe we could all just discuss it like gentlemen," suggested one of the attendants.

"I'm sure we could resolve our differences over a friendly drink," added a second.

"That's it!" bellowed the judge. "I'm having you *all* neutered!"

"Here's what Godzilla and I think of you and your orders!" snapped the handler. He unhooked the leash from the tiny dragon and pointed it at the judge, who took one look at the dragon's hate-filled little eyes, turned, and raced down the road. The dragon spread its wings and was soon in hot pursuit.

"I *like* training classes!" enthused Felina.

Suddenly everyone noticed Mallory's little party.

"Just passing through?" asked one of the attendants.

"Looking for a toy dragon, actually," replied the detective.

"How much are you willing to spend?"

"I don't know," said Mallory with a shrug. "How much is Fluffy worth?"

"You think *we* have Fluffy?" asked Godzilla's handler with a laugh.

"Beats me," said Mallory, pulling her photograph out of his pocket and displaying it. "Do you?"

"Put it away," said the handler. "You won't find a person on Fire Island who doesn't know what she looks like." He waved a hand around the island. "Look to your heart's content. Check every run, every house. Let me know if you find her."

"Perhaps you'll be kind enough to show us around," said Mallory.

The handler nodded, and led Mallory, Jeeves, and Felina on a brief tour of the kennel and pens. There were bold dragons, seeking to terrify the visitors; hungry dragons, begging for small tidbits of food, living or dead; sweet dragons who only wanted to be praised and petted; and even a few cowardly dragons who hung back and refused to leave their asbestos houses, which looked exactly like dollhouses to Mallory's untutored eye. Many of the dragons had companions kenneled with them to keep them happy and placid; they included goats, cats, gryphons, and a very unhappy-looking elf.

"Well?" said Mallory, looking at Felina. "You know her scent. Is she here—or *has* she been here?"

"No, John Justin."

"You're sure?"

She gave him a look of such withering contempt that he decided to accept it as an affirmative.

"Sorry to have put you to the trouble," said Mallory to the handler.

"No problem. I hope you find Fluffy. I'd hate to see a chimera win the show."

Mallory and his team returned to the beach. He stopped by a bait shop, which specialized in water buffalo and moose. It made him wonder just what people went fishing for around here. He asked the proprietor where he could find a pay phone.

"Ain't got one," came the answer. "Got an old cell phone that someone left here. I'll sell it to you for ten dollars."

"Make it five," said Mallory.

"Can't sell you five. Only got the one phone."

"Five dollars."

"Split the difference," said the man. "Nine-fifty and it's yours."

Mallory laid a ten-dollar bill on the desk.

"Got no change," said the man. "I'll have to owe it to you."

He handed the phone to Mallory, who took it outside.

"My, what strong manly hands you have!" crooned the phone in a sultry voice.

Mallory stared at it without saying a word.

"The strong silent type," said the phone. "I *like* that in a man."

"Do you actually work?" asked Mallory.

"Try me, Big Boy," said the phone.

Mallory began tapping out Brody's number.

"Oh my! Oh my! *Oh my!*" moaned the phone.

"Are you all right?" said Mallory when he had one more number to enter.

"Oh, yes, baby!" purred the phone. "Was it good for you, too?"

Mallory looked around to make sure that Felina and Jeeves weren't paying any attention, then tapped in the last number.

"Any ransom demands yet?" he asked when Brody picked up the receiver.

"None," came the answer. "Are you making any progress?"

"We've eliminated Fire Island, if that counts."

"Where are you going next?"

"I haven't decided," said Mallory. "I'll have a quick powwow with your assistant and make up my mind, then check in with you when I get back to Manhattan."

He broke the connection and was about to rejoin his companions when a single shot rang out and a bullet buried itself in the wall about an inch to the left of his head.

"What happened?" asked Jeeves.

"What the hell does it look like?" said Mallory, scanning the darkness. "Felina, did you see anything?"

"Yes, John Justin."

"What?"

"Someone tried to kill you," she said. Suddenly she frowned. "It's early in the evening for killing. I wish they'd wait a few hours."

"Thanks for that note of loyalty," muttered Mallory. "Did you see anything else?"

"I saw the cutest, fattest little bird . . ."

"Never mind." Mallory began walking, then suddenly stopped. "You two go ahead to the launch. I'll join you in a minute."

"Ah!" said Jeeves knowingly. "A sudden call of Nature. Discretion is my middle name."

"Felina is *my* middle name," said the cat-girl proudly.

"I thought it was your first name," said Jeeves.

"It is. I like it so much I use it for *all* my names."

Then they walked around a corner. Mallory waited for a moment, then cleared his throat.

"All right," he said without raising his voice. "I know you were watching. Who took that shot at me?"

"You must know by now that it is against my nature to reveal such things to you," said the Grundy's disembodied voice.

"You want me to find this damned dragon or not?" said Mallory irritably. "I won't be of much use with a bullet in my head."

"I made the assassin miss," said the Grundy. "That should constitute enough help."

"Did you kill him?" asked Mallory.

"Certainly not."

"Then he'll probably try again."

"Well, you *are* in a dangerous profession," said the Grundy.

"You could make it less dangerous if you'd just—"

"This interview is at an end," interrupted the Grundy, his voice fading on the wind.

"Thanks a lot," said Mallory bitterly. He began walking toward the boat, then realized he was still holding the cell phone and put it in his pocket.

"It's dark and stuffy in here!" complained the phone.

"Be quiet," said Mallory.

"I thought I meant something to you," whined the phone. "I thought we shared something beautiful."

"We shared a phone call," said Mallory. "If you'll shut up and stop bothering me, someday we may share another one."

"Go ahead!" cried the phone. "Break my heart! See if I care!"

"You don't have a heart," said Mallory. "You're a telephone."

"I know which of us doesn't have a heart," said the phone. "Just you wait. Someday you'll need me, someday it'll be a matter of life and death, and maybe I'll put your call through and maybe I won't."

"I'm starting to remember why I don't like cell phones."

"Go ahead, insult me," said the phone. "Cast me aside now that you've had your way with me. I'm never speaking to you again."

"I can live with that," said Mallory, increasing his pace to join Felina and Jeeves just before they all climbed onto the launch.

"Hey, Good-Looking," said the phone. "Want to dial one more number, just for old times' sake?"

"What was that?" said Jeeves.

"Don't ask," growled Mallory as the boat left the dock and began making its way back to Manhattan.

"How many fish are in a river, John Justin?" asked Felina, leaning far over the side of the boat.

"Lots."

"How *many*?" she persisted.

"Twenty-seven trillion and eight," said Mallory.

She reached down suddenly. Mallory heard a bite and a gulp, and then she straightened up and smiled at him. "Twenty-seven trillion and seven," she corrected him, and then leaned over the side again.

"*Bon appétit*," said Mallory. He turned to the gremlin. "Tell me again: What is a win at Eastminster worth in prize money?"

"There isn't any prize money," answered the gremlin. "Just a satin rosette and a trophy."

"Is the trophy solid gold?"

"Silver-plated," said Jeeves.

"Something's wrong," said Mallory.

"Yes," said Jeeves. "Someone's stolen Fluffy."

Mallory shook his head impatiently. "There's something wrong with this whole setup."

"I don't understand."

"Somebody just tried to kill me," said Mallory. "You don't risk getting caught for murder or attempted murder for a piece of ribbon and a silver-plated trophy. There's got to be more involved. Lord knows I'm not worth much, but I'm worth more than a ribbon and a trophy."

"Twenty-seven trillion and six," announced Felina.

"I'm lonely," said the cell phone.

Jeeves stared at Mallory's pants. "Is that your gun talking?" he asked.

"I don't carry a gun."

"A detective without a gun—isn't that unusual?" asked the gremlin.

"No," said Mallory. "Walking around in the middle of the night looking for an eleven-inch dragon named Fluffy is unusual. Not carrying a gun is merely eccentric."

"Twenty-seven trillion and fourteen," said Felina.

"You found eight fish on the boat and threw them in?" asked Mallory, surprised.

"No, I caught and ate another."

"Then why is it twenty-seven trillion and fourteen?"

"Because I don't know what comes before twenty-seven trillion and six," answered the cat-girl.

Mallory grimaced. "I'm going to give you a B-plus for that answer. It makes as much sense as anything else this evening."

"Is a B-plus good to eat?" asked Felina.

"Only with mustard and whipped cream," replied the detective.

"Eighty-three trillion and ninety-two!" cried Felina, holding up another fish. Suddenly she frowned and threw it back into the water.

"Too small?" asked Mallory.

"Too dead," she replied. "I like to play with them first."

"Yeah," concurred Mallory, "I can see where the dead ones hardly play at all."

"They cheat," agreed Felina.

"Do me a favor," said Mallory. "You see better in the dark than the rest of us. Go to the back of the boat and see if anyone is following us."

"For two macaws, a parrot, and a musk ox," she replied.

"How about: for not throwing you overboard right now?" said Mallory.

She considered for a moment, then nodded her agreement. "Okay, I'll go look."

"Why do you think we're being followed?" asked Jeeves.

"Someone took a shot at me. Whoever it was knows we've left the island. It makes sense that he has no further business there. If he's following us, maybe we can arrange a little surprise for him when he lands."

"He might not land where we do," said Jeeves.

"And there might be a typhoon in the next thirty seconds," said Mallory. "I can only plan for what I can control."

"I thought contingency plans were for what you *couldn't* control," said the phone.

"Once upon a time I thought so too. I even thought cell phones couldn't talk. You live and learn." Mallory turned and walked to the back of the boat. "Anyone following us?" he asked Felina.

"Just the swimmer," said the cat-girl.

"Swimmer?" repeated Mallory. "Where?"

She pointed to a spot in the water.

"Stop the boat!" snapped Mallory.

The boat came to a halt.

"Now where is he?"

"He's a she," said Felina.

"Okay, where is *she?*"

"She'll reach us in another minute," said Felina, pointing to a spot about two hundred yards distant. Mallory peered into the darkness and finally saw a steady ripple in the water, a ripple that was clearly approaching them.

In another thirty seconds he could make out the shape of a muscular woman, her arms and legs covered with grease, her bathing cap sporting a British Union Jack, swimming directly toward the boat.

"Avast there!" said a strong female voice. "Are you from the *Match?*"

"I beg your pardon?" said Mallory.

"The *Paris Match*," she said. "You know—the newspaper!"

"I'm afraid not."

"Damn!" said the swimmer, who now came up alongside the boat. "Well, do you see any members of the press in the area?"

"There's nothing in the area except us," said Mallory.

"And twenty-seven trillion and seventy-three fish," added Felina helpfully.

"Were you expecting the press?" continued Mallory.

"Of course," said the woman. "Whenever you swim the English Channel, you expect the press to greet you at the other end."

"The English Channel?" repeated Mallory.

"All right, all right," she said irritably. "I know I went a little off course, but they set me straight at Brisbane."

"Not as straight as you think," said Mallory. "This is New York."

"Are you quite sure?" she asked. "It smells just like Liverpool."

"Not as sure as I was when I first arrived here," answered Mallory. "But pretty sure."

"Damn!" said the woman. "I'm getting really tired of all this swimming."

"Let me give you a hand into the boat."

"Oh, I couldn't do that," she replied. "Not at all cricket. Hardly the British thing to do." She paused. "Well, I must be off. Treading water is a total waste of energy. Is Maggie Thatcher still the prime minister?"

"I'm afraid not," said Mallory.

"What a shame! What Brit does Ronald Reagan confide in these days?"

"Hardly anyone since he died," replied Mallory.

"My goodness!" she said. "Who's left to face the Soviet Union? I'd best be off immediately," she said. "I'll stay in France only long enough to give the press their interviews and have dinner at Maxim's, and then, if we haven't subdued the Falkland Islands yet, maybe I'll swim down there and lend a hand."

"Is there anything I can do for you?" said Mallory.

"Apologize to the New York press for me," she said, starting to swim away. "I hate to disappoint them, but I really must get to France. I hope they have a soufflé at Maxim's; I'm getting rather tired of fish."

"Those are *my* fish!" Felina yelled after her, but she was already out of earshot.

"Every time . . ." said Mallory.

"Every time?" repeated Jeeves curiously.

"Every time I think I'm starting to understand this Manhattan, something like that happens."

"*This* Manhattan?"

"Never mind. If I try to explain, we'll both wind up with headaches."

"*I* don't have a headache, darling," said the cell phone.

"I thought we weren't on speaking terms," said Mallory.

"I forgive you," said the phone.

"Hey!" hissed Felina, staring angrily at Mallory's pants. "It's *my* job to forgive him!"

"Lose the bimbo," said the phone. "I'll be waiting for you."

They reached shore in another few minutes, and Mallory pulled out the phone.

"I want the same number I dialed before," he said.

"Kiss me first," said the phone.

"I haven't got time for this nonsense."

"No kiss, no call," pouted the phone.

Mallory put the phone back in his pocket and walked into a nearby drug store.

"You got a phone?" he asked the goblin behind the counter.

"Hey!" said the cell phone. "*I'm* a phone!"

"I want one that doesn't talk back," said Mallory.

"Wouldn't you rather have a condom?" asked the goblin, staring at Mallory's pants.

"No," said Mallory.

"You sure?" persisted the goblin. "I've never heard one of them talk before. If you're on friendly enough terms to have a conversation with it, the least you can do is protect it."

"Just a phone."

"We got blueberries, orangeberries, redberries," said the goblin. "We got phones that play the Star-Spangled Banner when they ring, we got phones that cast a holographic image of Voluptuous Vanessa doing her specialty act (with or without the snake), we got phones that play the fourth quarter of the 1967 Super Bowl, we got—"

"I don't want to *buy* a phone," said Mallory, struggling to get a word in edgewise. "I just want to *borrow* one."

The goblin stared at him. "How do I know you'll bring it back?"

"I'm not taking it anywhere. I just need to use it right now."

"That's what they all say," replied the goblin. "Then they call Madam Bolero's House of Spanish Pleasures in Madrid and I'm stuck with the bill."

"I want to make a local call."

"Madrid isn't local."

"I'm not calling Madrid."

"You're not?" said the goblin. "Are you sick or something?"

"Something," answered Mallory, trying to control his impatience.

"All right," said the goblin, placing an old-fashioned dial phone on the counter. "Give me ten dollars and you can make a one-minute call."

"That's extortionate," said Mallory.

"That's business," replied the goblin with a smile.

"Are you open to a counteroffer?"

"Sure."

"One dollar for ten minutes."

"Out of the question," said the goblin.

"You're quite sure?" said Mallory.

"How dumb do I look?" said the goblin.

"Don't ask." He turned to the door. "Felina! Come in here." The cat-girl entered the store. "Would you like a new toy to play with?"

She grinned and nodded.

Mallory gestured to the goblin. "Here it is."

"On second thought, a dollar for ten minutes is a perfectly reasonable price," said the goblin quickly.

Felina took a step toward him.

"What the hell," said the goblin, standing absolutely motionless, "friends don't charge friends. Use it for free."

Felina took another step.

"I'll pay *you* a dollar a minute!" said the goblin desperately.

"I call that damned generous of you," said Mallory, picking up a phone. "Felina, stay right where you are." He dialed Brody's number.

"Yeah?" said Brody.

"This is Mallory again. Anything yet?"

"Still no," said Brody.

"Well, stay by your phone, though I'll be damned surprised if you actually get a ransom demand."

"Will do," said Brody.

Mallory broke the connection and handed the phone back to the goblin, who was trying unsuccessfully to ignore the fact that Felina was standing six inches from him and smiling hungrily.

"Are you sure you don't want it, old friend?" said the goblin. "Just say the word and it's yours—gratis."

"I'll cut my throat if you say yes," threatened the cell phone.

"Don't tempt me," muttered Mallory. He walked to the door. "Come on, Felina."

They walked out into the night. There was a cold wind and a few stray snowflakes, and most of the buildings were closed for the night. Jeeves was waiting for them outside the drugstore. "I assume he hasn't been contacted?" said the gremlin.

The detective shook his head. "I never thought he would be. I just had to make sure." He paused. "Well, where to next?"

Jeeves lowered his head in thought. "I'll have to give it some thought. We just eliminated the most likely place for dragons."

"You know," remarked Mallory, "it occurs to me that the very best way to hide something is to keep it in plain sight. I think I read that in a Sherlock Holmes story."

"I have a difficult time believing that would work with elephants or tubas," said the gremlin.

"No," said Mallory. "But I have a feeling I know where it'll work with an eleven-inch dragon."

"Where?" asked Jeeves.

"Where almost everyone has a small animal as a familiar."

The gremlin looked completely mystified.

"Next stop: Greenwitch Village," said Mallory.

CHAPTER 7

9:21 PM–9:48 PM

Mallory and his two companions emerged from the subway platform and stood in the chilly night air, staring at their surroundings.

"There must be two hundred coffee shops," commented Jeeves. "Do you come here often?"

"Not when I can help it," replied Mallory.

"And it's really filled with witches and the like?" asked the gremlin nervously.

Mallory nodded and pointed across the street, where an ogre had just emerged from a supermarket with a slab of raw, blood-covered meat under his arm. He turned left, almost bumped into a zombie, they growled at each other, and then they continued on their ways.

"I don't like it here," said Jeeves nervously.

"Neither do I," said Mallory. "Still, I don't suppose it's any worse than Greenwich Village back in my Manhattan."

"*I* like it," said Felina, sniffing the air. "There are lots of little animals here. Fat little, tasty little, juicy little animals."

"Most of those little animals aren't what they seem," said Mallory.

"If they're big animals in disguises, there'll just be that much more to eat," said Felina.

"Just stay close," said Mallory.

"What do we do now?" asked Jeeves.

"Now we hunt up someone who can help us," said Mallory, walking down a street that led him deeper into the Village.

After they'd gone a block, a goblin stuck his head out from between two decrepit buildings.

"*Pssst!*"

"We're not buying any," said Mallory.

"But you don't know what I'm selling," said the goblin.

"Whatever it is, we don't want any."

"Not even the hottest pornography ever printed?" said the goblin.

"Go away," said Mallory.

"Uh . . . let's not be too hasty," said the cell phone. "Ask how much he wants for it?"

"For you, seventy-three dollars," said the goblin.

"That's outrageous!" said the cell phone.

"Okay, keep your shirt on," said the goblin. "Since it's after closing time, thirty-four dollars."

"Forget it," said Mallory.

"And because it's Valentine's Day, I'll knock the price down to four dollars. Share it with a loved one." The goblin paused. "In fact, you'd better bring her along."

"Why?" asked Jeeves curiously.

"It'll take two people to carry it."

"A porn book?"

"Well, it's disguised as the Oxford Dictionary," said the goblin. "But all you have to do is pick out the right words and put them in the proper order, and *voilà!* you've got something that'll be even more outrageous than *Fanny Hill*, *The Autobiography of a Flea*, and even *The Congressional Record*."

Mallory turned to Jeeves. "Let's go."

"*Wait!*" cried the gremlin. "I've got a nude Raquel Welch calendar!"

"She never posed for one," said Jeeves.

"Triple your money back if I'm lying."

"Let me see it," said Jeeves.

The goblin held up a calendar with a photo of a dumpy redhead who was working on her second half-century.

"And that's supposed to be Raquel Welch?" demanded Jeeves.

"Absolutely."

"They ought to arrest you for fraud."

"I never said it was *the* Raquel Welch," said the goblin defensively. "It's *a* Raquel Welch. In fact, she was my fifth grade geography teacher before she became Raquel Glubowitz."

"Are you quite through annoying us now?" asked Mallory.

"Hey, Mac," said the goblin. "This is a capitalist society. I'm simply fulfilling my function."

"Fulfill it with someone else," said Mallory, starting to walk off again.

"Sex toys from Paris!" cried the goblin.

Mallory turned and glared at him.

"Well, *sept* toys, actually," said the goblin, "but *sex* sounds so much better, don't you think? And this way I get to toss in the seventh toy for free.

"Felina?" said Mallory.

"Yes, John Justin."

"If he says another word, kill him."

"Socialist!" screamed the goblin, darting between two buildings and vanishing from sight.

"Are the goblins this annoying in the Manhattan you come from?" asked Jeeves.

"Yes," replied Mallory. "But we don't call them goblins back there."

He commenced walking again, studying the signs as he passed a row of shops, and finally came to a halt.

"Madame Fatima's," he read. "Spells, curses, hexes, and conjurations." He shrugged. "First store in the whole block that isn't offering either cappuccino or erotic massages."

"You didn't read the small type," said Jeeves, pointing to it.

"Well, let's get on with it," said Mallory, reaching for the door.

"Are you sure you don't want to reconsider?" asked Jeeves nervously. "After all, she's a witch."

"Who better to tell us if someone's passing Fluffy off as a familiar?" said Mallory, entering the storefront, followed by Jeeves and Felina.

A gorgeous brunette with an hourglass figure and a revealing black satin gown emerged from a back room to greet them.

"Welcome to Madame Fatima's, John Justin Mallory," she said.

"I hate her already," whispered the cell phone.

"You've been here before," said Jeeves to Mallory.

"Never."

"Then how does she know who you are?"

"Madame Fatima sees all and knows all," replied the witch. Suddenly she frowned. "Unless it comes up muddy at Belmont. Then I'm only thirty percent accurate." She stared at Mallory. "I intuit that you've bet on Flyaway sixty-one times in a row." She stifled a guffaw. "You're a very slow learner."

"It's only fitting," offered Felina. "Flyaway's a very slow runner."

"I'm not here about horses," said Mallory. "I'm after a dragon."

"Try the Yellow Pages," said Madame Fatima. "I understand there are a lot of hobby breeders in Westchester."

"Don't go understanding me so fast," said Mallory. "I'm a detective, here on a case."

"I knew that," said Madame Fatima. He stared at her. "Sort of," she added lamely.

"A toy dragon's been stolen, and I have to find it and return it to its rightful owner by tomorrow afternoon."

"All this fuss is because some kid lost a toy?" she demanded.

"By definition a toy dragon is a dragon that's less than twelve inches at the shoulder," said Mallory. "This one happens to be the favorite for Eastminster."

"Ah! Now I understand," said Madame. "All I'll need is one of the dragon's scales."

"I don't have one."

"A tooth, perhaps?"

"No."

"Are you sure you wouldn't rather have some cappuccino and an erotic massage?"

"No."

"Have you at least got a photograph?"

Mallory produced it.

"Ugly little bastard, isn't he?" remarked Madame Fatima.

"Fluffy is absolutely beautiful!" snapped Jeeves.

"Fluffy?" she said, stifling another guffaw. "A *dragon*?"

"The most beautiful, feminine dragon in the world," said Jeeves. "Her eyes are—"

"Save it," said Madame Fatima. "All dragons look alike."

"I beg your pardon!" snapped Jeeves.

She sighed. "How many eyes has it got?"

"Two."

"Wings?"

"Two."

"Legs?"

"Four."

"Well, there you have it," she said. "You've seen one dragon, you've seen 'em all." She turned to Mallory. "What exactly do you want me to do for you?"

"See if anyone's shown up with a dragon today, probably claiming that it's a familiar," answered the detective.

"Twenty bucks," said Madame Fatima, holding her hand out.

Mallory dug into his pocket, pulled out a pair of tens, and handed them to her.

"I'll toss in the massage for five more," she said.

"Just the dragon."

She shrugged, then lit a pair of candles, closed her eyes, and began uttering a chant in a language Mallory couldn't identify. She spun around three times, stood rigid for a full minute, and finally opened her eyes.

"Well?" asked Mallory.

"There are fifty-seven familiars appearing as dragons just within a mile of us," she answered. "At least thirty of them are small enough to be the one you're after."

"How many of them showed up today?"

"It doesn't work that way," replied Madame Fatima. "A familiar can take any shape it desires. So it might well have been a banshee or a harpy yesterday and a dragon today."

"So if you tell me that there are a dozen, or twenty, dragons that weren't here yesterday . . ."

". . . they may well have been here yesterday in different forms," concluded Madame Fatima. "I suppose you'll have to check them out one by one."

"I haven't got time to track all of them down," said Mallory. "Besides, this is just a hunch. Fluffy might not be in Greenwitch Village at all. I just thought passing her off as a familiar made sense."

"Bring me a scale, and I'll pinpoint her whereabouts," said Madame Fatima.

"If I could pick one of her scales off her, I'd know her whereabouts," said Mallory.

"Well, yes, there *is* that," acknowledged Madame Fatima.

"Thanks for your time," said Mallory, "but we'd better get back to work."

"Let me give you a tip," said the witch.

He looked at her questioningly.

"Talk to Blind Boris."

"Blind Boris?"

"They call him the Wizard of Christopher Street. You can usually find him on the corner of Christopher and Remorse."

"Thanks," said Mallory.

"Let me give you another tip."

"I'm all ears."

"Stop betting on Flyaway if you want to stay out of the poorhouse."

As they were leaving, Jeeves stopped in front of a small gilt-framed photo on a counter and stared at it.

"Is something wrong?" asked Madame Fatima.

"No," said Jeeves. "There's just something very familiar about this fat ugly old lady. I was wondering where I've seen her before."

Madame Fatima picked up a cappuccino cup and hurled it at his head, barely missing him.

"What was *that* for?" demanded Mallory.

"I won't be insulted in my own establishment!" she snapped.

"What are you talking about?"

"*This*," she said, gesturing up and down her lithe, sexy body, "is my business outfit. *That*," she continued, "is the real me!"

"I'm sorry," said Jeeves.

"Well, you'd damned well better be!" she snapped, as her face and body began to broaden, wrinkle, and droop. "Now get out of here while I regain my self-control."

Mallory held the door open for Jeeves and Felina. As they left, he turned to Madame Fatima.

"He didn't mean any harm," said the detective.

"They never do," she replied, a single tear trickling down a pudgy cheek. "But it hurts just the same."

Then he was out on the street with his companions.

"I know it's a rare commodity around here," he said to Jeeves, "but try to display a little tact, will you?"

"What do I know about tact?" answered the gremlin. "My entire life has been devoted to dragons."

"What happens when you enrage a dragon?"

"It attacks you," said Jeeves.

"Same thing with a woman," said Mallory. "See that you remember it." He paused. "All right, let's get over to Christopher Street."

"Have you heard of this Blind Boris before?" asked Jeeves.

"No," said Mallory. "But how hard can it be to spot a blind wizard on the corner of Christopher and Remorse?"

They began walking, and soon came to a street filled with painters and paintings.

"An art fair," observed Jeeves. "But no one seems very excited about it."

"They have about three hundred a year down here in the Village," said Mallory. He looked around. "Where the hell did she go this time?"

"Felina?" asked Jeeves.

"Yeah," said Mallory, looking down the crowded sidewalk.

"Hey, mister," said a young bearded man in a paint-spattered smock. "Does *this* belong to you?"

He dragged Felina up to Mallory.

"She's mine," he acknowledged, staring at her suddenly multicolored face. "What the hell happened?"

"I was painting the most glorious bald eagle . . ." began the bearded man.

"It wasn't real!" muttered Felina.

"And she pounced on it and tried to eat it."

"It was a cheat!" said Felina.

"It was a cinch for the Nobel Prize before she ruined it," complained the man.

"They don't give a Nobel Prize for art," said Mallory.

"They certainly do!" said the young man heatedly. "Every year Harvey Nobel gives a prize for the best avian painting."

"I stand corrected."

"And now your cat-thing has ruined my masterpiece," continued the young man. "I want restitution. Failing that, I demand that you buy my painting." He frowned. "Though it's only worth about ten dollars now that it's all smeared."

Just then a small white-haired woman walked up to him and handed him a blue ribbon.

"What's this for?"

"My name is Hortense Picasso," she said, "and I'm awarding you the prize for the Best Nonrepresentational Painting. I love the way you incorporated the easel and the sidewalk into your art, to say nothing of the cat-girl."

She turned and walked away, leaving the surprised artist clutching his ribbon. Finally he turned to Mallory. "I guess we can forgo the restitution," he said. "And if you want to purchase the painting, it's twelve thousand dollars now. I'll toss in the easel and the sidewalk for free."

"You keep the painting, I'll keep the cat-girl," said Mallory.

"Deal," he said, walking back to his display.

"You think you can stay by my side and keep out of trouble for the next few minutes?" Mallory asked Felina.

"Yes, John Justin," she said.

"You're sure?"

"No, John Justin."

He grimaced. "Serves me right for not settling for the answer I wanted."

They walked two more blocks, turned right, and soon found themselves at the corner of Christopher and Remorse, where they saw half a dozen people lined up in front of a makeshift booth. Inside it a small, slender man, wearing dark glasses and a suit that had seen better decades, was speaking briefly to each of them.

"Get in line," said a woman irritably as Mallory approached the booth. He did as she said, and was joined by Jeeves and Felina.

The flow of advice from the raggedy man seemed to cover all subjects.

"Tell her you're sorry and buy her at least half a pound of chocolates."

"Sell Anaconda Copper short and take a spread on Worldwide Wickets."

"Next time try a two-iron instead of a three-wood, and watch out for the sand trap just beyond the dogleg."

"Not a good enough base at Aspen this year. Go to Barbados instead."

"Flyaway? You've got to be kidding!"

"The Dusenburg is a nice automobile, but for your needs I recommend a Tucker."

Suddenly Mallory was first in line.

"Well, bless my soul, it's John Justin Mallory, the famous detective!" said Blind Boris.

"How do you know that?" asked Mallory.

The raggedy man smiled. "What's the point of being a wizard if I *don't* know who I'm talking to?"

"You're solving everyone else's problems," said Mallory. "Can you take a shot at mine?"

"Yours is a little more complex than doping out the market or choosing the right club to use at Pebble Beach," said Blind Boris. "But buy me something to drink and we'll discuss it."

"What would you like?"

"Anything but cappuccino," said the Wizard of Christopher Street.

"Whiskey for me and coffee for my friends here," said Boris as the four of them sat down at a small table.

"Make that two coffees and one cream," said Mallory.

"You mean one with cream and one without?" asked the waiter.

"I mean what I said: two cups of coffee, one cup of cream."

The waiter shrugged and went to transmit his order to the bartender, as Mallory surveyed his surroundings. He'd been in taverns that had paintings of nudes over the bar before, but this was the first one that displayed a nude with four breasts, four eyes, an eagle's beak, and one leg. He'd been in bars that had fish on display in a tank, too, but until now he'd never seen one with a bunch of four-inch-tall men playing water polo. Finally, he'd been in many bars that catered to a mixed clientele, but as he surveyed horns, tails, hooves, and snouts, he concluded he'd never seen quite as mixed a clientele as this bar possessed.

At last, he turned back to Blind Boris. "So is Fluffy being hidden as a familiar?" he asked.

"*Fluffy?*" said Boris. "What a name for a dragon!"

"I didn't name her," said Mallory. "I'm just trying to find her."

"She's not posing or being presented as a familiar, and she's not in Greenwitch Village," said Boris.

"Okay, she's not here and she's not being passed off as a familiar," said Mallory. "What else can you tell me?"

"That you've got yourself a complex problem."

Mallory nodded. "Trying to find a dragon the size of a cat in a city of eight million with a twenty-hour deadline. I know."

"You don't begin to know," said Blind Boris. "Everything is not as it seems."

"You want to explain that?"

"I just did," answered Boris. "Everything is not as it seems."

"How about a more useful explanation?"

Boris frowned. "How about: There are enigmas inside of puzzles inside of riddles?"

"That's even less helpful," said Mallory.

"My fault," said Boris. "I did it wrong. How about: There are riddles inside of puzzles inside of enigmas?"

"You start making a little more sense or that's the only drink I'm buying you," said Mallory as the waiter arrived with coffee for himself and Jeeves, whiskey for Boris, and a cup of cream that Felina began slurping noisily.

"I'm *trying*, damn it!" snapped Boris. "But I have to obey the rules of the Wizards' Guild. I *am* Third Vice President of the Lower South Manhattan Chapter, after all."

"Does the Wizards' Guild tell you to sound mystical and all-knowing and not say a thing worth listening to?"

"In essence," answered Boris. "They never do anything directly. It would spoil the mystique."

"I noticed you didn't have any trouble giving straight answers to all the people who were in line ahead of me," complained Mallory.

"They had simple problems, so I gave them simple answers."

"What is so fucking complex about *my* problem?" demanded Mallory. "A dragon was stolen. I'm trying to get it back."

"Ah . . . but *why* was it stolen, and by whom?" replied Boris. "The only logical reason to steal it would seem to be for ransom, yet no demands for ransom have been made."

"How do you know?"

"I'm a wizard. I know almost everything."

"Almost?" repeated Mallory.

"I still don't know why all the elevators arrive at once, or how to open a childproof bottle, or why Fifi Malone refuses to hop into the sack with me . . . but I know almost everything else."

"Including who stole Fluffy?" persisted Mallory.

"I said *almost*," replied Boris.

"I think I want my drink back," said Mallory.

Boris clutched his glass. "I'll make a deal with you, Mallory," he said. "If I give you three hints, will you buy me another drink and stop hassling me?"

"Three clues for one drink?"

"I said *hints*, not *clues*."

"What's the difference?" asked Mallory.

"Clues are tangible."

Mallory stared at him for a long moment. "Deal," he said at last.

"Fine," said Boris.

There was a momentary silence.

"Well?" said Mallory.

"I didn't hear you order the drink."

"I didn't hear the clues."

"Hints, damn it."

"I didn't hear them either."

"Okay," said Boris. "Your first hint is the literature of the unshaven."

"What?"

"You heard me: the literature of the unshaven."

"That's *it?*" demanded Mallory. "That's the whole clue?"

"Hint, not clue."

"And it really has something to do with the case I'm on?"

"Of course."

"What the hell does it mean?"

"That would be telling," replied Boris. "And we wizards always put a little spring on the ball."

"You mean 'spin.'"

"I know what I mean."

"I'll be damned if *I* do," said Mallory, thinking about the first hint. "All right, what's the next one?"

"I gave you one as a sign of good faith," said Boris. "Now I want my next drink."

Mallory signaled to the waiter and ordered it.

"Thank you," said Boris. "You next hint is: All is not gold that glitters."

"Are you giving me hints or platitudes?" said Mallory irritably.

"What's the difference as long as they're valid?" retorted Boris.

"Fine. What's the third one?"

"After my drink arrives and I taste it to make sure you're not duping a trusting old man with flavored water."

Mallory stared at Blind Boris. "You know," he said, "I liked you about five minutes ago."

"I have that effect on people."

"But right now I'd like to strangle you."

"I have *that* effect, too," said Boris. "Usually on attractive women."

"I get the distinct impression that all they have to be is alive," said Mallory.

"Well," replied Boris, "it's a start."

The waiter arrived and handed Boris his drink. He took a sip, uttered a satisfied "Ahhh!" and put the glass down.

"My third hint?" said Mallory.

"What's three inches long, possessed of a minimum of eight legs, and has a painful bite?"

"That's my hint?"

"No," said Boris. "That's what just started crawling up my leg." He reached down and brushed it off. "Okay, Mallory, your hint is as follows: four plus nine times two minus one divided by five."

"That's *it?*" demanded Mallory. "That's my last clue?"

"Your last *hint*," said Boris. "And don't sound so annoyed. There's more to it than you think."

"There damned well better be," muttered Mallory.

A tall cadaverous man dressed all in black entered the bar with a raven on his shoulder. The bird took one look at Felina, who stared at it with rapt attention, and uttered a single word: "Nevermore."

"Nice bird," cooed Felina. "Pretty bird. Pudgy bird."

"Nevermore," repeated the raven as a note of desperation crept into its voice.

"Cute bird," said Felina getting to her feet. "Plump bird."

"Uh . . . boss?" said the raven nervously.

"Tasty bird."

"Boss, either turn around and walk right back out, or at least change me into a Rottweiler," said the raven.

The tall man turned to Mallory. "Can't you control your familiar?"

"I haven't got a familiar," said Mallory.

"*Oh, shit!*" cried the raven. It began flapping its wings, and took flight just before Felina launched herself through the air at it.

"*Nevermore!*" it screamed as it flew out the door.

The cadaverous man glared at Felina, uttered an obscenity, and went out after his familiar.

Mallory stared disgustedly at the cat-girl. "I'm starting to understand why Winnifred always suggests you come with me whenever we split up."

"She's right, John Justin," said Felina with a happy smile. "I would have saved you."

"From the animated corpse?" said Mallory. "I doubt it."

"From the bird," she corrected him.

"I'll give you a fourth hint, on the house," said Blind Boris.

"What is it?" asked Mallory.

"Put that damned cat-girl on a leash before she gets you into even more trouble than you're facing."

"I'm not facing any trouble."

"The night's young yet," said the Wizard of Christopher Street.

Mallory checked his watch as they walked out of the tavern.

"We're due to meet Winnifred in twenty minutes," he announced. "We'd better get up to Central Park." He raised his voice. "Unless someone would like to make my life easier and tell me where the damned dragon is."

"Making your life easy is not part of my job description," said the Grundy's disembodied voice.

"What was that?" asked Jeeves nervously.

"The owner of tomorrow's likely winner, if we don't find Fluffy," replied Mallory.

"Then he must be the culprit," said Jeeves.

Mallory shook his head. "No, he's not."

"*That's* a relief!" said Jeeves. "How do you get something back from the Grundy if he doesn't want to release it?"

"He's not a bad guy for someone who's Evil Incarnate," said Mallory. He raised his voice again. "But he could be a little more helpful."

He thought he heard an amused chuckle floating on the cold night air, but there was no reply.

"Where the hell's the subway?" asked Mallory. "I must have gotten turned around."

"We *did* walk a few blocks before we found the wizard," said Jeeves.

"*I* know where it is," offered Felina.

"Okay, where?" said Mallory.

She smiled. "I'm hungry."

"What else is new?" said the detective.

"I'll lead you for three sardines, a goldfish, a blue jay, and a hipponoceros."

"I think I'll just ask the first person I see," countered Mallory. An unkempt young man whose nose was crusted with white powder and whose eyes possessed wall-to-wall pupils staggered past. "Okay, the second person," Mallory amended.

A little old lady wearing a woolen shawl around her head and shoulders approached them, carrying a basketful of poppies in bloom.

"Excuse me, ma'am," said Mallory. "Could you tell me where to find the subway?"

"I didn't know it was lost," she said, uttering a toothless cackle at her own joke. "Just go past the art fair and the folksinging fair. Then turn right at the drug fair, left at the sex fair, and when you come to the panhandlers' fair you're there."

"I saw the art fair," said Mallory, "but I don't remember all those others."

"Ah," she said, nodding her head knowingly. "You probably turned left at the Young Republican."

"There's a Young Republicans fair?" asked Mallory, surprised.

"No, just a Young Republican," she replied. "Unless a second one has moved into the Village."

Then she was gone, and Mallory and his little group made their way to the subway entrance, took an escalator down to the platform, and waited for the train to arrive.

"Uh . . . what are *those?*" asked Jeeves nervously, pointing to a trio of dark, hulking shapes some fifty feet away.

"Gnomes of the Subway," said Mallory. "Don't worry about them. They're just scrounging for food."

"Aren't *we* food?" asked the gremlin.

Mallory smiled and shook his head. "They feed on subway tokens."

"Really?"

Mallory nodded. "They damned near starved to death a few years back when the subways were so dangerous almost nobody rode them. But they're both making a comeback these days—the subways and the Gnomes."

A train pulled up, and Mallory and his party got on.

"I've never ridden the Manhattan subway before," remarked Jeeves, looking around. "It's nicer than I thought."

"It's nicer than the ones I grew up with, that's for sure," said Mallory. "There's a dining car, an observation car, even a sleeper car for commuters who are going all the way out to Queens or Brooklyn."

"A sleeper?" repeated Jeeves, frowning. "But Brooklyn can't be forty-five minutes from here."

A couple passed through the car, hand in hand, and Mallory gestured to them. "If truth be known, mighty little sleeping gets done in the sleeper cars. On the other hand, it makes for a very happy commute."

"Oh," said Jeeves.

"Try not to blush," said Mallory. "It doesn't go with green skin."

"By the way, what do you see from the observation car in a subway tunnel?" asked the gremlin.

"You'd be surprised what you can see down here if you know where to look," replied the detective. "Now that we've got a minute or two, tell me a little more about Fluffy."

"What do you want to know?"

"Anything that might prove useful," said Mallory. "For example, how long can she go without food, and if she gets desperate enough, will she eat something besides elephant-shaped chocolate marshmallow cookies?"

Jeeves shrugged. "I don't know. She's been pampered her entire life and never goes more than a few hours without her cookies."

"Okay, how long can an unpampered toy dragon go without food?"

"That depends."

"On what?"

"On what you mean," said Jeeves.

"I thought I was perfectly clear. How long can a toy dragon go?"

"It's not that simple," said Jeeves. "How long can he go before he loses his flame? Before he can't fly? Before he dies?"

"Forget it. Let me try another one. How far can Fluffy fly?"

"With or against the wind currents?"

"Goddammit!" snapped Mallory. "Can't you answer *anything?*"

"I'm trying to," said Jeeves.

Mallory glared at him and remained silent while Felina busied herself looking at all the obscene graffiti scrawled on the door to the next car. A minute later they came to the Central Park stop and left the car, ascended to ground level, and stepped out into the park.

"Where am I?" said a familiar voice.

"Who was that?" asked Jeeves.

"Oh, God! I found him and now I've lost him!" said the cell phone.

"Your pants are talking again," said Felina.

"Mallory?" said the phone. "Is it you? Is it really you?"

"Shut up," said Mallory.

"It *is* you!" cried the phone. "Then it wasn't a dream!" A pause. "Where are we?"

"In Central Park," said Jeeves, staring at Mallory's pants with rapt attention.

"Lift me out of here so I can see," said the phone.

"You don't have any eyes," said Mallory.

"Let *me* worry about that," said the phone.

"If I put you in my lapel pocket and let the top of you stick up an inch over the top, will you be quiet then?"

"Yes, darling."

Mallory withdrew the phone and moved it to his lapel pocket.

"Oh, this is much better!" said the phone.

"Fine."

Suddenly the phone began weeping softly.

"What now?" said Mallory.

"After all we've been to each other, you haven't even asked me my name."

"What's your name?"

"Belle."

"Why am I not surprised?" said Mallory.

"What a team we're going to make!" said Belle.

"If one half of this team says another word before we reach the dragon pond, it's going to get left in the park."

"*She!*" Belle corrected him. "I'm a she, not an it."

"I'll take it under advisement," said Mallory. "Now be quiet." He stood still and surveyed his surroundings.

"Do you know where we're supposed to go?" asked Jeeves.

Mallory nodded. "There's a stable straight ahead. What we want is off to the right."

"It looks deserted that way," remarked the gremlin.

"You'd be surprised," said Mallory.

"Is it dangerous?" asked Jeeves.

"Only to your wallet. We'll be lucky if we run into less than half a dozen goblins selling things nobody could possibly want."

"Actually, if you're going to the dragon pond, there are eight," said a voice from behind them.

Mallory turned and found himself confronting a goblin wearing a loose-fitting karate outfit.

"It's shameful the way they harass innocent passersby," continued the goblin. "I'm surprised you don't hate the entire goblin race."

"*I* hate the entire goblin race," offered Felina happily.

"You see?" said the goblin. "That's what a few thousand bad eggs will do to you."

"You, of course, have nothing to sell us," said Mallory sardonically.

"Only my services," said the goblin.

"Why am I not surprised?" said Mallory.

"I am Chou En-lai Smith, of the Vietnamese Smiths," said the goblin. "Master of karate, kung fu, judo, jujitsu, fisticuffs, kickboxing, and the off-putting snide remark." He proudly gestured to the sash around his waist. "Fifth-level puce belt. Hire me, and I'll rid you of any goblin who accosts you with useless trinkets to sell."

"That's fine," said Mallory. "But who'll rid me of you?"

The goblin threw back his head and laughed. "I admire your sense of humor!"

"I wasn't being funny," said the detective.

"Of course you were," said the goblin. "You *need* me. You don't know it, but lurking ahead is my cousin Hymie, of the Brooklyn Smiths, just waiting to sell you all twelve 1962 issues of *Playboy*, and three of them don't even have their center spreads. Further up the park, lurking under that big tree off to your right, is Billybob, of the Alabama Smiths, preparing to pounce on you and sell you copper-plated fishing hooks."

"Why copper-plated?" asked Mallory, curious in spite of himself.

"They fell out of his pocket into a vat of molten copper when he was rob-bing the Denver mint. By the time he reached them, they weren't the only thing that was copper-plated. If you should ever get in a fistfight with him and I'm not around to save you, watch out for his left."

"Thanks for the tip," said Mallory. "Now go away and leave us alone."

"I thought we were engaging in an honest negotiation!" said the goblin.

"You thought wrong."

"What are you, some kind of bigot?"

"I'm the kind who's not going to hire you," said Mallory.

"Goblin hater!" screamed Smith. "Hey, everyone, we got a goblin hater here!"

Half a dozen goblins suddenly appeared from behind trees and shrubs, brandishing blackjacks and brass knuckles.

"Is that right, Mac?" said one of them. "Do you hate goblins?"

"Just this one," said Mallory, indicating Chou En-lai Smith.

"Oh. Well, that's okay, then," said the goblin, turning his back and walking away. "Can't say that I blame you."

The other goblins all followed suit.

"They're just jealous," said Smith.

"You mean they want to be hated too?" asked Mallory.

"I've a good mind to break your kneecaps, pulverize your Adam's apple, rip your head off, and spit down your neck," said the goblin. "What do you think of that?"

"It sounds messy," said Mallory.

"It does, at that," agreed the goblin. "Maybe I'll just cave your chest in with a spinning kick."

"You're absolutely bound and determined to fight?" asked Mallory.

"Damned straight," said the goblin. "I'll tear you apart. I'll dissect you with such grace and skill that they'll award me both ears and the tail. I'll—"

"Felina?" said Mallory.

The cat-girl moved in front of him and opened her hands. An instant later each finger sprouted a two-inch razor-sharp claw.

"She's my surrogate," said Mallory.

"I don't give a damn about your sex life!" snapped the goblin. "Let's fight!"

"You're fighting *her*."

"I can't hit a girl," said the goblin. "It's against the rules. Everybody knows that."

"Felina," said Mallory, "do you know of any rule that says you can't remove a goblin's face?"

She smiled a predatory smile and shook her head.

"You're sure you want to do this?" demanded Smith. "You're facing the guy who single-handedly stood off a village of three hundred rabid Chinese leprechauns back in Shanghai." He paused. "Of course, it helped that I had a submachine gun and they were unarmed peasants, but still . . ."

Felina took another step toward him.

"All right, cat-thing," said the goblin, "prepare to die!"

He bent over into a fighting stance and suddenly uttered a piercing shriek.

"You aren't going to scare her by screaming," said Mallory.

"That wasn't a scream of attack," rasped the goblin. "It was a scream of pain!"

"Oh?"

"I threw my back out," he moaned. "I can't straighten up."

"Ripping his face off is no fun if he can't fight back," said Felina.

"When did it ever bother you that your prey couldn't fight back?" asked Mallory curiously.

"You're right, John Justin," she said apologetically. "I wasn't thinking clearly. I'll kill him now."

"No!" cried Chou En-lai Smith.

"Some other time," said Mallory to the cat-girl.

"Thank you," said the goblin.

"My pleasure," said Mallory, starting to head off toward the dragon pond.

"You're not going to just leave me here, are you?" demanded the goblin.

"Well, you *were* going to kill me, remember?"

"My passionate nature got the better of me. It was rude of me to want to tear off your head and spit down your neck, and I truly regret mentioning it."

"You're forgiven," said Mallory. "And now we're late for an appointment, so . . ."

"Take me with you!" cried the goblin.

"Like that?" asked Jeeves, who had been a fascinated observer of the little scene.

"Help me straighten up and I'll be fine."

Jeeves walked once around the bent-over goblin. "How would you suggest?" he asked. "I suppose I could put a knee in your back and pull your arms behind you and . . ."

"The cure sounds worse than the problem," complained the goblin.

"Well then," said Jeeves, "I could tie your arms over your head, and hang you from a tree until you stretch out—but I don't have any rope with me."

"Felina," said Mallory, "go straighten him out."

Still smiling, the cat-girl approached Chou En-lai Smith, extended a forefinger, slid it just beneath the point of his chin, and pressed upward—and as she pressed, he straightened up until a few seconds later he was standing erect.

"Thank you," he said. "She's quite a weapon, that cat-thing."

"You just have to know how to aim her," said Mallory.

"So can I come along with you?" asked the goblin.

"What the hell," said Mallory with a shrug. "They've already taken a shot at me. Who knows? I may need two bodyguards before this case is over."

"Case?" repeated the goblin.

"I'm a detective."

"Have you got an oversexed secretary called Velma? I'm told they go with the job."

"No," said Mallory. "I have a partner who's addicted to romance novels and shooting things, an office cat who's a walking appetite, and a magic mirror with an attitude."

"Pity," sympathized the goblin. "What kind of case are we on?"

"We're after a stolen dragon."

"Good!" enthused the goblin. "Finding dragons is one of the very best things I do."

"Right up there with fighting, is it?" said Mallory.

"I won't tease you about not having a Velma, and you don't tease me about my slipped disk, okay?"

"Deal," said Mallory. He checked his watch. "And now we've really got to get going." He began walking toward the dragon pond. "What should we call you?"

"All my friends call me Chou," replied the goblin.

"Joe it is," said the detective.

"Just one moment," said Joe the goblin. He stepped ahead of Mallory and shouted: "This man and his friends are under my protection. Be warned that anyone who threatens or even hinders us faces my fierce and righteous wrath." He turned to Mallory. "Okay, we can go."

"Now?" asked Mallory. "Or should we wait for all the laughter to die down?"

"I think I see it," said Jeeves, peering into the darkness.

"Either that, or someone is playing with matches," said Mallory as small flames briefly darted out.

"Not to worry," said Joe, moving to the front of the procession. "I'll protect you."

"From the pond's attendants, or from my partner?" asked Mallory dryly.

"It's not easy being a superhero," said Joe in hurt tones. "The least you can do is not make fun of me."

"Do you really come from Vietnam?" asked Jeeves.

"Almost," said the goblin.

"Almost?"

"I come from the Vietnamese section of the Bronx," replied Joe.

"That's only a block or two long," noted Mallory.

"Even so, we have our heroes," said Joe.

"For example?"

"Danny Diem," said Joe. "He moved to Hollywood ten years ago. Whenever you see Jet Li or Jackie Chan kicking the shit out of someone, odds are it's Danny."

"Why not root for a winner?" asked Mallory.

"He's from the neighborhood," answered the goblin. "We used to cut classes together and sneak off to watch Slinky Sally and Her Educated Snake at the Rialto."

"Well, that puts a different light on it," said Mallory.

Joe smiled happily. "I knew you'd understand."

"John Justin!" called Winnifred. "Is that you?"

"Yeah," said Mallory, looking around until he spotted her standing near the extensive structure that formed the dragon pond. "Any luck?"

"Not so far," she said. "And you?"

"Well, I know a few places where he isn't."

"And who is this?" asked Winnifred, indicating the goblin.

"Joe En-lai Smith at your service, ma'am," was his response. "Villains defeated, armies destroyed, enemy strongholds laid waste to."

"Forget all that," said Winnifred. "How are you at finding dragons?"

"I don't know," he answered honestly. "I've never lost one."

"I'm glad you're here, John Justin. Let's get on with the inspection."

"Who is this . . . this *female?*" demanded Belle.

"What was that?" asked Winnifred.

"You wouldn't believe me if I told you," said Mallory.

"Try me."

Mallory pulled the cell phone out of his lapel pocket and held it up.

"You're kidding, right?" said Winnifred.

"Do I look like a joke?" demanded Belle.

"The mind boggles with questions," said Winnifred.

"Let's look at the pond," said Mallory. "You can ask them later."

"All right," said Winnifred, opening the front gate and walking through into the large interior. She was followed, in order, by Felina, Jeeves, and Joe.

"Lose the cat-thing and the fat broad, Big Boy," purred Belle as Mallory put her back in his pocket. "I'm all the woman you'll ever need."

"I can't tell you how comforting that is," said Mallory as he closed the gate behind him.

The interior of the pond reminded him of a cross between a kennel and a zoo. There was a row of small runs with tops on them to prevent the small dragons within from flying away . . . but there were also large open areas, filled with trees, ponds, asbestos toys the size of horses, completely fenced off from onlookers, where huge dragons, some fully as large as dinosaurs, were kept. One of them noticed Mallory's little group, opened his mouth, and shot out a flame that would have incinerated them, but it bounced off a transparent fireproof barrier that they hadn't seen in the darkness.

"What stops them from flying away?" Mallory asked Jeeves.

"I don't know," answer the gremlin.

"I thought you were the dragon expert."

"I'm the *toy* dragon expert," explained Jeeves.

"Look," said Joe, pointing to a nearby behemoth's back leg. A chain was attached to it.

"I wonder how they got it on him?" mused Mallory.

"Probably just poured some salt on his tail and that nailed him to the spot for a minute," said Joe.

"I think that only works with fawns, not ten-ton dragons," replied the detective.

"It doesn't work with fawns either," said Winnifred. She raised her voice. "May we please have some help here?"

Suddenly lights came on in a small building at the back of the compound, and a troll emerged wearing a nightshirt.

"We're closed," he said irritably.

"Your gate was open."

"The fact that I'm careless doesn't give you the right to intrude and wake me up," said the troll.

"We have a few questions to ask," said Mallory.

"Come back tomorrow and I'll be happy to answer them."

"We need answers now."

"Well, I need my sleep now," said the troll.

"Joe?" said Mallory. "Can you encourage him to be more helpful?"

The goblin struck a karate pose, moved his hands back and forth rapidly, and uttered some intimidating screams.

"Sorry," said the troll. "I don't speak French."

"I think we're going to go with the old standards," said Mallory. "Felina, if he doesn't answer our questions, he's all yours."

Felina grinned, stepped forward, and displayed her claws. "Please don't answer," she said.

"Perhaps I was being hasty," said the troll promptly. "What do you want to know?"

"We're looking for a dragon that went missing this afternoon. How many new arrivals have you got?"

"Well, let me see," said the troll. "Daisy's back again."

"Daisy?"

"The big girl off to the left. Keeps killing her keepers and coming here because she likes the food we serve." He shook his head sadly. "She could save us all a lot of trouble if she'd just eat her keepers."

"Dragons are clearly thoughtless creatures," said Mallory. "We're not looking for anything like Daisy. We're after a toy dragon that went missing this afternoon. Eleven inches at the shoulder." He pulled out the photo, but it was too dark for the troll to see it.

"Hey, Percy!" yelled the troll. "We could do with a little light."

Another huge dragon, confined about fifty feet away, roared and emitted a brilliant flame that shot out almost to Mallory's group. The troll had time to study the photo before the flame vanished.

"Thanks, Percy," said the troll. "He's my pet," he added confidentially. "Sweetest little fifteen tons of love and devotion you ever saw."

"So did you get a toy dragon in today?" persisted Mallory.

"Got three of 'em, but I don't think yours was one of them."

"Do you mind if we look anyway?" asked Winnifred.

The troll cast a quick sideways glance at Felina, who was staring unblinking at him, her pupils mere vertical slits. "Not at all. Let me point them out to you." He led them to the small runs. "The first three."

Three small dragons walked up to greet the visitors, each with a please-take-me-home-with-you look on its face.

"Well?" said Winnifred to Jeeves.

The gremlin shook his head. "She's not here."

Mallory turned to the troll. "Sorry to have bothered you. Are there any other dragon ponds in Manhattan?"

The troll shook his head. "There's one up in Westchester, and I think New Canaan over in Connecticut's still got one."

"Okay, thanks," said Mallory. His group walked out through the gate. He expected to hear it lock behind him, but when he turned to check he found it swinging open and the light in the troll's building already extinguished.

"Well," said Mallory, "we've eliminated Fire Island, Greenwitch Village, and the dragon pond." He checked his watch. "It's almost eleven, and we're no closer to finding him than when we started."

"Who cares about dragons?" said Belle. "You found me, and that's all that matters."

Winnifred frowned. "We can't stop looking. Where next?"

"I think it makes sense to split up again," said Mallory. "We've got a lot of ground to cover, and only one clue."

"A clue?" she said. "You didn't mention one."

"It's not much of a clue," he said.

"Well?"

"Someone took a shot at me."

"Where were you?" asked Winnifred.

"Out in the open. Easy target. They missed."

"They were lousy shots," said Jeeves.

Mallory stared at the little gremlin for a moment. "Tell him, Winnifred."

"If they wanted to kill him, they'd have taken more than one shot," said Winnifred. "They wanted to scare him off."

"I never thought of that," said Jeeves.

"You're not a detective," said Winnifred.

"Well, nobody had better try again," said Joe. "Or they'll have *me* to answer to."

"I don't believe you heard a word," said Mallory. "They weren't trying to hit me."

"A poor shot could try to miss and bury a bullet between his eyes," said Joe. "You got to think these things through."

"I'll take it under advisement," said Mallory.

"You know," said Winnifred, "there are a number of upscale pet shops on the Upper West Side. No one over there ever goes to bed before two in the morning, so some of the shops may still be open. As long as you have Jeeves, why not give me one of the photos and I'll check them out?"

"She's worth thousands!" protested Jeeves. "Whoever stole her knows that. They won't be selling her for peanuts."

"Not selling her," said Winnifred. "Stashing her until the show's over. Where better than right out in front of everyone?"

"Good idea," said Mallory. "As for me, I think I'd better get back to Seymour Noodnik's and see if he's got any answers for me."

"You think someone sold her as meat?" asked Joe.

Mallory shook his head. "He's finding out what stores carry her favorite food."

"When and where shall we meet?" asked Winnifred.

"One thirty?" suggested Mallory.

"Sounds good," she said. "Where?"

"I don't know where I'll be," said Mallory. "Wait a minute. I'm carrying a cell phone. Call me when you're ready and we'll decide on a place to meet then."

"Fine," said Winnifred. "I'll need the number."

"Belle, what's your number?" said Mallory.

"I'm not telling *her*," said Belle.

"You're telling *me*," said Mallory.

"And then you'll tell her," whined Belle. "You're mine, damn it! I'm not sharing you."

"Joe," said Mallory, "you want a cell phone?"

"*No!*" screamed Belle.

"Then give my partner your number."

"And then we can be together?"

"Until tomorrow, anyway," said Mallory.

"I want more than a one-night stand," said Belle.

"Joe?" said Mallory, pulling the phone out of his pocket.

"But I'll settle!" said Belle quickly. She rattled off her number to Winnifred.

"All right," said Winnifred. "I'll walk to the west side of the park, and then start scouting out the pet shops." She stared at Mallory's entourage. "You're not going to sneak up on anyone with that crowd, John Justin."

"I view it as three alternate targets in case the shooter gets new orders," said Mallory.

"Four," said Belle.

"Four," amended Mallory.

"I'll check in with you in two hours," said Winnifred, heading off into the darkness.

"What if someone attacks that poor old woman in the dark?" asked Joe, staring after her.

"If they do, I feel very sorry for them," said Mallory. "Especially if the emergency rooms are full."

"You're kidding!"

"Am I smiling?" said Mallory.

"That's some partner you've got yourself," said Joe, "if she's able to walk alone through Central Park in the dark."

"She's got the easy job," said Mallory as he began walking south across the grass. "I may need all of you to protect me from Noodnik's notion of salesmanship."

As Mallory's little group approached Seymour Noodnik's Emporium they were greeted by the outraged screams of a woman who was arguing with the proprietor.

"But I don't want brontosaur!" she yelled. "I just want a pound of hamburger!"

"Diplodocus, then," said Noodnik. "Three cents a pound. You can't beat that price anywhere in the city."

"All right, all right," said the woman. "I've got to make Marvin his dinner. Give me a pound, you thief!"

"I can't break up the cut," said Noodnik. "You'll have to take it all."

"How much are we talking about?" demanded the woman. "Two pounds? Two and a half?"

"Eighty thousand."

She stormed out of the store, almost knocking Jeeves over. "I'll be damned if I'll ever shop here again!" she thundered.

"I'll bone it for you," Noodnik shouted after her.

"You're sure this is the place?" asked Joe. "Personally, I wouldn't pay more than two cents a pound for diplodocus, and I'd want it delivered."

"I can tell you're going to be right at home here," said Mallory. He walked to the door and entered the store.

"Any lewd women in the case yet?" was Noodnik's greeting.

"Not yet."

"Any naked ones?"

"I just said—"

"Not all naked ones are lewd," interrupted Noodnik. "And not all lewd ones are naked, though they usually wind up that way. Can I sell you some zebra horns?"

"Zebras don't have horns," said Mallory.

"*This* one doesn't, at least not anymore," said Noodnik as he wiped his hands on his bloodstained apron. "Or better yet, how about some Easter eggs?" He pointed to a nearby carton of eggs in a refrigerated unit.

"They're white," noted Joe.

"That's right."

"So what makes them Easter eggs?"

"They've been sitting there since early last April," answered Noodnik.

Joe made a face, and Noodnik turned back to the detective. "Some dognip for your cat-thing?"

Mallory frowned. "Dognip?"

Noodnik suddenly snapped his fingers. "Damn! I forgot! The cops took Fido away for rabies testing today after he nipped old Mrs. Satterfield."

"Seymour, will you shut up for a minute?" said Mallory.

Noodnik checked his wristwatch. "Okay, you got it. Sixty seconds."

"I'm not here to buy anything."

"Then why are you wasting my time?" demanded Noodnik.

"You were supposed to get some information for me, remember?"

"Of course I remember. Just because I climbed into bed with Troubles McTavish last night instead of the beloved Mrs. Noodnik doesn't mean I have a bad memory," said Noodnik. "A bad sense of direction, maybe . . ."

"Seymour, did you get the information or didn't you?" demanded Mallory.

"Of course I did!" snapped Noodnik. "I'm Seymour Noodnik, aren't I?"

"Are you?" said a shopper with an amused smile. "I heard you telling your wife that you blacked out and thought you were Angus McTavish."

"Well, I had to tell her *something*," said Noodnik.

"Was that before or after she emptied her shotgun into your car?" asked a female shopper.

"Hey!" said Noodnik to the store at large. "Do I pry into *your* private affairs?"

"All the time," came an answer.

"Besides," said another shopper, "what's so private about running down the block with your pants off at three in the morning while your wife is shooting at you?"

"Special on carrier pigeon eggs!" yelled Noodnik, cupping his hands to his mouth. "A dollar a dozen."

Nobody moved.

"Tenderloin steaks, eight cents a pound. Fresh cuts of tenderloin, eight cents a pound."

There was a mad rush to the meat section.

"You were saying?" said Noodnik, turning back to Mallory.

"Are you actually going to honor that price?"

Noodnik grinned. "If they can find it, they can have it at eight cents a pound."

"You haven't changed," said Mallory.

"Just my socks. And maybe my bedmate."

"So who sells elephant-shaped chocolate marshmallow cookies?"

"Buy a dozen pickled bats' wings and we'll talk," said Noodnik.

"I haven't got any time to waste," said Mallory. He turned to the goblin. "Joe?"

Joe En-lai Smith leaped forward, struck a martial arts position, and screamed.

"Is he sick?" asked Noodnik.

"I'm intimidating you, damn it!" snapped Joe.

"You are?" asked Noodnik curiously. "How can you tell?"

Joe screamed again, chopped the air with his fists, and delivered a devastating spinning kick that missed Noodnik by a good eighteen inches.

"Is that the best you can do?" asked Noodnik.

"I'm nearsighted," answered Joe. "There's no call for you to belittle me."

"Why aren't you wearing glasses?"

"It doesn't go with being an action-adventure hero," answered Joe.

"I got a special on 'em," said Noodnik enticingly. "Ten bucks an eye, and the price drops to seven for three or more."

"We're getting off the point here," said Mallory. "Seymour, I'm on a tight schedule. Are you going to tell me what I want to know or not?"

"Are you going to buy a dozen pickled bats' wings or not?" shot back Noodnik.

"What if I report you to the city health inspector?" said Mallory.

"Be my guest," said Noodnik. "He's laid out there with the frozen ham in Aisle Three."

"Men!" snapped a feminine voice. "I'm sick of all your macho threats and posturings!"

"Who was that?" asked Noodnik, looking around.

"Belle, keep out of this," said Mallory. "I have enough problems as it is."

"Belle?" demanded Noodnik. "Who's Belle?"

Mallory pulled the cell phone out of his pocket and held it up "Seymour, say hello to Belle."

"Your phone?"

"Stop looking at me as if I'm just some mere *object*!" demanded Belle.

"But you *are* just some mere object," said Noodnik reasonably.

"Watch your mouth, Mac!" said Belle. Suddenly her voice softened. "God, I love the feel of your hands on me! You want me to solve your problem, Lover?"

"Can you?" said Mallory.

"If he doesn't tell you what you want to know, take me to Mrs. Noodnik. I'll tell her I belong to Troubles McTavish, and I want him to stop calling and talking dirty at all times of the night and day."

"You'd do that to *me*?" demanded Noodnik. "A peaceable, decent guy who'd never hurt a fly. Except for the candied ones in Aisle Seven, that is."

"You heard me," said Belle.

"But what am I going to do with a dozen pickled bats' wings?" complained Noodnik.

"You're a clever man," said Mallory. "You'll think of something. Now my information, please?"

"You know where that new zillion-dollar building is, the one populated by all the rich divorcées and widows with no taste?"

"Are you talking about Frump Tower?" asked Mallory.

"Where else?" said Noodnik.

"On Fifth Avenue, right?" said the detective.

"Right. The fancy gift shop there sells elephant-shaped chocolate marshmallow cookies."

"Anyone else?"

"Do they sell anyone else?" said Noodnik. "How the hell do I know?"

"Does anyone else sell the cookies?"

"Not that I've been able to find. Buy the bats' wings and I'll spend another day looking."

"By tomorrow afternoon it'll be too late," said Mallory.

"Then we're done, and I can go back to making an honest living?"

"Well, we're done, anyway."

"Okay—and thanks for not bringing the cat-thing this time," said Noodnik. "She's always so disruptive."

Which was when Mallory discovered that Felina was nowhere to be seen. He made a beeline to the fish section, found her reaching into a tank where Noodnik kept his prize South Dakota Fighting Fish, pulled her away, and headed for the door.

"She ate seventy-three fish, Mallory," said Noodnik as Mallory was walking out. "I'll add it to your tab."

Mallory stopped and stared at the grocer. "Seymour, I've never seen more than six fish in that tank."

"Today is the commencement of the breeding season," replied Noodnik. "They multiply like crazy. Seventy-three."

"Mallory, have we got time to call Mrs. Noodnik?" asked Belle.

"I suppose so," said the detective.

"How many fish?" said Belle.

"Two," said Noodnik.

Mallory smiled and walked out the door with Felina, followed by Jeeves and Joe.

"Welcome to the team, Belle," he said as the turned left and headed toward Fifth Avenue.

CHAPTER 12

11:20 PM–11:51 PM

Some people said it was a seventy-three-story monument to bad taste. Others said that was an understatement.

It was the glittering self-proclaimed crown jewel of Fifth Avenue, a mostly shining needle piercing the Manhattan sky with an outer epidermis of polished (and occasionally tarnished) brass, a metal the architect seemed to have fallen in love with. The interior decorator, on the other hand, appeared to have an ongoing affair with red flocked wallpaper and cheap Oriental rugs. The shops, selling everything from tasteless lingerie to fake furs to designer knockoffs, all of which could be purchased for a third of the asking price on the Internet or a few blocks away in the garment district, did not seem out of place . . . and neither did the residents.

The builder, who had abandoned his first four wives in pursuit of younger and cheaper bimbos with more impressive silicon implants, was finally visited by an enormous sense of guilt at just about the same time his erectile dysfunction pills finally stopped working. He declared that the policy of the Tower would be to rent only to widows, divorcées, and single women over the age of forty. In fact, its official name was the Brass Edifice, but the press and public got one look at the residents and promptly dubbed it the Frump Tower, a name that stuck despite one lawsuit on the part of the builder and seventeen more brought by various residents. The lawsuits stopped only when the Manhattan press started describing the plaintiffs with a nasty relish usually reserved for Republican politicians and the Boston Red Sox.

As Mallory and his group approached the garish front entrance, the detective noticed two liveried guards bowing obsequiously to a rather dumpy woman who entered ahead of them.

"She must be someone very important," whispered Jeeves.

"I think probably the most important thing about her is that she pays her rent on time and her checks don't bounce," replied Mallory.

The doormen paid no attention as Mallory approached, and remained motionless except to shoot Felina a pair of disapproving glances.

The entire ground floor, as well as the mezzanine, was filled with shops that made every effort to appear exclusive. Most failed miserably. Which is not to say that there were no unique shops (all of which preferred to call themselves "shoppes"), but rather that they were usually unique for the wrong reasons.

The first store they passed was a rental agency, and it rented just a single commodity: butlers. It differed from most of its competitors—Mallory was inclined to think *all* of its competitors, but this Manhattan had conditioned him never to think in absolutes—in that the butlers it was renting were displayed in the store's windows. Not photos of them, or models, but the actual butlers, all standing at attention except for the occasional twitch of an eyebrow or the wrinkle of a nose.

Take Frothingham home with you, said a sign next to a balding butler. *He's brave, loyal, always laughs at your jokes, promises to pinch you when no one's looking, and hardly ever passes out from exhaustion. $75.00 a day takes him away.*

Oglethorpe's the butler for you, said another sign next to another butler. *Charming, articulate, mixes a dynamite vodka martini, death and taxes on dirty carpets and smudged windows, and he's always there with an intimate suggestion whenever your visitors are close enough to overhear.*

Try Reginald! claimed a third sign, this one next to an underweight butler who had clearly seen better days, if not decades. *He cooks, he cleans, he'll scrub your back in the shower, he'll read* Fanny Hill *aloud to you while you're in bed, and best of all, you can feed him for less than $5.00 a day!*

"I want that one," said Felina, pointing to Reginald.

"No you don't," said Mallory.

"Why not?" she asked curiously.

"You're a growing girl, and he'd barely make dessert," answered the detective.

"Then get me two of him," she said after a moment's thought.

"Let's concentrate on finding the cookies," said Mallory, moving on to the next store, which specialized in selling and delivering greeting and holiday cards. There was a huge display of valentine cards in the window, and a discreet sign noting that there was no postage needed because obviously the cards would never leave the building, and delivery could be made within five minutes of the seller receiving a phone call telling him which apartment to deliver them to.

"Now you're *sure* you can deliver them at precisely eleven forty-five tonight?" a dumpy middle-aged woman was asking the man behind the counter.

"Absolutely," he assured her.

"That's seventeen valentines, all addressed to me?"

"Right," said the man. "Six from Secret Admirer, seven from Lovelorn in Brooklyn, three from You Know Who, and one with just a question mark for a signature."

"Okay," said the woman, slapping a pair of fifty-dollar bills on the counter. "I'd better get back to my mahjong game." She lowered her voice. "They think I'm in the bathroom."

"It'll be our secret," the man assured her as she left the store and headed to an elevator.

"Sad," said Belle, from within Mallory's lapel pocket. "Very sad." Then: "Thank God I found you before I was like that."

Mallory looked from the cell phone to the woman and back to the phone. "You were never going to be like that."

"I know," said Belle. "It was fated that we should meet and spend all eternity together."

"Do you have a second topic of conversation?" asked Mallory.

"Sex."

"Forget it."

They passed a bookstore that sold nothing but *Cliff's Notes* and *Reader's Digest*, a dress store that had meticulously removed the first digit from their dress sizes, so that sizes fourteen, sixteen, and eighteen miraculously became four, six, and eight, and a florist who sold only artificial flowers (and whose slogan was: "You're a busy woman of the world. Why buy something that needs constant care, and which you must eventually throw out?").

"I don't like the way some of these women are looking at me," growled Joe as a trio of residents passed by.

"Like you're intruding?" asked Mallory.

"Like they *wish* I'd intrude," complained Joe. "One of them even blew me a kiss!"

"It could be worse," said Jeeves. "See that gray-haired one in the print dress and the shawl?"

"Yes."

"She whispered something to me as she walked by."

"What?" asked Joe.

"It was so filthy I can't repeat it out loud," said Jeeves.

"That's okay," said Belle. "You can whisper it to me."

"Now *that's* interesting," said Joe, who was staring at Jeeves. "I've never seen a gremlin blush before."

"Are you sure you don't want to tell us about it?" persisted Belle. "Some obscene propositions are better shared."

Jeeves shook his head. "Besides, it was a physical impossibility."

"Don't be so sure," said Belle. "I majored in human geometry. Just whisper it to me and I'll tell you if it can be done, and if I don't know, why, my Sugar Daddy here and I will find some private alley or storeroom and field-test it."

"One more remark like that and you're back in the pants pocket."

"Closer My God to Thee," intoned Belle.

"And one more like *that* and I give you to Felina."

"After everything we've been to each other?" she demanded.

"You heard me."

"Wait till you turn down one of these frumps and she hollers 'Rape!'" said Belle. "Maybe I'll testify and maybe I won't."

"I'll just have to live with the doubt," said Mallory.

"We could sneak off for an hour and then everyone would *know* you're too tired to rape anyone," said the phone.

"You're all heart," replied Mallory.

"Not *all*," said Belle seductively. "Want me to prove it?"

"Not just now."

They passed a second bookstore, this one dealing exclusively in paranormal romances—in fact, the manager was in the process of ejecting a woman who'd had the temerity to refer to them as vampire sex books—and since it dealt in such a rigidly defined commodity, there were only about fifteen thousand different titles in the store.

Posters announced the newest dramas, especially produced for residents of the Tower. There were *Hamlet*, *Macbeth*, *A Long Day's Journey into Night*, and *Our Town*, each condensed to a thirty-minute one-act play so as not to bore anyone. (*Three Guys Naked from the Waist Down*, with a larger orchestra than the original Broadway production, was of course playing at its normal length.)

The busiest shop of all was one that seemed to specialize in lingerie exclusively designed for the Tower's residents. There were padded bras, waist cinchers, corsets that looked like they'd be more at home in medieval torture chambers, and the pièce de résistance—a row of funhouse mirrors that took fifty pounds off anyone who stood in front of them.

"Can't keep 'em in stock," confided a salesgirl to Mallory, who was staring into the store.

"Can't keep what?" he asked. "The bras or the waist cinchers?"

She chuckled. "The mirrors. We must sell an average of twenty a day."

"Makes sense," said Mallory. "Your clientele consists of a bunch of overweight residents, I take it?"

"And a bunch of underweight ones, too," she said. "But of course they buy different mirrors."

"Let's stick with the overweight ones for a minute," said Mallory. "I presume a lot of them have a taste for candies and cookies?"

"Who doesn't?"

"If I wanted to buy a chocolate marshmallow cookie without leaving the building, where would I go?"

"Probably to Satan's, up on the seventy-third floor."

"That's the top floor, right?"

"Yes," she said. "Everything between the mezzanine and the penthouse is condominiums, but the penthouse has a restaurant, a bar, a couple of other things . . . and of course Satan's."

"Thanks," said Mallory, heading off toward an elevator.

"Uh . . . sir?" she called after him.

"Yes?"

"They're pretty liberal-minded up there," she said. "They'll serve goblins and gremlins, and I think they'll even tolerate a cat-thing as long as you keep her under control."

"But?" said Mallory. "I sense a 'but' in there."

"But your cell phone just winked at our janitor."

"Belle?" said Mallory.

"I was just kidding around," said Belle innocently. "You know you're the only one for me."

"Thanks for the warning," Mallory told the salesgirl. He pulled Belle out of his pocket. "Felina, hang on to this." He tossed the phone to the cat-girl.

"Suddenly I'm a *this*?" demanded Belle. "I'm not even a *her*?" Her voice softened. "I was just fooling around, killing time, honest I was. I couldn't even tell you anything about him, except that he has brown hair, is probably about five foot ten, maybe one hundred and sixty-five pounds, blue eyes, straight teeth with no more than five fillings on the lower molars, and his suit was starting to wear out at the elbows. Oh . . . and he hasn't shaved since yesterday."

"Maybe *he* needs a phone," said Mallory.

"*No!*" screamed Belle. "Just put me back in your pants pocket, and pay no attention to my piteous, body-wrenching sobs."

"Deal," said Mallory, taking the phone back from Felina and putting it in a pocket. "Now let's get this show on the road." He led Felina, Jeeves, and Joe to an elevator, where the obviously annoyed operator was speaking on his cell phone.

"Come on!" he was saying. "You're my union steward. You have to stick up for me." He listened for a moment. "I'm telling you: I goosed her twice, and she only tipped me once. I want to make an official complaint. If I'm going to go around pinching and goosing women for free, they're going to be women *I* want to touch, not the frumps who live in this joint . . . Yeah, you bet your ass I will!"

He put the phone in a pocket and turned to face his passengers.

"I remember when being a member of a union *meant* something," he said.

"I remember when elevator operators said 'Which floor?'" replied Mallory.

"Okay, okay—which floor?"

"The seventy-third."

"Is it all right with you if I just hit the seventy-third," came the sarcastic reply, "or do you want me to say 'Going up' too?"

"Just hit it before *I* hit *you*!" snapped Joe.

"You think I'm scared of a goblin?" said the operator contemptuously.

Joe screamed and aimed a karate kick at the side of the elevator, which caved in. "*Are* you?"

"How did you know?" said the operator, promptly pressing the button for the seventy-third floor. "I'm sorry if I offended, sir," he continued. "I'll pinch your cat-thing for free if you'd like."

"Why not?" said Mallory as Felina hissed and spat at the operator. "You'll still have one hand left for pushing buttons." He smiled at the operator's discomfiture. "Maybe we'll just stand still, be quiet, and ride up in silence."

"That's a very good suggestion, sir," said the operator as the elevator began ascending. "I couldn't have said it better myself. In fact—"

"Joe," said Mallory, "pull your sword out, and if he finishes that sentence, cut his tongue off."

They rode the rest of the way in silence, and a moment later they stepped out onto the seventy-third floor of the Frump Tower.

The first thing Mallory saw was the restaurant. He'd seen a lot of rooftop restaurants that revolved left to right, or right to left, but this was the first one he'd ever seen that revolved top to bottom. Tables had been nailed to the floor, their magnetic surfaces held the metal dishes and glasses motionless, the chairs were affixed to the floors and the diners strapped into the chairs, and attentive if officious waiters covered each dish and wine goblet as its table tilted enough for them to begin spilling over the sides. The diners, about ninety percent of them women, chattered on, paying no attention to the waiters *or* the room.

"Odd," said Jeeves, staring in through a window. "Very odd."

"But original," Joe noted.

"Originality is a greatly overrated virtue," said Mallory. "The first case of nausea was original, too."

He noticed a discreet sign in the window:

Help wanted: Waiters lacking in social graces. Must be French (or at least must be able to approximate French accents). Arrogance and condescension essential. No prior experience needed.

"Why am I not surprised?" muttered the detective.

"I think I see what we're looking for," announced Joe, pointing to a shop just past the restaurant.

Mallory looked where Joe indicated. It was a store called Get Thee Behind Me, Satan, and given the goodies in the window, Mallory concluded that that was precisely where most of the calories were going to wind up. He walked over, entered the store, decided that although he was in perfect health it would be completely understandable if he lapsed into a diabetic coma in the next sixty seconds, and looked around for elephant-shaped chocolate marshmallow cookies. He found them right between the candied dinosaur eggs and the fruit-flavored malted milk balls.

"May I help you?" asked a young man from behind the counter.

"I have a question about these," said Mallory, indicating the elephant-shaped cookies.

"I can assure you that no elephants were harmed in the creation of these cookies, sir," said the young man, smiling at his own joke.

"Have you sold any in the past seven or eight hours?"

The young man looked into the display case. "All right, so they're not that fresh. I'll give you three percent off."

"Just answer the question."

"Fifty percent off?"

Joe leaped onto a nearby counter and withdrew his sword. "Answer the question!" he yelled.

"Not in the last seven or eight hours, no sir."

"How about the past two days?" Mallory turned to Jeeves. "Whoever stole her may have known this is what she eats, and planned ahead."

"Someone bought some yesterday," said the man.

"Who?"

The man shrugged. "He paid cash, so I don't have a record of his name."

"Can you describe him?" said Mallory.

"A large man, with horns growing out of his head."

"Brody," said Mallory.

"No, my name's Irwin."

"Not you," said Mallory. He turned to Jeeves. "How long can she go without eating?"

"Toy dragons have a very high metabolic rate," said the gremlin. "She has to eat every two or three hours. If she tried to sleep the night through, she'd be very sick and very weak by morning."

"And no one's bought any of these things except Brody," mused Mallory.

"She'd get the same nutrition value out of *any* chocolate marshmallow cookie," said Jeeves. "She just prefers these."

"But if she's starving, she might eat one of a different shape?" persisted Mallory.

"Yes, but . . ."

"Yeah, I know," said Mallory. "If the thief knows she eats these things, he'd get them for her . . . and if he doesn't know, then he won't think of getting her a chocolate marshmallow rhino or lion either."

"So where to next?" asked Joe.

Mallory turned to the young man behind the counter. "You got a phone book I can borrow for a minute?"

"Hey, you've got me, Hot Lips," said Belle. "Just tell me what you want and I'll ring up Information for you—providing you press your lips *very* close to me when you're speaking."

"Cancel the phone book," said Mallory, as he pulled Belle out of his pocket.

"Okay, Big Boy," she said in her best Mae West accent, "what can I do for you, other than the obvious?"

"I know there's a Bureau of Missing Persons," said Mallory, "because my first case took me there. I know it's going to sound crazy, but I'm wondering if *this* Manhattan also has a Bureau of Missing Creatures?"

"Checking . . ." said Belle.

"I don't want to be rude," said Jeeves, "but time is running out, and that may be the silliest suggestion I've heard all night."

"I heard two sillier ones when I was a teenager," Joe chimed in, "but that was before I learned what you could and couldn't do inside a small phone booth with a naked goblin girl."

"Probably the same thing I couldn't do with a gremlin girl in a null-gravity bathysphere," said Jeeves.

"I'll bet it's not as silly as what I suggested to Sally Ann McDermitt after she had three drinks last night," said the young man behind the counter. He paused thoughtfully. "All I got out of it was a slap in the face. I'll bet she'd have tried it if I could have just gotten her to have that fourth drink."

"Anyway, Mallory," said Jeeves, "it's silly, and that's all there is to it."

"I sadly concur," said Joe. "We need another plan of action."

"Even I agree," said the young man, "and I have no idea what's going on."

"Excuse me for interrupting," said Belle, "but do you need the phone number of the Bureau of Missing Creatures, or will the address be sufficient?"

The old, dilapidated building was one of Manhattan's many deserted high schools. This one had miraculously avoided being burned to the ground by students who resented homework or parents who resented their illiterate teenaged children being given mediocre grades for sub-mediocre work. Since those halcyon days as a (theoretical) institution of learning, it had been a flea market, a crack house, and an auxiliary of the City Morgue, but now it sported a sedate, tasteful sign on what had been the gymnasium, stating that it indeed housed the Bureau of Missing Creatures.

Mallory and his party walked up to the reception desk, where a tall, exceptionally thin man with scaly skin and large unblinking eyes watched them approach.

"Welcome," he said at last in a sibilant voice. "We take deliveries around back."

"Deliveries?" said Mallory, puzzled.

"A goblin, a gremlin, and a cat-thing," said the clerk. "I assume they were scavenging in your yard and you brought them here."

Mallory shook his head. "You misunderstand," he said. "They're friends."

"Ah!" said the clerk, his face lighting up. "Now I comprehend! You wish to find paramours of the goblin and gremlin race, and a tomcat for the cat-thing. I call that damned generous of you, sir."

"Try not to comprehend quite so fast," said Mallory. "I'm looking for a toy dragon."

"Have you tried F.A.O. Schwarz?" suggested the clerk. "They're the biggest toy store in the city."

"Just listen to me," said Mallory.

"Or how about Macy's? They may not tell Gimble's where they keep their toys, but they'll tell you."

Joe leaped up onto the counter, sword in hand. "Just shut up and listen!" he snapped.

The clerk made the motion of turning a key to lock his lips, then throwing it away. Felina dived through the air to catch it, and landed empty-handed with a puzzled expression on her face.

"He cheated!" she complained. "Everybody hates me."

"That's not so," said Mallory.

"It isn't?"

"Only people who know you hate you."

Felina's face brightened. "I never thought of that." She turned around. "Skritch between my shoulder blades."

"Don't you touch that hussy!" shouted Belle. "You're mine!"

"Who said that?" asked the clerk, looking around.

"*I* did," replied Belle.

He still couldn't spot her, so Mallory pulled her out of his pocket. She giggled girlishly.

"Move that finger, you naughty boy, you!" she said.

The clerk stared harder. "*Madre de Dios!*" he whispered.

"Pay no attention to her, John Justin," said Felina. "You know you love to skritch my back."

"I've seen men with complicated love lives before," said the clerk, "but I've never seen a man who was having simultaneous affairs with a cat-thing and a cell phone!"

Mallory stared at him for a long moment. He was considering staring him down until he noticed that the clerk didn't have any eyelids. "Now listen to me and don't interrupt," he said in clipped tones. "We are looking for a toy dragon. By definition, that is a dragon that is less than twelve inches at the shoulder. She went missing in midafternoon, so I'm only interested in toy dragons that showed up here after, say, three o'clock. Now, do you have any?"

"Any what?" asked the clerk.

"Toy dragons, idiot!" screamed Joe, bringing his sword down and stopping it an inch from the top of the clerk's head.

"Now look what you've made me do!" complained the clerk.

"What?" said Joe.

Felina leaned over the counter and smiled. "Small puddle," she announced.

"My arm's getting tired," said Joe. "I can't hold the sword up much longer. Are you going to answer the question or not?"

"Larger puddle," said Felina.

"I don't know what's come in today," said the clerk. "I just greet the public and talk them into making donations. Just walk back to the pens and you can see what we've got for yourself."

Joe sheathed his sword. "You'd better be telling the truth." He paused and glared at the clerk. "I'll be back." Suddenly he smiled at Mallory. "That's a great line. Maybe they should use it in a movie someday."

He hopped lightly to the floor, and then Mallory and his party went through the doorway indicated. They soon found themselves surrounded by chain-link pens, each housing some creature that had been found wandering the streets and brought here by public-minded citizens.

As they passed the first pen, a catlike creature with a man's face approached them.

"What the hell is that?" asked Mallory.

"A mantichora," replied Jeeves. "Very scarce, except in upstate Vermont. My guess is that this one's a pet who got lost."

The mantichora gave them an ingratiating smile, sat up on its haunches, and hummed a sweet, lilting melody.

"Begging for treats," said Jeeves knowingly.

The next pen held two Gnomes of the Subway, who simply glared at Mallory and stayed at the far end of the enclosure.

"Help!" said a human-sounding voice, and Mallory walked down to where he had heard it.

A small, dapper, balding man with a three-piece suit, horn-rimmed glasses, and an umbrella hanging from a forearm walked up to the gate of his pen.

"Was that you?" asked Mallory.

"Yes," said the man, clearly upset. "I am Marvin Finkelstein of 429 Castlebury Drive in Westchester, and I don't know what I'm doing here!"

"Waiting to be claimed," offered Joe.

"You make me feel like a racehorse," protested the man.

"More like an object in the Lost and Found."

"I am *not* an object, no matter what Sylvia says!" yelled the man. "I'm a bookkeeper for Penworthy & Smythe, and if I'm not back at work by eight o'clock tomorrow morning I'll be fired!"

"Oh, you poor thing!" said Belle.

The man frowned and finally said, "I know this is going to sound strange, but your chest is talking to me."

"He has a very compassionate chest," said Joe.

"But he's in love with mine," added Belle.

The man blinked very rapidly. "Your chest seems to be capable of independent thought, and it's clearly a different sex from the rest of you."

"They don't get much different," agreed Mallory. He stared at the little man. "How the hell did you wind up here?"

"It's that yenta's doing!" said the man. "Just because I complained about her matzo ball soup . . ."

"That's hardly considerate," said Belle.

"You didn't taste the soup," said the man. He shuddered. "I hate to think how many matzos were gelded to make that hideous concoction."

"I think you're laboring under a false impression," said Mallory.

"Go ahead," sniffed the man. "Take her side. Everyone does."

"I feel sorry for you," said Belle. "I think a roll in the hay would ease your tensions and make you forget about your problems."

"With this gentleman's *chest*?"

"Oh, no," she said promptly. "I'm reserved for the studmuffin here. I thought we'd give you the cat-thing."

Felina hissed and displayed her claws in front of Mallory's lapel pocket.

"You don't scare me," said Belle.

Felina swiped at the pocket, shredding some material just next to it.

"Cut it out, both of you!" said Mallory.

"Don't worry, Sweetmeat," said Belle. "I'll protect you."

"One more word out of you and I'll leave you here," said Mallory.

"But I'm already here," said the man.

"I was speaking to my cell phone."

The man shook his head. "And I thought my nephew Morris was weird!"

"Give him time," said Joe. "He's young yet."

"Joe, you might as well let Mr. Finkelstein out of there," said Mallory. He turned to the man. "You can come with us."

"With *all* of you?" said the man.

"Yeah."

"Including the phone and the cat creature?"

"Yes."

"You know," he said, "I'm sure Sylvia's on her way to claim me right now. I think I'd better just stay in here and wait for her."

Mallory shrugged. "Have it your way."

He resumed walking down the row of pens.

"One question," said the man.

"What is it?"

"I've got to know. You and the cell phone—how do you . . . ?"

Mallory stared at him. "You have a low mind." He turned and continued walking.

"*Psst!*" said Joe.

The man leaned down to the goblin's level.

"I haven't watched them, mind you," said Joe. "But since she's a cell phone, I'd be surprised if they didn't do it orally."

"That's either a horrible pun or a profound observation," said the man. "I'll have to consider and decide which."

The next pen contained a small pool, and as Mallory was watching it a slimy green serpent stuck its head out.

"It's getting so one can't go skinny-dipping in private anymore," complained the serpent in perfect English.

Mallory made no comment, but simply looked at it, frowning.

"Something bothering you, buddy?" demanded the serpent.

"I have the feeling that I've seen you before."

"You go to the movies?"

"From time to time," said Mallory.

"Ever see *Creature from the Mauve Lagoon?*"

"A long time ago."

"That was me."

"What are you doing here?" asked Mallory.

"My unemployment benefits ran out," said the serpent. "You'd be surprised how few job openings there are for a twenty-seven-foot sea serpent, even one that can speak five languages and sing in the key of H. So the city lets me stay here."

"Maybe they'll make a sequel," said Joe sympathetically. "These days the definition of an endangered species is a book or a movie with no sequels."

"My agent's working on it," said the serpent. "Last year he got me a tryout for the remake of *Moby Dick*." He uttered a mournful sigh. "But I didn't get the part."

"Not big enough?" suggested Mallory.

"No, that wasn't it," said the serpent. "I simply couldn't walk on that damned peg leg."

"I don't suppose you've seen a small dragon today?"

"Sorry," said the serpent. "Usually I only see them after I eat some bad chili."

"Then I think we'd better be moving on," said Mallory.

"If you see Cecil or Otto, tell them I'm available."

"I think they've been replaced by George and Stephen," said Mallory. "Or maybe Clint."

They passed three zombies, a gorgon, a chimera, two unicorns, a banshee, a harpy (Belle insisted Mallory avert his eyes until the harpy started wearing a bra), a phoenix, and two miniature dragons which each stood about fifteen inches at the shoulder. Mallory was able to speak to about a third of the creatures, and questioned them closely about Fluffy, but no one had seen any dragon answering to her description.

"It's a big city, and a very small dragon," said Mallory to Jeeves. "Maybe I should talk to your boss again, and see if he's got any personal enemies, someone who might want to see him lose the show for some reason other than to have their own entry win."

"No," said Jeeves adamantly. "Buffalo Bill Brody hasn't got an enemy in the world. Time's getting short. We have to keep looking."

"Okay," said Mallory, "but I'm running out of ideas. We've tried the pond, and Greenwitch Village, and this place . . ."

"And Frump Tower," said Joe. "Don't forget Frump Tower."

"I'm trying my best to," said Mallory sardonically. He turned to Jeeves. "You're the expert. What's next?"

The gremlin lowered his head in thought for a moment, then looked up.

"There *is* one place where dragons are objects of respect, not to say study. We might be able to come up with a clue or a lead there."

"I'm game," said Mallory. "Where is it?"

"Chinatown."

They walked down the darkened street, their footsteps echoing off the pavement.

"We must be getting close," said Mallory. "There's a Chinese carryout every half-block."

"There's a Mexican carryout every half-block too," said Belle. "I can smell it from in here."

"You'd better let me go first," said Joe, stepping forward and brandishing his sword. "Tong members don't scare me. I'm ready for anything."

"Joe, put your sword away," said Mallory.

"Why?" asked the goblin.

"If you saw a stranger walking through *your* neighborhood with a sword in his hand, what would you think—that he's looking for a dragon, or that he's looking for a fight?"

"No problem," said Joe, sheathing his sword. "My hands are deadly weapons, and are registered with the police departments in Saigon, Macao, Hong Kong, Manhattan, and Chinquapin, North Carolina."

"Chinquapin?" repeated Mallory, curious.

"There was this girl . . ." said Joe wistfully.

They saw an ancient, bald, bent-over Oriental man emerge from a hotel, walking unsteadily with a cane.

"I'll handle this," said Joe.

"Handle *what?*" asked Mallory.

"Canes can be deadly weapons. Leave him to me."

"Joe, if he swings that cane, or even picks it up off the ground, he'll fall over."

"That's what he wants you to think," said Joe suspiciously.

"What makes you think he knows anything about Fluffy?"

"We have to start somewhere," responded the goblin.

"Let's start with someone who has a fifty-fifty chance of still being alive at ring time," said Mallory.

Joe shrugged. "You're the boss."

"I'm glad someone remembers that," muttered the detective.

They passed a row of gift shops filled with cheap presents and cheaper tourists, and Felina told Mallory which fifteen items she wanted from each. Next came a trio of Chinese restaurants, and finally a small building with a sign in the window that this was *Tong Headquarters, Local 84*. Mallory turned to Jeeves.

"All right, we're in Chinatown. What now?"

"I don't know," admitted the gremlin. "I just know that the Chinese are partial to dragons."

"Even when it isn't New Year's?"

"Absolutely," said Jeeves. "The dragon is the Chinese pet of choice."

"Are you saying you think someone stole Fluffy to keep as a pet?" asked Mallory.

"No."

"Then what *are* you saying?"

Jeeves shrugged. "Just that this seems a likely place to look for her."

"I thought you were supposed to be the expert on dragons," said Mallory irritably. "I need more input than that."

"I *am* an expert on dragons," said Jeeves defensively. "But *you* are supposed to be the expert on criminals."

Mallory glared at him for a long moment, then turned to Felina. "Do you remember what Fluffy smells like?" he asked.

"Like a dragon," answered the cat-girl.

"I'm surrounded by experts," said Mallory dryly.

"Forget them, Sweetie," said Belle. "I'm all you'll ever need."

"I'm open to suggestions," said Mallory. "What's your take on the situation?"

"Kiss me first."

Mallory pulled out the phone and stared at it. "Where?"

Belle uttered a high-pitched giggle. "I'll let you decide."

"You'd better have something interesting to say," said Mallory, bringing the phone to his lips and briefly kissing it. A pudgy Oriental woman on the other side of the street, who had been watching him suspiciously, almost fell over laughing.

"That's *it?*" demanded Belle. "Where was the passion? Where was the romance? Where was the *je ne sais quoi?*"

"I left them in my other suit," said Mallory. "Now what's your suggestion?"

"There's a sign on the next block," said Belle. "Can you see it?"

"Yeah."

"Well?"

"'The Dragon Lady Sees All, Knows All, Tells All,'" read Mallory. "Are you seriously suggesting I should go to a Chinese fortune-teller?"

"Why not?"

"Fortune-tellers are all phonies."

"Not in *this* Manhattan," said Belle.

"She's right, you know," said Joe. "I lost my dagger two months ago. I looked everywhere and couldn't find it. So I went to Madame Markoff, and she solved my problem."

"She told you where the dagger was?" asked Mallory.

"She told me to bet on Blarney Stone in the fifth race at Aqueduct."

"What the hell has that got to do with a missing dagger?"

"Blarney Stone paid eighteen-to-one, and I used the money to buy a new dagger and treat myself to dinner."

"So was she a fortune-teller or a tout?" asked the detective.

"What difference does it make?" replied Joe. "I paid her to solve a problem. She solved it." He patted the hilt of his dagger.

"Did she also tell you where to look for the damned thing?"

"She told me that Slippery Stanley had a fine dagger for sale in his window, and to remember to give her an extra five-spot if Blarney Stone won."

"I don't want a substitute Fluffy," said Mallory. "I want the original item."

"It can't hurt to ask," said Joe. "I mean, ordinarily I'd be very leery of anything an oversexed cell phone said . . ."

"Well, I like *that!*" snapped Belle.

". . . but when she gives you battle-tested advice like this," continued Joe, "how can you go wrong?"

"I'm sure Will Shakespeare could give you an answer," said Mallory.

"He could?"

"'Let me count the ways,'" quoted the detective.

"So you're not going to give it a try?"

"I haven't heard any better suggestions," said Mallory, heading off toward the little storefront on the next block. "Belle, you'd better be right."

"I am," said the phone. "Though for a kiss like that, it'd serve you right if all she directed you to was a dead cat."

Felina stopped peering into store windows long enough to hiss.

"No offense intended, cat-thing," said Belle. "Make it a dead dog instead."

"Well," said Mallory as they approached the shop, "she's called the Dragon Lady. At least that's encouraging."

"I don't know," said Jeeves. "The sexiest girl I ever knew was called Herman."

"It sounds like at least one of you was very confused," said Mallory.

They reached the storefront and found that the windows had been blackened.

"I don't like the looks of this," said Joe.

"It's probably just a way to provide privacy," said Mallory. "If you're here to find out if you're wife's cheating on you, or what the odds are of her finding out if you decide to cheat on her, a little privacy isn't a bad idea. And if she's selling tips on the races, you don't want someone looking in with binoculars or a telescope in case you write the name down or circle it in the *Racing Form*."

"Just the same, I'd better enter first," said Joe, pulling out his sword again.

"You wait here," said Mallory. "Felina, you too. And don't wander off."

"Yes, John Justin," she said with a feline smile.

"I mean it."

"Yes, John Justin."

"Can I trust you?"

"Yes, John Justin."

"I couldn't trust you this afternoon," he said. "What's changed since then?"

"Yes, John Justin."

Mallory sighed and turned to Jeeves. "You come in with me."

"Me?" said the gremlin, startled.

"We're looking for *your* dragon," said Mallory. "If she needs to know anything about it—its habits, what it answers to, anything more than she can learn from a photo—you're the one who's going to have to tell her. Unless she's a mind reader, too—then she can just take a peek and get what she needs."

"What if there are villains in there just waiting to pounce on you?" asked Joe.

"I'll protect him," said Belle.

"How?" asked Joe.

"If nothing else works, I'll offer myself to them and let them satisfy their carnal desires while my Sweetums makes his getaway."

"The mind boggles," said Mallory wryly.

"Turns you on, does it, Big Boy?" said Belle.

Mallory found himself hoping that the Dragon Lady was a little more grounded in reality than the members of his party. He opened the door, waited for Jeeves to enter, followed him in, and turned to Joe.

"Make sure Felina doesn't wander too far."

"I can't leave my post at the door," protested the goblin.

"Sure, you can."

Joe shook his head. "Nobody enters until you emerge."

"Joe, this is a place of business. Anyone can enter."

"Oh. Right." Then: "So why can't I come in?"

"It's a small shop, you're wearing a sword and a dagger, and I want her full concentration on the dragon."

"You mean I might terrify her?" asked Joe hopefully.

"Anything's possible," said Mallory, who thought it equally likely that she might fall over laughing and hurt herself.

"Makes sense," said Joe. "I'll stay out here with the cat-thing."

Mallory closed the door behind him, and found himself and Jeeves in a small, dark room, lit solely by a half dozen candles. There was an ornate desk and chair at the back, and three less impressive chairs facing it. There were a number of framed pictures on the wall, but it was too dark to make them out.

"Sit down," the detective said to Jeeves.

"Where?" asked the gremlin.

"There are three empty chairs and a floor," said Mallory. "How hard a choice can it be?"

Jeeves shrugged and sat down on a chair. Mallory sat on another, leaving the one between them empty. A moment later a tape recorder played "Hail to the Chief" and the theme from *Rocky*, and then a woman entered the room. Her skin was green and covered with scales, she sported a truly impressive tail, the nails on her hands were as long as Felina's and didn't appear to be retractable, and her face, while clearly feminine, was nonetheless reptilian, topped off by green shoulder-length hair. She wore a red velvet gown, but the shoe had never been created that could cover her splayed feet, and so she was barefoot.

"You may sit," she said in a harsh voice.

"We *are* sitting," replied Mallory.

She frowned. "Who gave you permission to sit?"

"You did, eight seconds ago."

"Well, that's all right then," she said. "I am the Dragon Lady. I see all, know all, predict all, and am never wrong except on certain unique occasions which we never refer to."

"I'm John Justin Mallory, and this is Jeeves."

She stared at them for a moment. "Jeeves, your family will disown you. Still, if you're set on it, I suggest a honeymoon at the Passionfire Motel just outside Natick, Massachusetts. Free breakfast, mirrors on the ceiling, a heart-shaped tub, and they never ask any questions. Say I sent you and you'll get a discount."

Suddenly she smiled. "I trust that solves your problem, and I predict that you will be very happy together."

"I'm afraid not," said Mallory. "We came here with a different problem."

The Dragon Lady closed her eyes and pressed her fingers to her temples. Suddenly she looked at Mallory. "Not to worry. No matter what the doctors tell you, it's benign."

"Would you like to hear what we came for, or are you just going to keep guessing all night?"

She glared at him for another moment, then shrugged. "All right. You talk, I'll listen."

"A dragon went missing this afternoon," said Mallory. "A very valuable dragon." He pulled out one of Fluffy's photos and tossed it onto the desk. "She stands eleven inches at the shoulder."

"Are you the fuzz?" asked the Dragon Lady.

He shook his head. "I'm private."

She studied the photo. "Pretty little feminine thing."

"Jeeves can answer any questions you may have about her." Mallory paused. "And there's a time limit."

"Oh?"

"She's due in the ring at Eastminster at four o'clock this afternoon."

The Dragon Lady turned to Jeeves. "What does she eat?"

"Elephant-shaped chocolate marshmallow cookies," replied the gremlin.

"Sounds tasty," said the Dragon Lady. "What name does she answer to?"

"Fluffy."

"Does she fly, or are the wings just for show?"

"She flies very short distances."

"How short?"

Jeeves frowned. "Maybe ten feet. Unless she's jumping off the top of the Vampire State Building. Then she can fly a couple of thousand feet. But she lands with a splat."

"Any habits I should know about?"

"Well," said Jeeves, "I snore, and I bite my nails, and—"

"Not you, idiot—the dragon!" she snapped.

"She's never been alone long enough to develop any habits."

"Poor little thing," said the Dragon Lady. She began rummaging through her desk drawers. "Now where the devil is it?" She began tossing papers, pens, rulers, small liquor bottles, and pencils onto the floor. "Ah!" she said with satisfaction after a couple of minutes. "I've got it!"

She pulled a crystal ball out of a drawer and set it on the desk in front of her.

"Stay back," she warned. "This could be dangerous."

Jeeves tensed and got ready to race for the door. Mallory looked unimpressed.

"Boil and bubble, cauldron of trouble!" she intoned, then looked up. "That's just for effect, you understand. Crystal balls hardly ever boil."

"We'll take your word for it," said Mallory. "Could you get on with it, please?"

She quoted stanzas from "The Face on the Barroom Floor," "Casey at the Bat," and "The Charge of the Light Brigade," followed by two of the more salacious verses of "The Ring Dang Doo," then peered into the crystal for a long moment.

"Well," she said when she looked up again, "I can give you bad news or no news."

"You want to explain that?" said Mallory.

"There's no live dragon in Chinatown that fits Fluffy's description. Either she's been processed and served at Ming Toy Epstein's Kosher Chinese Eatery down the street, or she never got to Chinatown." She paused. "I wish I could help you further, but I never leave the premises and I don't have a phone."

"Use mine," said Mallory, pulling out his cell phone.

"Finally an acknowledgment!" exclaimed Belle. "I *am* yours, just as you are mine!"

"Does it bite?" asked the Dragon Lady, staring at Belle.

"I only bite the superstud here," said Belle. "Little love bites. It drives him crazy."

The Dragon Lady picked up the phone as if it was a loaded bomb that might go off any second, quickly punched out the numbers as Belle cried "Ouch!" at each touch, and then held it a few inches from her ear.

"Hello?" she said. "Yes, this is me. I need to know: Have you got any dragon on the menu today? No. How about a few hours ago? Thanks. And as long as you ask, yes, send over a pig, a chicken, and a duck. No, don't kill them; I like them fresh. Yes, I'll be waiting."

She handed the phone back to Mallory.

"No dragon?" he asked.

"None."

"Thanks for your trouble."

"Thanks for your fifty dollars," she said.

"For *that*?" he demanded.

"Okay, three ninety-five."

He pulled out four ones and placed the on the desk. "Keep the change."

"Maybe it isn't benign after all," the Dragon Lady yelled after him as he and Jeeves rejoined Joe and Felina out on the street.

"Where to now?" asked Joe.

"Doesn't make much difference," said Mallory. "Winnifred's due to call in a few minutes, and we'll see where she wants to meet." He shrugged. "She's sure as hell not going to want to traipse all the way down to China-town, so I suppose we might as well start heading back to Brody's place."

"Doesn't it make more sense to meet at your office?" asked Jeeves.

"Why?" asked Mallory.

Jeeves shrugged. "She might not be able to find Mr. Brody's building."

"She was there just a few hours ago," said Mallory, "and she knows her way around this Manhattan better than I do." He began walking. "Let's go." He raised his voice. "I hope you're enjoying all this."

"I most certainly am not," said Jeeves.

"I wasn't talking to you."

"I am, now that we're together forever, Sweetcakes," said Belle.

"I wasn't talking to you, either." He raised his voice. "Are you just going to sit on your ass, or are you going to give me a little help?"

"I am ethically forbidden from helping you, even when you are toiling in my service," said the Grundy's disembodied voice.

Joe pulled out his sword and looked around for the voice's owner. Jeeves started trembling. Felina merely yawned.

"It's been seven or eight hours, and I haven't turned up a single lead," said Mallory. "If you want her found by ring time, screw your ethical system. Hunt up a higher categorical imperative and tell me where to look."

"You're a bright man, John Justin Mallory," said the Grundy. "You know almost everything you need to know. You'll figure it out."

"What the hell are you talking about?" demanded Mallory. "I don't know a goddamned thing!"

He waited for a reply, but none came.

"I just hate know-it-all demons!" he muttered.

A single amused laugh floated toward him on the cold night wind.

"What was *that*?" asked Jeeves.

"The Grundy."

"Why are you conferring with *him*? Surely he's responsible for the theft."

Mallory shook his head. "It's too difficult to explain, but he wants me to find Fluffy as much as you do."

"That doesn't make any sense," said Jeeves.

"It doesn't make any sense to a rational mortal," said Mallory. "It makes perfect sense to a demon who considers himself a sportsman."

"He's the most powerful demon on the East Coast," continued Jeeves. "If he wants her found, he must know where she is."

"He does. But he won't tell me."

"Why not?"

"If you want my opinion," answered Mallory, "he took too damned many philosophy courses in college."

"Do demons *go* to college?" asked Joe. "I mean, other than to eat professors and make out with gorgeous coeds?"

"How the hell do I know?" said the detective.

"You just said—"

"Forget it."

"Just trying to be helpful," said the goblin.

"I know," said Mallory. "I'm just frustrated. It's been a pretty unproductive evening." He paused. "Well, what the hell—maybe Winnifred will have unearthed a couple of leads to the dragon."

"Bird," said Felina.

"No, dragon," said Mallory.

"No, *bird!*" she repeated, her face pressed against the window of a building they were passing.

Mallory stopped to see what she was looking at and found himself staring into the interior of a wax museum. There were Errol Flynn and Douglas Fairbanks wielding swords, Gary Cooper reluctantly drawing his gun, Mae West asking Cary Grant if he was carrying a pistol in his pocket or if he was just glad to see her, Jean Harlow chewing gum and announcing to general disbelief that she had just read a book, Marilyn Monroe breathing deeply, Bette Davis declaring that the place was a dump, and highlighted in the center were Humphrey Bogart, Peter Lorre, and Sydney Greenstreet, all gathered around a table and examining the Maltese Falcon.

"I want it!" said Felina, rushing into the museum.

"Hey, mister," said the doorman, who looked exactly like Lionel Barrymore, "get your cat out of here or pay me twenty-five cents for her admission."

"Only a quarter?" said Mallory.

"Raised our prices in 1946. No one's told us to raise 'em again."

"Here's a dollar for the three of us and the cat-girl," said Mallory, handing him a bill.

"Thanks, mister," said the doorman. "It gets mighty lonely around here. These days everyone wants Brad Pitt and Julia Roberts and Leonardo whatever-the-hell-his-name-is. Tradition doesn't mean anything to them anymore."

"Maybe it'll come back."

The doorman shook his head. "Not a chance. They even tore down Yankee Stadium. Nothing's sacred these days."

Mallory couldn't think of anything comforting to say, so he simply entered the museum, followed by Joe and Jeeves. Felina, crouching and silent, was stalking the falcon. She was just about to pounce when Bogart suddenly looked up.

"I wouldn't do that if I were you, sister," he said with a slight lisp.

Felina drew back and hissed at him.

"Hey, fella," Bogart said to Mallory, "if you can't control your woman, get her out of here."

"She's not exactly a woman and she's not exactly mine," replied Mallory.

"Good!" said Belle. "Hold that thought."

Bogart turned to Felina and pulled a revolver out of his pocket. "You touch the dingus, sister, and I'll ventilate you."

"No!" said Lorre's high nasal voice. "Let *me*!"

"Felina, get away from there," said Mallory. "It's not real anyway."

"Yes it is," she insisted. "It's a big black bird."

"It's a phony," said Mallory.

"A phony?" laughed Greenstreet. "By gad, sir, you are a card! Do you know how many years it took me to get my hands on this bird, how many men I had to cheat out of it? A phony indeed!"

"I hate to disillusion you," said Mallory, "but the bird is just lead."

"And why should we believe you?" demanded Lorre. "You just want to cut yourself in!" He pulled a knife out of his pocket. "If there's any cutting to do . . ."

"Don't kill him," said Bogart.

"Why not?" asked Lorre.

"We need a fall guy. He looks like he fits the frame."

"You don't want me," said Mallory. "I'm a shamus, just like you."

"Yeah?" said Bogart with a slight grimace. "You know, I'm in the market for a new partner."

"Some other time, perhaps," said Mallory. "I'm after a dragon at the moment."

"It could be worse," said Greenstreet jovially. "The dragon could be after you."

"Not this one," said Mallory. "It's as small as the falcon."

"Bring it by," said Bogart. "If you're right about the dingus, maybe the stuff's hidden under the dragon's skin."

"The dragon has a prior commitment," said Mallory.

"Well, think about it," said Bogart. "And about hiring on as my partner. The last one got himself shot."

"Too bad," said Mallory.

"When a man's partner is killed, he's supposed to do something about it," continued Bogart.

"You're sending the girl over, right?" asked Mallory.

"A honey like that?" said Bogart. "You've got to be kidding! What I'm doing about it is hiring another partner."

"*I'm* available starting a week from Tuesday," offered Joe.

"Come by then," said Bogart. "We'll talk."

The three men went back to examining the falcon, and Mallory began looking around the museum. There was no Indiana Jones, but he spotted Jones's predecessor, Charlton Heston, in leather jacket, khaki pants, and battered fedora from *Secret of the Incas.* There was no *Star Trek* or *Star Wars* either, but off in a corner Walter Pidgeon was being menaced by his id in *Forbidden Planet*. Elsewhere Clark Gable seemed just on the verge of telling Vivien Leigh that he didn't give a damn.

"So where are Mickey Rooney and Judy Garland?" asked Mallory of no one on particular.

"They're preparing a musical in the old barn," said Marjorie Main.

"Oh, my God—another one?" complained W. C. Fields.

Suddenly Mallory was momentarily blinded by a flashlight.

"Quick, Watson!" said Basil Rathbone, shining the light in the darkest area of the museum. "The game's afoot!"

"No," said Fields. "The game's at Ebbets Field. A foot is what's at the end of your leg."

Mallory looked around for Felina. "Now where the hell did she go?" he muttered.

"Not another step, pilgrim!" said a masculine voice, and Mallory turned to see John Wayne throwing a protective arm around Felina, who was struggling to get loose.

"She doesn't belong to you," said Clint Eastwood, wearing a pancho and smoking a small bent cigar.

"I'm a man of few words, pilgrim," said Wayne. "Walk away while you still can."

"I'm a man of one word," said Eastwood. "Die!"

"*Stop!*" yelled Mallory as they both went for their guns. The two figures froze. "Felina, get away from there!"

"I just wanted to see if he had anything to eat in his saddlebags," said the cat-girl.

Mallory grabbed her by the wrist. "You stay with me. We're getting out of here." He turned toward the door, and saw that Bogart, Lorre, and Greenstreet were still in their original positions—but now the Marx Brothers were blocking the way.

"One morning I got up early and shot a detective in my pajamas," said Groucho. "What he was doing in my pajamas I'll never know."

Chico nudged Mallory. "That'sa some joke, huh, boss?"

Harpo merely made a face.

"An old one but a good one," said Mallory. "Let us pass, please."

"I'm tired of the old ones," said Groucho. " Is there a town in Alabama called Tusksatighta?"

Chico sat down at a small piano.

"Señor Ravelli will now play for you," said Groucho. "Señor, what's the first number?"

"One," said Chico.

"And in base eight?"

"You can'ta fool me, boss," said Chico. "They only got-a four bases."

Harpo feigned riotous laughter and honked his horn.

"You're not laughing," said Groucho to Mallory.

"I'm not in a laughing mood," said the detective. "If you don't mind stepping aside, we're on our way out of here."

"Not until you laugh," insisted Groucho.

"You want me to chop them down to size?" asked Joe, swinging his sword.

"Yes," said a voice from the shadows.

They turned and saw a handsome, well-dressed young man.

"Who the hell are you?" said Joe.

"I think I know," said Mallory. "Zeppo Marx, right?"

Zeppo nodded. "I was the funniest of them all. Groucho even said so in his autobiography. But I was the youngest. By the time I joined the act, all the funny parts were taken."

"But you always got the girl," said Groucho.

"After you three pawed her for all but the last two minutes of the film," said Zeppo bitterly. He turned to Joe. "Go ahead, chop them to bits."

Joe turned to Mallory with a questioning expression. "Boss?"

"Hey, that'sa *my* line," said Chico.

"Put the sword away," said Mallory.

"That's more like it," said Groucho. "One laugh and you're out of here. Harpo, make him laugh."

Harpo approached Mallory and gingerly tried to tickle his armpits. Felina hissed and showed her claws.

"You guys want to keep it quiet over there?" demanded Bogart. "We're examining the black bird here."

"Let us by," said Mallory. "I'm getting good and tired of this."

"Goodness had nothing to do with it," chimed in Mae West.

"To be or not to be, that is the question," said Laurence Olivier from the far corner of the museum.

"Oh, God, not Shakespeare again!" muttered Groucho, and suddenly all the figures froze.

"Now," said Mallory, leading his party out into the street. He side-stepped a sleeping drunk, two panhandlers, and a very overweight hooker. "Yeah, we're back in the real world again," he muttered.

"Interesting place," remarked Joe, "even if Bruce Lee wasn't there."

"Darling?" said Belle.

"Don't call me that," said Mallory.

"Sweetie-Pie?"

"What?" he replied irritably.

"The fat broad's calling you."

Mallory pulled the phone out of his pocket and held it to his ear.

"Forceful," said Belle. "I like that in a man."

"Hello, Winnifred?" said Mallory.

"John Justin," said Winnifred Carruthers. "I'm been trying to get through to you for the past ten minutes. I kept getting a busy signal."

"We *were* busy," Belle chimed in.

"Any luck?" asked Mallory.

"Nothing at this end," said Winnifred. "How about you?"

"Zip. Where do you want to meet?"

"I suppose it makes the most sense to go back to Brody's and see if there's anything we overlooked."

"My feelings precisely," replied the detective. "And we can find out if anyone's made a ransom demand. How long will it take you to get there?"

"Maybe ten minutes."

"Same here," said Mallory. "See you then." He examined the phone in the dim light. "How the hell do I hang up?"

"Push the button that's glowing," said Belle.

He did so.

"*Wow!*" shrieked Belle.

"What the hell happened?" asked Mallory, staring at the phone.

"I lied to you," said Belle. "And it was worth it!"

"Okay, you had your fun. Now how do I disconnect you?"

"I'm already disconnected, Honeylamb. My God, you sure know how to turn a girl on!"

"I don't think I should be listening to this," said Joe.

"I don't think *I* should be either," said Mallory, putting the phone back in his pocket.

They walked past a block of condemned buildings. Joe used his sword to scare off the omnipresent beggars, and Felina, after half a block of jumping over sidewalk squares without touching the lines, began jumping over sleeping drunks and addicts instead.

Finally Jeeves tugged at Mallory's sleeve. "Can you call your partner back?" asked the gremlin.

"No," said Mallory. "I don't know where she is. Why?"

"I just think going back is a waste of time," said Jeeves. "You can phone Brody and see if anyone's contacted him. Why go all that way to ask him?"

"We'll also want to examine the premises again. There might be something we missed."

"I doubt it," said Jeeves. "We were only there for a day."

"And JFK was only in Dallas for a few hours, and they're still finding evidence almost half a century later," said Mallory, sidestepping two more hookers and their business manager, a leprechaun decked out in a thousand-dollar suit and chewing on a solid gold toothpick.

After they'd gone another half block and the panhandlers were getting more numerous and aggressive, Mallory felt a sharp claw tapping him on the shoulder. He turned to find himself facing Felina.

"What is it?" he said.

"I just want you to know that I'm not talking to you, John Justin," said the cat-girl.

"And to what do I owe this rare treat?"

"It's not a treat!" she snapped. "It's a punishment!"

"Okay, to what do I owe this cherished punishment?"

She frowned. "Is 'cherished' good or bad?"

"Yes," said Mallory.

"I'm not talking to you because you wouldn't let me eat that bird."

"You'd have broken all your teeth on it," said Mallory.

"I'm used to eating raw things."

"Not *that* raw," said Mallory.

"Well, I just wanted you to know that I'm never speaking to you again for as long as I live."

"Thanks for informing me."

"I mean it, John Justin. These are the last words I'll ever speak to you."

"I'll just have to live with the disappointment," said Mallory.

"Don't worry about the cat creature," said Belle. "*I'll* never desert you."

"I can't tell you how comforting I find that," said Mallory in bored tones.

Suddenly an anguished scream came to his ears, and Mallory turned to see Jeeves lying on the sidewalk, clutching his knee.

"What the hell happened?" asked the detective.

"I tripped," grated the gremlin. "And I felt something pop when I hit the ground."

"Can you walk?"

"I don't think so. Where's the nearest hospital?"

"About five blocks," said Mallory.

"I'll never make it," said Jeeves. "You'd better carry me."

Suddenly a grim smile crossed Mallory's lips. "I'm in a hurry. But I'll leave Joe here with you while I have Belle call an ambulance."

"But—"

"It's okay. Joe's happy to stay. After all, I wouldn't want you running off the second I was out of sight."

"What are you talking about?" said Joe. "He just blew out his knee."

"Then he won't be needing it, will he?" said Mallory. "Joe, count to five, and if he isn't standing, bury your sword in his knee." He turned to the cat-girl. "Felina, if he tries to run, he's all yours to play with for as long as you want."

Joe frowned. "Are you sure?"

Mallory looked down at Jeeves. "Well, *am* I sure, or are we about to cripple you for no good reason?"

Jeeves got to his feet. "I don't like any of you very much."

"What did *I* ever do to you?" asked Belle.

"What's going on?" asked Joe.

"That's what we're going to find out," said Mallory. "He's supposed to be an expert on dragons, and for all I know he is. But in the course of the whole evening he never asked a question that I couldn't have asked, never gave any information I didn't know by the time we'd left Brody's place. And for the past couple of hours, every time I suggest going back there, he tries to talk me out of it. He even faked busting up his knee."

"What does it mean?" asked the goblin.

"I don't know, but I'll give plenty of ten-to-one that when we get to Brody's place, he's not there."

"Well," said Jeeves, "since you know all about Brody, you won't be needing *me* anymore, so I'll just take my leave of you."

He started walking back the way they had come, only to find Joe confronting him with his sword.

"Not just yet," said Mallory. "I think we'd like to enjoy your company a little longer. Joe, you're in charge of him."

"Right," said the goblin.

"Let's go," said the detective.

They began walking toward Brody's again. When they got within half a block, Mallory felt a familiar tapping on his shoulder.

"I'm hungry, John Justin," said the cat-girl who was never going to speak to him again.

CHAPTER 16

1:48 AM–2:06 AM

The lobby of the Plantagenet Arms was filled with marble-topped little tables serving latte to well-dressed if not well-conditioned women wearing a variety of minks and sables, and looking down their noses as anyone gauche enough to be wearing cloth or even sealskin coats. Winnifred stood at the edge of the area, waiting for her partner to arrive.

"You have an inscrutable expression on your face, John Justin," she noted as Mallory and his party entered the hotel.

"Let me ask you a riddle," said Mallory. "What's the difference between a wild-goose chase and a tame-dragon chase? And before you spend too much time thinking about it, let me suggest that the answer is: nothing."

She stared at Jeeves. "*He's* the culprit?"

Mallory shook his head. "Him? He's just the flunkie."

"I resent that!" said Jeeves.

"Resent it all you like," said Mallory. "Just don't deny it, or your nose might start to grow."

"So you've solved it?" said Winnifred with a smile. "That's good news indeed!"

"I haven't solved a damned thing," answered Mallory. "But at least I know who the bad guys are. What I don't know is *why*." He turned to the goblin. "Joe, you wait here. And Jeeves doesn't leave, no matter what."

"Got it," said Joe.

Mallory walked to an elevator, waited for the door to slide open and for Winnifred to enter it, then turned to Felina.

"You, too," he said.

"I'm not talking to you forever and ever," said the cat-girl.

"Forever and ever ended three minutes ago," said Mallory.

"Oh," she said, entering the elevator and smiling. "Then I'll come."

They emerged at Brody's suite and looked around.

"Neat as a pin," said Mallory. "Every cushion is plumped up, every glass washed, everything spick-and-span. I'll bet he flew the coop four or five hours ago and tipped the maid to clean the place tonight, just to make sure he hadn't left any clues behind."

"Still, we might as well check each room to make sure he's not hiding. He could have tipped her so we'd see it like this and *assume* he's gone."

"There's an easier way," said Mallory. "Felina, is anyone else here?"

The cat-girl sniffed the air, then walked a few feet in each direction and sniffed again. "No, John Justin."

He walked to a closet and opened it. It was empty. He then went to the bedroom, checked the closet there, and got the same result.

"Well, that's that," he said, returning to the main room. "A stone cold trail."

"He's pretty distinctive in appearance," noted Winnifred. "There must be ways to track him down."

"There are," agreed Mallory. "But we've got to find him—and we especially have to find Fluffy—by midafternoon at the latest. Let's not forget that he may be the culprit, but retrieving Fluffy is the object of the exercise."

"Maybe we should just turn the case over to the police," suggested Winnifred. "I mean, you can hardly expect him to pay us for apprehending him and getting Fluffy to the show on time."

"Not *him*," said Mallory. "But the Grundy offered to double what Brody was paying us."

"That's right!" said Winnifred. "I forgot!"

Mallory walked to a window and opened it, oblivious of the noise of the traffic and the odors wafting to his nostrils. "Now that we're working exclusively for you," he said in a loud voice, "I don't suppose you'd like to help us earn our fee?"

"Nothing would make me happier," answered the Grundy's voice.

"Good!"

"Unfortunately, happiness is denied to me," continued the demon.

"You can destroy buildings, kill thousands of people, cause the city to freeze in midsummer just by blowing on it, and you can't help a man you've just employed to solve a problem for you," said Mallory. "Exactly what the hell kind of ethical system is that?"

"Mine, for better or worse," answered the Grundy. "Use your brain, John Justin Mallory. You know what your next step has to be."

"The hell I do!"

"Then you'd better consider it very carefully or your fee will fly away to the four winds."

"Look," began Mallory, "can't you just—?"

"I can't be bothered now," said the voice. "I have to groom Carmelita."

"Thanks a heap," said Mallory bitterly.

There was no reply, nor did he expect one.

"All right," he said wearily, shutting the window and turning back into the room, "how many more dragon ponds and missing-creature kennels *are* there in this town?"

"We've been to all the major ones," said Winnifred. "Besides, she's more likely to be in some hotel room, of which this city possesses about two hundred thousand."

"I know," he said. "And checking with the Prince of Whales and some of the other fences won't help. As good as Fluffy's supposed to be, you can't just buy her, change her name, and show her in your colors; as Jeeves kept saying, she's the most recognizable dragon in the country."

"If we had time, we could get out to Brody's ranch, talk to his associates, check into his finances," said Winnifred. "We may still, but we can't do it by midafternoon."

"Why does that damned demon keep telling me I know everything I need to know?" muttered Mallory. "You could fill a book with what I don't know about this case. Add in what I don't know about dragons and you've got a trilogy."

"Don't berate yourself, John Justin," said Winnifred. "We haven't failed yet."

"No," he said, checking his wristwatch. "We have fourteen more hours in which to fail." He shook his head. "Damn! We could have used that money, too."

"Yes, we could," agreed Winnifred. "I hate to point fingers, but if you just didn't bet on Flyaway every time he runs . . ."

"He *never* runs," said Felina. "That's his problem."

"Shit!" exclaimed Mallory. "That's it!"

"What is, and how many legs has it got?" asked Felina eagerly.

"That's what the Grundy was telling me!"

"I don't follow you, John Justin," said Winnifred.

"Flyaway!" replied Mallory. "Hell, he said it plain as day: our fee will fly away."

"I'm still confused."

"It's as close as that idiot ethical system of his will let him come to pointing me in the right direction!" said Mallory.

"It has something to do with that poor horse you're always betting on and losing on?"

He shook his head impatiently. "No. He couldn't be *that* direct."

"Then I don't understand," said Winnifred.

"Think about it," said Mallory excitedly. "There's no money for winning Eastminster, just a trophy and a piece of ribbon. And we know there's no money in stealing the dragon; you can't sell her because she's too easy to recognize. So where *is* there money?"

Winnifred looked puzzled. "All right—where?"

"In betting on the outcome!" he replied. "We've been using the terminology all night without even thinking about it: Fluffy is the favorite, Carmelita is the second choice, and so on."

"But that doesn't make any sense, John Justin," said Winnifred, frowning. "The Grundy has the defending champion, right?"

"Yes."

"And if Fluffy hadn't been entered, the Grundy's chimera would be a heavy favorite to win?"

"Very likely," said Mallory. "No, scratch that. Certainly."

"Then I just don't see it," said Winnifred. "If Fluffy was an odds-on favorite, and Brody faked her kidnapping so he could bet on someone else, then Carmelita becomes as heavy a favorite as Fluffy was, so how can he show more of a profit by betting on her?"

"I don't know the answers yet," said Mallory. "But I sure as hell intend to find out."

"How?"

"I'm going to talk to the one man who can answer my questions—my bookie."

Joey Chicago's Three-Star Tavern looked like it belonged in the 1950s. Some of the customers were dressed as if they didn't know that it *wasn't* still the 1950s.

Mallory and his party entered the place. The wall was lined with a row of leather booths. There were a few tables, a pair of pinball machines, and a long bar with leather barstools that had seen better days. The wall behind the bar was covered with the photographs of great Americans: Babe Ruth, Al Capone, Man o' War, and Voluptuous Vanessa.

The detective turned to Joe. "Find a booth or a table and sit there with the gremlin until I call you or tell you it's time to leave."

"And if he tries to escape?" asked Joe.

"That would make me very unhappy," said Mallory.

Joe smiled and patted the hilt of his sword. "Not as unhappy as it'll make *him*," he assured the detective.

"Joey," said Mallory to the man behind the bar, "give my ladyfriend here"—he indicated Felina—"some milk."

Joey Chicago made a face. "You want milk, go to a dairy."

"You got cream for a brandy alexander?"

"Ah, Brandy Alexander," said a short man at the bar. "She belongs in the Ecdysiasts' Hall of Fame. I knew her well. And often. What a dish!"

"I'll have to charge you for the whole drink," said Joey Chicago.

"That's fine. Felina, drink what the man gives you and try to behave yourself."

"How come you never give me anything easy to do?" she complained.

"Okay, here's an easy one. Go out in the street without the cream and wait for me."

"I'll behave," she said, walking to the bar. "Give me a tall one."

"You talking drinks or tomcats?" asked Joey Chicago.

"Yes," said Felina with a catlike smile.

Mallory looked around and spotted the man he was after: normal height and weight, dressed in a white suit, a black silk shirt, a silver necktie, a black handkerchief in a breast pocket, a straw hat in February, and two-toned shoes that looked like they should have spikes on the bottoms. The detective and Winnifred walked over to the third booth and sat down opposite him.

"Hi, Harry," said Mallory. "Let me introduce you to my partner, Winnifred Carruthers."

Harry the Book tipped his hat. "Pleased to meet you, ma'am. Any friend of Mallory's is"—he considered it for a moment—"a friend of Mallory's."

"I've heard a lot about you," said Winnifred, extending her hand.

Harry studied the hand, then chose to ignore it when he determined there was no money in it. "I would not believe a word the cops say, ma'am," said Harry. "They have riotous imaginations." He turned back to Mallory. "Six, two, and even that you are not here to lay a bet at two in the morning, but I would love for you to prove me wrong."

"Are you ever going to rent an office again?" asked Mallory.

"You're sitting in it," replied Harry. "Most of my clientele winds up in here, and besides my personal mage has staked out the men's room as *his* office. Beware of all the black candles should you pay it a visit," he added confidentially. He folded his hands on the table between them. "Now what can I do for you? After all, it is my understanding that Flyaway is not running this week. Well," he added, "not in a *real* race, anyway."

"What do you mean?" asked Mallory, momentarily distracted.

"You know how they hold publicity stunts for charity from time to time, like having a football player or a track star run against a horse?"

"Yeah, but those are exhibitions," said Mallory. "The racetracks don't allow betting on them."

Harry the Book smiled. "Do I look like a racetrack?"

"So Flyaway's in a race against a man?" said Mallory. "Who's he up against—that wide receiver for the Mauve Devils? Or maybe that kid from Miskatonic University who set the record for the hundred-yard dash?"

"They disallowed it," said Harry.

"The record?" asked Mallory. "Why?"

"I guess you did not see what was chasing him," answered Harry.

"So who's Flyaway up against?"

"A former mountain climber by the name of Lester Glover."

"Fast?" asked Mallory.

"Well, it is said that he went down Pike's Peak pretty damned fast," allowed Harry. "I understand he will make the next edition of Mr. Guinness's record book."

"He must be very sure-footed," offered Winnifred. "Those mountain paths can be tricky."

"I do not believe he ever saw one," said Harry. "He slipped on a ledge and went top to bottom in twenty-two seconds flat."

"It sounds painful," she said.

"He didn't feel a thing the first twenty-one seconds," said Harry. "Anyway, they amputated both his legs, and he's on oxygen, and of course he's in a wheelchair, and I seem to remember that his left arm doesn't work very well."

"And *he's* what Flyaway has to run against?" said Mallory. "It'll be a slaughter."

"Most of the oddsmakers agree with you."

"So what *are* the odds?" asked Mallory.

Harry grimaced. "The best I can offer is eighty to one," he said.

"A nickel for a four-dollar bet?"

"No, three hundred twenty dollars for a four-dollar bet."

Mallory shook his head in frustration. "You don't understand: I'm not betting on Glover. I'm betting on Flyaway."

"I know."

"And he's an eighty-to-one longshot to beat a legless man who's on oxygen?"

"Those odds sound about right to me, John Justin," said Winnifred.

"I will be honest with you, Mallory," said Harry. "You can get better than a hundred to one from most of my competitors."

Winnifred glared disapprovingly at Mallory as he pulled out a twenty and forked it over. "On Flyaway's nose."

"Done," said Harry, taking the bill and stuffing it in a pocket. "I hope your day was going well before this terrible misfortune befell it."

"I almost forgot what we came here for," said Mallory. "We need information."

"Certainly," said Harry. "The first thing I can tell you is that anyone who bets on Flyaway is not the brightest bulb on the lamp."

"Let me ask my questions first, then tell me how dumb I am, okay?" said Mallory.

"The floor is yours," said Harry. There was an angry inhuman growl from beneath the table. "The table is yours," he amended.

"I have a client who owns the favorite for the Eastminster show tomorrow. Well, today."

"Good," said Harry. He signaled to Joey Chicago. "I assume you are on retainer, so you're buying."

"The dragon is missing," continued Mallory.

"What dragon?"

"The favorite for the show. I have a feeling that my client faked its kidnapping, but I don't know why. I thought you might throw a little light on the subject."

"I'd like to help," said Harry. "but you could write a book about what I don't know about dragonnapping. In fact, I'm sure someone already has."

"He offered me a lot of money to find it . . ." began Mallory.

"Then why do you think he stole it himself?"

"Because he's flown the coop and saddled me with an assistant who's been less than useless."

"Hey, Gently," said Harry to a morbidly obese balding man in a plaid suit. "Come over and say hello to John Justin Mallory and his partner."

The pudgy man approached them. "The famous detectives?"

"Well, the detectives, anyway," said Winnifred.

"And this is Gently Gently Dawkins, one of my employees," said Harry.

"Everyone calls us Harry's stooges or his lackeys," said Dawkins. "But we're not."

"No?" said Winnifred.

"No," said Dawkins, with a look of pride. "We're his flunkies."

"That'll do, Gently," said Harry. "I think I see some candied peanuts over on the bar."

Gently Gently Dawkins backed away, then turned and raced to the bar, and grabbed a handful of the peanuts.

"What was that about?" asked Mallory.

"I'll match my useless assistants against yours any day of the week," said Harry. "At least he's as honest as the day is long, especially this time of year." He paused. "Now what is it that you two wish to know?"

"Why would our client fake a kidnapping, and then pay us five thousand dollars if we can find the dragon and get her to Eastminster by ring time?" asked Winnifred.

"Five large?" said Harry, clearly impressed. "Maybe he really wants her back."

"He doesn't," said Mallory. "I'm convinced of that. Winnifred and I are just for show."

"I thought he was showing the dragon."

"He's *not* showing the dragon. There has to be money involved. I need to know what's going on."

"The dragon is the heavy favorite," said Harry, pulling out a small note-book. He flicked a wand at it, and it turned to the page he wanted. "The morning line has her at six to five."

"If she loses," said Mallory, "the second choice is the Grundy's chimera."

"Three to one right now," said Harry, checking his book, "but I would expect her to go down to two to one or even nine to five by post time."

"Post time?"

"Ring time," amended Harry.

"And if Fluffy—that's the dragon—doesn't make it to the ring?" asked Mallory.

"Then she will be odds-on, maybe three to five. There is not supposed to be anything else that can give her a run for the money."

"Then it still doesn't make any sense!" muttered Mallory. "If one of the two is missing, the other's got a lock on it. Why fake the kidnapping when you'll make even less betting on the Grundy's chimera if Fluffy's not there?"

"Not necessarily," said Harry.

Suddenly Mallory was alert. "Why not?"

"It depends on when he makes—or made—his bet or bets," said Harry. "Go on."

"Well, if he bets today, he might get three to one if he is exceptionally lucky, or more likely two to one. Tomorrow, it will be even shorter odds, and his three to one will be but a distant memory. *But*," continued Harry, "if he laid his money down three months ago, on a future book . . ."

"What's a future book?" asked Winnifred.

"You know how you can go to Vegas, or even on the Internet, and get the odds on any upcoming event—ballgames, races, elections, everything?" asked Harry.

"So I've been told."

"Well, you can get them on dog shows too," said Harry. "And I seem to remember a few months back there was a rumor that the Grundy's chimera was pregnant and would not make the show, and for a week or two, until the rumor proved to be false, her odds shot up to forty to one."

"So what?" asked Mallory. "She'll be odds-on tomorrow."

Harry shook his head. "With a normal bet, you would be right. But if you lay down your money on a future book, you get the odds that your pick is at the moment you make the bet."

"Even if she drops from forty-to-one to even money?" asked Winnifred.

"Even so," said Harry. "But if she breaks a leg, or retires, or even dies, you are still stuck with the bet."

"So if our client knew the chimera wasn't pregnant," said Mallory, "if he maybe even started the rumor himself and laid his bets with a future book, he stands to get a forty-to-one return if she wins tomorrow."

"That is correct."

Mallory wrote Brody's name down on a napkin and shoved it across the table. "Can you find out if this guy placed some big money bets around town, or even out of town, on Carmelita—the Grundy's chimera?"

"It will take some work, but I can do it—for, shall we say, half of your retainer?"

"Only half? You're all heart, Harry," said Mallory bitterly.

"You are mistaking him for a human being," said Gently Gently Dawkins from the bar. "He is a bookmaker."

"But a bookmaker with a heart, as you suggest," said Harry. "To that end, I will take your marker."

"I'll pay cash," said Mallory, pulling out his wallet and peeling off five hundred dollars of the thousand Brody had given him. "But this is the end of it. No more later."

"This is very strange," said Harry. "The stars have not stopped in their courses and the rivers are not flowing upstream, and yet you are in possession of five yards, and it looks like you have even more than that. It causes me serious pain to suggest it, but maybe you should quit while you are ahead of the game."

There was a horrible grating noise coming from the back of the room.

"What was *that*?" asked Winnifred nervously.

"Oh, that is just Dead End Dugan," said Dawkins. "He is another of Harry's flunkies."

"He sounds horrible," she said.

"He differs from Benny Fifth Street and myself in that he is dead, and somewhat bigger than a mountain, but other than that we are alike as peas in a pod."

"Mighty few pods have zombies in them," noted Mallory.

"Well," said Dawkins, "the truth of the matter is that he has not fully adjusted to being a zombie yet. For example, zombies cannot metabolize food or drink, but he is always munching on a pizza or pouring himself an Old Peculiar from the bar."

"Fascinating," said Mallory, who was considerably less than fascinated. He turned to Harry the Book. "Okay, can you get going on this right away?"

"This may take some time," replied Harry. "There are more than two hundred local bookies, and that is before we cross the river to New Jersey or sojourn up to Connecticut, and of course there is always Vegas."

"We need to know before tomorrow afternoon," said Mallory.

"You can start with this," said Harry. "The biggest future book in town is run by Hot Horse Hennigan over on the corner of Greed and Gluttony."

"Hot Horse Hennigan," repeated Mallory. "Got it. I'll need some more names soon."

"Perhaps if you will let your partner help me . . ." suggested Harry.

"With both of us manning phones, or at least me manning one and her womaning the other, we can get through this twice as fast."

"I don't know," said Mallory. "That's going to leave me shorthanded."

"Shorthanded for what?" asked Harry. "We will find out if this Brody made any bets, never fear."

"We have a second client," explained Mallory. "It's worth another ten thousand to us if we can find the dragon and get it into the ring on time."

"The goblin with the sword belongs to your entourage, does he not?" asked Harry.

"I want him to stay here and guard our prisoner until we catch his boss," said Mallory, indicating Jeeves. "All that leaves me is Felina."

"Let me consider this," said Harry.

"Don't consider it long," said Mallory. "The clock is ticking."

"No, that is just Dean End Dugan picking his teeth," said Harry. He was silent a moment longer. "I have it. We will make a trade until ring time. I will loan you Gently Gently Dawkins and Dead End Dugan, and you can leave the goblin here with me." He paused. "I use Dugan for *difficult* collections. Your sword-carrying flunkie can fill in for him."

"Then who will watch the prisoner?" asked Winnifred.

"Hey, Joey?" shouted Harry.

"Yeah?" asked Joey Chicago.

"Are you in possession of an empty beer keg?"

"At the rate things are going, I'll have one in ten minutes."

"Fine," said Harry. He turned back to Mallory. "If I have to send the goblin out to make a collection, we will simply nail the gremlin inside a beer keg until he comes back."

"Why don't we *not* trade and we'll nail him in right now, and I'll take Joe En-lai with me?"

"Think about it, John Justin," said Winnifred suddenly. "Who's more likely to get people to talk to you—a little goblin with a sword who looks like a refugee from a cartoon, or a six-and-a-half-foot zombie?"

"Six of one, half a dozen of the other," replied Mallory.

"But you will also have Gently Gently Dawkins," noted Harry. "The more bodies you have, the more ground you can cover." He shot Mallory a quick glance from under the brim of his hat. "You of course will pay for all his meals while he is with you."

"Does he do anything but eat?" asked Mallory.

"Not to worry," said Harry. "Dugan can go months without eating, so it evens out."

"And if they're keeping the dragon underwater," added Dawkins, "why, Dugan's your man. He never breathes."

"If they're keeping the dragon underwater," said Mallory, "she drowned."

"I never thought of that," admitted Dawkins.

"Why am I not surprised?" muttered Mallory.

"You seem less than thrilled with our arrangement," noted Harry.

"Let's be honest," said Mallory. "Dawkins is not going to outwit any suspects, and the only way he'll intimidate them is by eating them out of house and home." He signed. "Okay, let me take a look at the other one."

"Dugan, come over here!" called Harry.

The zombie walked over and stood in front of their booth.

"Well?" asked Harry.

"He looks like Primo Carnera with eczema," said Mallory approvingly. "I'll take him."

"Check in by phone every couple of hours, John Justin," said Winnifred. "Brody doubtless made the bets under a phony name. If we can find it, and match it with an address, it might save you a lot of legwork."

"Right," said Mallory, getting up from the booth. He turned to Harry. "The zombie knows he's coming with me?"

"Dugan, go with this guy," said Harry. He smiled. "Now he knows."

"Does he owe us money?" asked Dugan.

"No, he is a Good Guy. He will aim you at the Bad Guys."

"I'm thirsty," said Dugan.

"No you're not," said Harry. "You're dead."

"I forgot," said Dugan. Then: "I'm dead *and* thirsty."

"Concentrate on being dead, and worry about thirsty later," said Harry.

"Yes, boss," said Dugan.

"You see?" said Harry to Mallory. "You just have to be firm with him."

"And what about Dawkins?" asked Mallory.

"Sweetest guy in the world. Salt of the earth. Loyal as a hound dog." He paused briefly. "Just don't get your fingers too near his plate when he's eating."

"Felina, are you ready?" asked Mallory as he walked to the door.

"For what?" she asked. "And did you know you have a dead man and a blimp following you?"

"Oh, well," said Mallory as she joined him, Dawkins, and Dugan, and they headed toward Hot Horse Hennigan's. "I never could spell incognito anyway."

CHAPTER 18

2:33 AM–3:08 AM

"So where do we find Hennigan?" asked Mallory, as they walked out into the street.

"In his office," said Dugan.

"I'd never have guessed," said Mallory. He turned to Dawkins. "Where's his office?"

"The Met," replied Dawkins.

"The Metropolitan Museum of Art?"

"No."

"The Metropolitan Opera?"

"No."

"We could play guessing games all night, or you could just tell me," said Mallory.

"The Metropolitan Five-Star Map Store, Luggage Shop, and Burlesque Emporium."

"An interesting combination," remarked Mallory.

"Oh, it makes perfect sense," said Dawkins.

"Yeah?"

"Absolutely," Dawkins assured him. "Say your wife catches you tossing money at Voluptuous Vanessa or Slinky Sally while they're onstage. What could be handier than a map store and a luggage shop, just in case she didn't bring her pistol with her? And you can get passports right next door."

"A government office is next to a strip show?"

"Not exactly," said Dawkins. "It's the Handy Dandy Quick Print Shop. They say they can get you a passport in two minutes, three if you don't have a photo."

"Yeah, I can see where that might come in handy."

"It's a necessary public service," continued Dawkins. "They estimate that

157

they save eight to nine hundred husbands a year. And of course, the Rest-in-Peace All-Night Mortuary is just across the street, for those husbands whose wives come prepared."

"It's that wild a show?" asked Mallory.

"Hot Horse Hennigan wouldn't use it for an office if it didn't attract people."

"What about women who want to bet?" asked Mallory.

Dawkins frowned. "Women don't bet. They're smarter than men. Everyone knows that." He paused briefly. "But for those who do, Fast Buck Flossie operates a very classy handbook out of the Lucretia Borgia Beauty Shop just up the street."

"Well, introduce me to Hennigan when we get there, and maybe we can figure out what name Brody used when he made his bet and where he's holed up now."

"I thought we'd watch the show first," said Dawkins.

"Why?"

The chubby man shrugged, a shrug that seemed to go all the way down to his toes. "You never know."

"You think Hennigan might be stripping between Voluptuous Vanessa and Slinky Sally?" asked Mallory sardonically.

"Well, when you put it that way, probably not," admitted Dawkins. "But you haven't lived until you've seen Lascivious Lezli the Lizard Girl shed her skin."

"We'll let Dugan watch for us," said Mallory. "Maybe he'd like to live again."

"I don't remember enjoying it that much the first five times," said Dugan.

"It's got to be better than dying," offered Mallory.

"Maybe," admitted Dugan. "Less restful, though."

"I can believe that," said Mallory.

They had to stop for a moment as they passed a cheap gift shop and Felina pointed out each of the sixty-eight presents she wanted for her birthday, once she remembered when her birthday was. They stopped again when they passed an all-night bakery and Dawkins felt compelled to buy a small chocolate cake and four eclairs to hold him until they reached Hennigan's headquarters, which was three blocks away.

"How about *you?*" asked Mallory of the zombie when they were on their way again. "Aren't you going to tell me what you want?"

"Should I?" asked Dugan.

"I don't know. Do you eat?"

Dugan paused the blinked his eyes very rapidly. "I can't remember."

"Good," said Mallory. "Hold that thought."

Dugan stared at his open right hand. "How?" he asked.

"I don't want to offend anyone," said Mallory, "but right now it is looking like Harry got the better of our trade."

"I take umbrage at that," said Dawkins.

"Will umbrage fit in your mouth with all those eclairs?" asked the detective.

"You never can tell when I'll need my energy," said Dawkins defensively.

"I think you left it in your other suit," said Mallory.

"You are a cruel, unforgiving taskmaster," said Dawkins with all the dignity he could muster.

"I thought Harry was the one without a heart."

"He is a bookie. What's your excuse?"

"Hey, Mallory," interrupted Dugan.

"Yeah?"

"Your cat-thing's gone."

Mallory looked around. "Again?" He raised his voice. "Felina!"

Felina emerged from between two buildings. "You ruin everything," she complained.

"It's one of my special talents," said Mallory. "What did I ruin this time?"

"There was the cutest little rat," she said. "He looked so lonely, and you scared him away. I was just going to—"

"Torture and eat him?" suggested Mallory.

"Well, I was going to cuddle him first."

"That makes all the difference," said Mallory.

"It might," agreed Dugan. "No one ever cuddled me when I died." He scratched his head. "At least I don't think so." A pause. "Well, definitely not the third time."

Mallory looked ahead and saw the flashing lights of the burlesque theater's marquee.

"Okay," he said, turning to Dawkins. "Where do I find him?"

"I told you: at the Metropolitan Five-Star—"

"Let me amend that," interrupted the detective. "Where inside the theater do I find him?"

"I don't know," said Dawkins. "If he's hungry, he could be at the candy counter. If he's thirsty, there's a bar. If he has to answer a call of Nature—"

"Let's pretend he's not hungry, he's not thirsty, and he either has no urge to visit the men's room or else he's incontinent. Now where do I find him?"

"He's got a private office."

"Where?"

"At the Metropoli—"

"Harry *is* going to take you back when we're done, isn't he?" growled Mallory.

"Oh, yes," said Dawkins proudly. "I am one of Harry's three favorite flunkies."

"How many has he got?"

"So far, counting all of us including Dugan, three."

"All right," said Mallory. "Clearly you're having difficulty telling me where to locate Hennigan, so why not just tell me what he looks like and I'll take it from there."

"He looks like a bookie," answered Dawkins.

They passed a taco vendor with a cart, and Mallory bought a pair of tacos, which he handed to Dawkins. "Here," he said. "Eat these. Maybe your brain just needs more calories."

"That's what Harry is always saying," replied Dawkins, taking the tacos and biting into one.

"I can't imagine why," muttered Mallory.

They reached the theater, and Felina immediately began giggling.

"What is it?" asked Mallory. "Is some small defenseless creature in distress?"

"This woman is so silly!" said Felina, pointing to a poster of Dressy Tessie Torso, who was wearing a pair of shining silver pasties. "Look where she's wearing her earrings!"

"I'm sure she'll realize the error of her ways and take them off before her act is over," commented Mallory dryly.

"Will you buy me some earrings like that?" asked Felina.

"If we find Fluffy and get her to the ring on time," said Mallory. "You think that'll help you concentrate? I would like one member of this party besides me to be thinking about what we're doing."

"Yes, John Justin."

"You're sure?"

"Yes, John Justin."

"You think you can behave yourself in the theater, or do I have to leave you out here?"

"Yes, John Justin."

He stared at her. "What year is it?"

"Yes, John Justin."

"Don't just stand there, gents," said the leprechaun that was selling tickets in a glass-enclosed booth. "You're taking up space. How many will it be?"

"Does Hennigan own a piece of this place?" asked Mallory.

"I don't know," said Dawkins. "Why?"

"Because if he does, he makes a tidy profit just from admissions before anyone can even lay a bet."

"That's not what most of 'em come here to lay," said the leprechaun with a leer. "How many tickets?"

"Is there a discount for cat-people?" asked Mallory.

"Not a chance."

"What about zombies?"

"Never."

"Are you sure?" said Dugan ominously, stepping up to the leprechaun's window.

"Change of policy!" announced the leprechaun. "All zombies are free on Saturday nights."

"This is early Tuesday morning," said Mallory.

"It's Saturday night on Betelgeuse," said the leprechaun quickly. He turned back to Mallory. "You owe me for four tickets."

"You just said he was free."

"He is," said the leprechaun. "But that one"—he pointed at Dawkins—"takes up two seats."

"Dugan, reason with him," said Mallory, starting to head into the theater.

"It's against my religion to argue with zombies on a Monday night!" shouted the leprechaun. "You're all in for free as guests of the house."

"Thank the house for us," said Mallory, entering the lobby. Half the people were balding men in raincoats, lining up to see the show, and the other half were studying *Racing Form*s and various tip sheets, ranging from *Guaranteed Greyhounds* to *Cockfighting Choices* to the *Wall Street Journal*, depending on their particular sporting obsessions.

"So where is he?" asked Mallory.

"Just get in line with all the plungers," said Dawkins. Suddenly a snare drum and shouts of *"Take it off!"* came to their ears. "I think I'll just slip into the theater just in case Hennigan's girlfriend is working tonight."

"His girlfriend is a stripper?"

"His girlfriend bets claimers who are moving up in class, which everyone knows is a losing proposition. This is the way she pays off her losses."

"She can't be too happy about it," remarked Mallory.

"It doesn't bother her at all, but Billy Pinsky is furious."

"Billy Pinsky?"

"He runs the strip show two blocks north of here. She used to work for him."

"Not that much!" yelled a voice.

"Lascivious Lezli," explained Dawkins, shaking his head sadly with the air of One Who Knows. "When she gets carried away she always takes off that extra layer of skin."

The snare drum started up again.

"Uh . . . Mallory . . . ?" said Dawkins.

"Go," said Mallory. "We'll pick you up when we're done."

"If you absolutely insist," said Dawkins, racing into the theater.

"I've never seen a fat man move so fast," commented Felina.

"You probably never saw one so motivated," said Mallory dryly. He looked around and saw a line forming at an unmarked door about seventy feet away.

"Dugan, come with me," he said. He turned to Felina. "You, too."

He walked past all the people waiting to see Hennigan and soon reached the door.

"Hey, fella," said a man. "There's a line, you know."

Mallory jerked a thumb in Dugan's direction. "Argue with him."

The man glanced at Dugan and gulped hard. "Well, if he wants to lay his bet and get back in time to watch Voluptuous Vanessa, who am I to tell him he can't? I mean, if we have to show sympathy to the dying, clearly we have to show even more to the dead."

"Good decision," said Mallory, as a small man wearing a bright plaid suit exited the office. The detective held the door open for Felina. He considered leaving Dugan outside to make sure they weren't disturbed, but decided the zombie probably couldn't retain that thought for more than half a minute, so he ushered him into the office.

"So what can I do for you, friend?" said a burly man sitting behind an ornate desk. He wore a sports jacket of brilliant, almost phosphorescent, gold, with a brown shirt, a gold tie, black tuxedo pants, and two-toned golf shoes.

"My name is Mallory."

"Harry phoned and told me you were coming," said Hot Horse Hennigan. "Something about the big show at the Garden tomorrow."

"Right. You run a future book here, right?"

"Straight or future, take your choice."

"About two or three months ago, when she was thirty or forty to one, someone plunked down a big wad on the Grundy's chimera."

"Fifty large at thirty-seven to one," said Hennigan. His eyes narrowed. "Are you going to tell me the hex is in?"

"Not the hex," said Mallory. "The fix. I need to know who made the bet and where to find him."

"*You* need to find him?" demanded Hennigan. "I could be out almost two million dollars!"

"Is that more or less than a quarter?" asked Felina.

"What name did he use?" asked Mallory.

"Let me see," said Hennigan, pulling out the notebook that seemed to be common to all bookies. He waved a small wand and the pages flipped by, finally coming to a stop. "Here it is: John H. Holliday, MD."

"Wonderful," said Mallory disgustedly.

"What's wrong?"

"That's Doc Holliday," said the detective. "Did he give his address as Tombstone, Arizona?"

"As a matter of fact he did," said Hennigan, frowning.

"Shit!" said Mallory. "Another dead end."

"Wait a minute," said Hennigan, still studying his notebook. "We're not giving up on my two million that easily. He said if he won to deliver the money to his friend William Masterson, who lives in Manhattan."

"Figures," said Mallory. "That's Bat Masterson. He spent his last few years here as a reporter."

"How do you know all this?"

"I watched eight zillion cowboy movies when I was a kid. Didn't you?"

Hennigan shook his head. "I watched Secretariat and Seattle Slew and Ruffian." Suddenly he snapped his fingers. "Now I've got it! You're Harry's third certainty!"

"What are you talking about?"

"He says there are three certainties in the world: death, taxes, and the fact that Mallory will blow a week's pay every time Flyaway runs." He paused. "*My* certainty is that when I get my hands on Brody or Holliday or whoever the hell he is, he's going to think the Death of a Thousand Cuts looks like a walk in the park."

"Could we get back to the subject at hand?" asked Mallory.

"Sure," said Hennigan. "What was it?"

"Masterson's home address?"

"That's curious," said Hennigan, frowning. "I never noticed it before. He's in an office building." Suddenly he shrugged. "Why the hell *should* I notice? If he wins, he'll be on my doorstep ten seconds later."

"What office building?"

"The World Jade Center."

"Thanks," said Mallory. He turned to Felina and Dugan. "Let's go."

They left the office and walked to the lobby. "You two wait here," said Mallory, who didn't want Dugan terrifying the strippers or Felina trying to collect pasties for her ears. "I'll get Dawkins."

"*Eight!*" cried the audience in unison through the closed doors. "*Nine! Ten!*"

Mallory opened a door and walked down the aisle, looking for Dawkins. "*Eleven!*"

He glanced at the stage, where Voluptuous Vanessa was showing the audience how many uses she could put a broom to that had nothing to do with sweeping floors.

"*Twelve!*"

Finally he spotted Dawkins, who was seated midway between two aisles, but was unable to get the fat man's attention until Voluptuous Vanessa had run through her repertoire at about the same time the audience ran out of fingers and toes.

"Come on," said Mallory when Dawkins finally noticed him. "I found out what I needed to know."

Dawkins got up and began making his way to the aisle, drawing grunts of pain and shouts of outrage as he stepped on various toes.

"You can't interrupt *my* act!" bellowed Voluptuous Vanessa. "I am a serious artiste! I don't have to put up with this shit!" She spotted the bouncer, who looked like a walking ad for steroid treatments. "Bruno, throw these bums outta here!"

Mallory and Dawkins made it to the lobby two steps ahead of Bruno, who took one look at Dead End Dugan and decided to seek new employment elsewhere, making a beeline out the main door.

"So what did you learn?" asked Dawkins.

"Brody's a cowboy fan, and we're heading to the World Jade Center," said Mallory. "I don't suppose you learned anything?"

"Nothing pertaining to the case," admitted Dawkins. "But if you ever have a case where a broom is among the clues . . ."

Suddenly alternating cries of "*Right! Left! Right! Left!*" came from the theater.

"I don't even want to think about what *that* means," said Mallory.

"I could find out for you," volunteered Dawkins.

"If you do, no more food tonight," said the detective.

"What are we dawdling for?" demanded Dawkins, suddenly hurrying toward the street. "The game's afoot!"

Chapter 19
3:08 AM–3:42 AM

The World Jade Center was seventeen blocks away from the Metropolitan Five-Star Map Store, Luggage Shop, and Burlesque Emporium. That meant Mallory had to pull Felina away from four lingerie shops, two fish markets, a jewelry store, three toy stores, and for reasons he would never understand, an all-night currency exchange. It was easier to predict Gently Gently Dawkins's distractions: one deli per block. He had no problem with Dead End Dugan lagging behind, but he did have to reintroduce himself every two blocks.

It was when they were within a block of the Jade Center that Mallory heard a "*Psst!*" off to his left.

"We're not buying any," he said without even looking in the sound's direction.

"Just as well," said a goblin, stepping out to block his way. "I'm not selling any."

"Good," said Mallory. "Then go away."

"Hey, keep a civil tongue in your head, fella," said the goblin. "This is a free country."

"Then we're free to ignore you."

"Hah!" said the goblin. "So you admit it's free!"

"Scram," said Mallory.

"Now that we've started a dialogue?" responded the goblin. "Don't be silly. And since we both agree that it's a free country, I am going to give you, absolutely free, seventeen 78 rpm records of Vaughn Monroe singing 'Racing with the Moon.'"

"What the hell do I want with a seventy-five-year-old record?" said Mallory.

"You're looking at it all wrong, pal," said the goblin. "Think of it as seventeen Christmas presents to your friends and relations, especially those who are tone-deaf."

"Not interested."

"I'll toss in a 1943 calendar with twelve—count 'em: twelve—pinups by Alberto Vargas and Gil Elvgren."

"If 1943 ever rolls around again, we'll talk," said Mallory, trying to step around the goblin, who managed to stay directly in front of him.

"You're a hard sell, Mac," said the goblin. "Okay, here's my best offer: everything I've mentioned so far, plus a monocle that—get this!—was once almost purchased by Teddy Roosevelt!"

"And that's everything?"

"You got it. Everything, and all of it free."

"Fine," said Mallory. "Now go bother someone else."

"Not so fast, fella," said the goblin. "You owe me forty-seven dollars and sixty-two cents."

"I thought it was all free."

"It is—when you buy a subscription to *Commode Manufacturers' Weekly*."

"But I'm not buying one."

"This is a capitalistic society," said the goblin. "You *have* to buy one."

"I don't want it."

"What's that got to do with anything?" demanded the goblin. "This is a society of conspicuous consumers. It's sacrilegious to be a nonconsumer."

"Oh, I'm a consumer, all right," replied Mallory. "I'm just an inconspicuous one."

"You are one hell of a hard sell, buddy," complained the goblin. "Okay, I'll toss in three thimbles, and a wristwatch that always reads 2:07."

"Forget it."

"And I'll cut the price on the subscription to thirty dollars."

"No," said Mallory, feinting left and walking by the goblin to the right.

"Eight dollars!" yelled the goblin as Mallory continued toward the World Jade Center.

"And give us three parakeets and a whale," said Felina.

"Be reasonable, cat-thing," said the goblin. "There are hardly any whales on the street at this time of night."

"Five parakeets, then."

"They don't come in pairs at this end of town," said the goblin. "How about five single keets?"

"And a macaw, and a cockatoo, and fourteen goldfinches, and a hipponoceros, and . . ."

The goblin held up an empty hand. "Would you settle for a 1933 issue of *The Shadow* pulp magazine?"

"There's nothing in your hand," said Felina.

"Sure there is," said the goblin. "It's such a powerful story that it's clouded your mind already."

"Leave that phony and start walking," said Mallory.

"How do you know he's a phony?" asked Felina.

"You don't have a mind to cloud."

"I never thought of that," she said, falling into step behind him.

"I can't imagine why," said Mallory.

"Last chance!" cried the goblin as they were almost out of earshot. "How about a candid photo of Bettie Page, and she's—hold on to your hat!—fully dressed? They don't come any rarer than that!"

Finally the World Jade Center loomed large before them, a huge, hundred-story edifice made entirely of third-rate metal alloys that had turned green after repeated exposure to the sunlight. When the cost of resurfacing or repainting the building was computed, the landlord decided that it was cheaper to capitalize on the sickly green color than replace it, and hence it became the World Jade Center.

Mallory walked up to the main entrance, nodded to the green-clad guard, and entered the lobby, followed by his ill-matched crew. They marched over to the building directory, and Mallory found that a William Masterson was in apartment 6317.

They entered a self-service elevator, and Mallory pressed the button for the sixty-third floor.

"I *like* elevators!" said Felina as she happily bounced up and down.

"I'm dying!" moaned Dawkins, clutching his belly. "I shouldn't have eaten those last eight knishes!"

Dugan, who was almost certain he had been shot with bullets rather than knishes, at least the last two times, simply kept silent until they reached the sixty-third floor and exited the small elevator.

"This way," said Mallory, checking the apartment numbers on the doors, and walking until he came to 6317. He rang the bell, got no response, and then knocked. There was still no answer.

"Okay," he muttered, pulling out a set of skeleton keys, "we'll do it the hard way."

His first two keys didn't work, and he uttered a low curse.

"I was a housebreaker once," offered Dugan. "Would you like me to help?"

"Why not?" said Mallory, holding out the keys to Dugan, who ignored them and smashed his huge fist against the door, which splintered and caved it. "Or you could do that," concluded Mallory, as he entered the small apartment.

The place was entirely unfurnished. Mallory walked to the kitchen and opened the refrigerator. It was warm and empty. He checked and saw that it wasn't plugged in.

"Felina, take a whiff," said the detective. "Has there been a dragon here in the past day?"

"There hasn't been anyone here forever and ever, for a trillion zillion years," said the cat-girl.

"A trillion zillion years?" repeated Mallory.

"Well, a month, anyway."

"And there's no food in the house," said Dawkins, choking back a manly little sob.

"Where the hell's the phone?" asked Mallory.

"What am I, chopped liver?" said Belle.

"I'm sorry," said Mallory, pulling her out of his pocket. "I forgot all about you."

"Go ahead, break my heart," she replied. "See if I care."

"Well, you *were* quiet for the past half hour or so."

"A girl's got to get her beauty sleep," said Belle.

"Dial Winnifred," said Mallory. "I need to talk to her."

"Say please."

"Please."

"Say I love you with all my heart," said Belle.

"Dawkins, see if this place has a phone," said Mallory.

"All right, all right, I'm dialing," said Belle.

"Thanks."

"Hold your lips a little closer to me."

"Just dial the goddamned number," growled Mallory.

"Has anyone ever told you you're beautiful when you're angry?" said Belle.

"Has anyone ever told you you're irreparable when you've been thrown against a wall?" shot back Mallory.

"Hello?" said Winnifred's voice.

"Hi. Mallory here."

"Any luck?" she asked.

"Not so's you'd notice it," he said. "Hennigan gave us Brody's phony name and address, but it's a dead end."

"Too bad," said Winnifred. "I've got four more bookies who booked future bets of ten thousand or more on Carmelita."

"Give 'em to Belle in a minute," said Mallory. "But first, I think there's a new line of inquiry to follow."

"Oh?"

"He's Buffalo Bill Brody, and so far he's used Doc Holliday and Bat Masterson as aliases."

"Ah!" said Winnifred. "You want me to check on William Cody?"

"No," said Mallory. "Too close to his own name. Besides, Cody made his reputation killing buffalo, and Brody looked like he was half buffalo himself."

"Then I don't understand."

"Try cowboys. Billy the Kid was born in Manhattan. He used the alias of William Bonney, and his real name was Henry McCarty. And try Wyatt Earp, John Wesley Hardin, Jesse James, Johnny Ringo, and Cole Younger while you're at it."

"I will," said Winnifred. "But some of those names are bound to belong to real people."

"I don't doubt it. And if you can contact any of them, they're eliminated. But see if you can find one that doesn't answer his phone at three in the morning. It'll be a start."

"If the house or apartment is empty, why would he have a phone in the first place?"

"He had to give an address and phone number when he laid down those big bets, or they'd have suspected something was fishy," said Mallory. "By the same token, he didn't want them all coming from the same name or the same address."

"All right," said Winnifred. "I'll get right on it, and let Harry concentrate on future books."

"Fine," said Mallory. "Now feed the information you have to Belle."

He waited for almost a minute, until Belle announced "Got it!" then tucked her back into a pocket, left the apartment, and ushered his team into the elevator.

"Where to now?" he asked Belle.

"William Hickok, southwest corner of Seventh and Lust."

"Wild Bill Hickok," said Mallory. "It figured." As the elevator began descending and Gently Gently Dawkins began moaning and clutching his stomach again, the detective came to a conclusion. "I think we'll skip it," he announced. "I'll give plenty of fifty-to-one that apartment's going to be as empty as this one. In fact, they're all going to be empty."

"Do you want me to call your partner back and tell her not to bother tracking down the empties?" asked Belle.

"No," said Mallory. "They're empty *now*, but if we don't turn up with the dragon before ring time, he's going to have *someone* in each place to call his various bookies and make arrangements to get paid."

"Why not just call from a—*ptui!*—pay phone?" asked Belle.

"Because he gave each bookie a different name and number so they couldn't spot the scam, and you can bet they've all got Caller ID to stop some phony from pretending to be a winning bettor and picking up someone else's payoff."

"So what do we do now?" asked Belle.

"I don't know," said Mallory as the elevator reached the lobby level and they all got off. "All he's got to do is lay low for another twelve hours. He's not going to leave wherever he's at or take a chance of Fluffy being spotted, and he's sure as hell not going to be in any room or apartment that he rented as a front for his bets. There's hundreds of thousands of hotel rooms in town, and a lot of them aren't very choosy about who or what they'll let in. Winnifred and Harry will get some more contacts, but they're going to prove as empty as this one." He paused and signed deeply. "I hate to admit it, but I'm stumped."

"Not you, Studmuffin," said Belle. "I have faith in you."

"I could do with a little less faith and a few more leads," said Mallory as they exited the World Jade Center and stood out on the street. Suddenly he looked around. "Where the hell did Dawkins go?"

Felina pointed into the building, where Gently Gently Dawkins was putting coins into a candy machine.

"Goddamn!" exclaimed Mallory. "We've been walking around with the clue we needed, and I didn't realize it until this very second!"

"What are you talking about?" asked Belle.

"You'll see," said Mallory. He opened the door. "Hey, Dawkins! Come out here!"

"In a minute," answered Dawkins, putting the last of his change into the machine for one last candy bar. The machine disgorged it, he picked it up, unwrapped it, and began eating it as he went outside. "What is it?" he asked when he had joined the others.

"I need your expertise," said Mallory.

"Do I have some?" asked Dawkins, patting his pockets as if it might be residing there.

"Based on our brief association, I'd say you are probably a greater expert on a certain subject than anyone else alive."

"Really?" said Dawkins, a happy smile on his round face.

Mallory nodded. "Really." He paused. "What do you know about elephant-shaped chocolate marshmallow cookies?"

"They're scrumptious," said Dawkins. "But they're very rare. You have to know who sells them."

"And do you?" asked Mallory.

"Oh, sure," answered Dawkins enthusiastically. "They're one of my favorites."

A smile crossed Mallory's face. "I think the case is open for business again."

CHAPTER 20

3:42 AM–4:29 AM

Mallory's little group trudged down the empty street. Darkened buildings loomed over them, and a few stray snowflakes floated down through the chilly air.

"You're *sure* there's a candy stand in the Holland Tunnel?" said Mallory.

"Absolutely," replied Dawkins. "It's one of my favorites."

"I don't remember seeing one," said the detective. "There are just traffic lanes in the tunnel, nothing else."

"When's the last time you drove through it?"

"Not since I came to this Manhattan," admitted Mallory.

"Well, that explains it." Dawkins pulled a candy bar out of his pocket and peeled the wrapper off it.

"If you don't care about your weight, you might consider what all that junk is doing to your health," suggested Mallory.

"You're looking at it all wrong," answered Dawkins. "Not only does this contain the three major food groups—chocolate, peanut butter, and sugar— but it's an energy food."

"You've consumed enough energy in the past two hours to light up Mexico City for a week," said Mallory.

"You're exaggerating," laughed Dawkins. Suddenly the smile vanished. "Boise, Idaho, maybe."

"Winnifred just checked in to say she located empty apartments for Cole Younger and William Bonney," said Belle.

"I didn't hear you ring," said Mallory.

"You turned off my ringer, remember?"

"Even so, aren't you supposed to vibrate or something?"

"Only *you* can make me vibrate, Hot Lips."

"Are you *trying* to embarrass me?" asked Mallory.

"No," said Belle, "I'm trying to excite you beyond all endurance."

"Excitement is another union, but you're fast reaching the endurance limit," said Mallory. "Try to just converse normally, okay?"

"Aye, aye, sir," said Belle. "Ten-four. Roger. Over and out." A pause. "Is that any better, Sweetmeat?"

Mallory decided it was easier to ignore her than argue with her, and he increased his pace. He had to slow it a moment later when Dawkins fell too far behind.

"This is fun!" enthused Felina. "We should go out in the middle of the night and do absolutely nothing more often, John Justin."

"We're not *doing* nothing," Mallory corrected her. "We're *accomplishing* nothing." He turned to Dawkins. "And it better come to an end pretty soon."

"I know about that," said Dead End Dugan, who hadn't spoken since they left the World Jade Center.

"You know about *what?*" asked Mallory, confused.

"About coming to an end," replied Dugan. "Coming to an end is one of the best things I do." He frowned. "Or at least one of the most frequent."

"Joe En-lai is looking better and better," muttered Mallory.

"Not as good as you, Cuddles," said Belle.

"It wasn't so bad in *my* Manhattan," said Mallory wistfully. "I couldn't pay my bills, and my wife ran off with my partner, and the courts kept putting the bad guys back on the street quicker than we could bring them in . . . but it all made a certain corrupt kind of sense."

"You have to think big here," said Dawkins knowingly. "Dealing in corrupt cents is for small-timers. We deal in corrupt dollars."

"Thanks for that cogent insight," said Mallory dryly.

"Here we are," said Dawkins, pointing to the entrance to the tunnel, a pitch-black hole in its near-black surroundings.

"How far?" asked Mallory as they entered it. "And what happened to the lights?"

"It's a cost-cutting measure," said Dawkins. "Hardly anyone drives the Tunnel at three in the morning."

"Watch out!" said Mallory, as a quartet of cars blinded them with their headlights and raced past.

"Well, *almost* hardly anyone," amended Dawkins as another car and two trucks zoomed by.

"You're *sure* it's here?" demanded Mallory after they'd gone another hundred yards.

"We're getting close," said Dawkins. "Trust me."

"What is it—a drive-through?"

"No, of course not," said Dawkins. "It's a regular shop. No *real* New Yorkers own cars." Suddenly the tunnel wall jutted out, forming a cozy and dimly lit alcove. "Here we are."

An old man with wild, unkempt white hair and a bushy white beard stood behind a counter. "Hi, Gently Gently. Long time no see."

"What are you talking about?" said Dawkins, frowning. "I was just here this afternoon."

"I was referring to that C-note you've owed me for two months," said the man. "Even you have to admit that's a long time."

"I'm working on it," said Dawkins. "You have to understand: Harry barely pays me enough to eat."

"Yeah, I suppose when you live alone and your food budget tops fifteen hundred dollars a week . . ."

"Speaking of food," said Dawkins, peering through the glass countertop, "what have you got?"

"The usual."

"Have you got any elephant-shaped chocolate marshmallow cookies?" asked Mallory.

"Who's your friend?" asked the bearded man.

"John Justin Mallory, say hello to Butcher Burstein."

"Butcher?" asked Mallory curiously.

"Candy butcher," replied the old man. "And in answer to your question, I'm out of the elephant-shaped ones. I could sell you some rhino-shaped ones to hold you until my next batch arrives."

"Did you sell them today?" asked Mallory.

"Matter of fact I did."

"To whom?"

"I run a candy counter in a tunnel," replied Burstein. "I don't keep records."

"The guy who bought them—was he a big man, real broad head, with a couple of horns growing out of it?"

"Now that you mention it, he was," said the old man.

"Did he have a dragon with him?"

"In a traffic tunnel? It wouldn't fit."

"This was a little one," said Mallory. "Maybe the size of a small cocker spaniel."

Burstein's eyes lit up. "A cocker spaniel?" he repeated in awed tones. "I've never seen anything that rare!"

Mallory stared at him for a moment. Finally he used his hands to indicate Fluffy's size.

"Nope," said Burstein.

"Damn!" said Mallory. "Then we still don't know where he's got her."

"I might be able to help," offered the old man.

"How?"

"I only had three of the cookies left, and he told me that wasn't enough, that he'd pay top dollar for them. He wouldn't take any substitutes, and he wasn't willing to wait until my new batch came in. So I sent him to Horrid Hubert's."

"Oh, shit!" moaned Dawkins.

"Who's Horrid Hubert?" asked Mallory.

"He's more of a what than a who," replied Dawkins. "As hungry as I get, I've never been so hungry that I was willing to go to Horrid Hubert's."

"But he sells the cookies?" persisted Mallory.

"Oh, no question about it," answered Burstein. "Mostly to little boys and girls who are never seen again."

"Where's he located?"

"Let me see now," said Burstein. "He used to be at the corner of Sloth and Gluttony . . ."

"That's where I first saw him," Dawkins chimed in.

"But now he's got a concession at the Arkham Spell and Curse Shoppe, a few blocks north of the Vampire State Building over on Despair Street."

"Okay, that's our next stop, I guess."

"You *sure*?" said Burstein. "I mean, they're good cookies, but nothing is *that* good."

"No choice," replied Mallory.

"Well, meaning no disrespect, I hope you ain't relying on Gently Gently to protect you."

"Do I *need* protection?"

Burstein shrugged. "I suppose it all depends on whether or not you want to wake up tomorrow."

"Well, if push comes to shove, I've got the zombie," said Mallory. "I don't suppose you can be afraid of anything once you're already dead." He paused. "Thanks for your help." He turned to Felina, Dawkins, and Dugan. "Okay, let's go."

"Where to?" asked Dawkins.

"Horrid Hubert's," replied Mallory.

"Oh, shit!" groaned Dead End Dugan.

CHAPTER 21

4:29 AM–5:16 AM

Mallory's little group turned onto Despair and headed toward the Arkham Spell and Curse Shoppe.

"Do we really have to do this?" asked Gently Gently Dawkins. "I mean, what are the odds that Brody actually sought out"—a slight shudder—"Horrid Hubert, when so many others sell the same thing?"

"Almost nobody else sells the same thing," said Mallory. "If you're frightened, you can wait outside."

"Me, frightened?" said Dawkins in a shaky voice. "Silliest thing I ever heard." A pause. "Terrified, maybe."

"What's he like?"

"He's exactly like . . . like someone who would be called Horrid Hubert."

"Thanks a lot," said Mallory. He turned to Dead End Dugan. "Have you got anything to add to that?"

"What kind of thing?" asked Dugan, checking his pockets for things.

"Forget it," said Mallory.

"Forget what?" replied Dugan.

"I *like* you," said Felina, purring and rubbing her hip against Dugan. "You're the only one who makes sense. Besides me, that is."

"Did I hear someone mention scents?" said a goblin, stepping out from the shadow of a tall building. He turned to Dugan and inhaled deeply. "Just in time, too."

"Go away," said Mallory.

"Not so fast, friend," said the goblin. "I have a license to peddle scents on Gluttony Street."

"We're on Despair."

The goblin shrugged. "Just as well I sold it, then. Now, let's be perfectly honest: Your friend isn't likely to attract the girl of his dreams smelling the way he does now."

"I have a feeling that is precisely the way he'll attract the girl of his dreams," said Mallory.

The goblin threw back his head and laughed. "What a kidder! I like that in a client." The laugh ended as quickly as it began. "Now to get serious, sir—I happen to have rose, violet, jasmine, daffodil, jack-in-the-pulpit, My Sin, Your Sin, Their Sin, Chanel Number Three X Squared, fudge, mozzarella, and pistachio, all in two-ounce spray bottles."

"Leave us alone."

"I've also got Tomcat and Mighty Numa for the lady cat-thing," continued the goblin.

"Fine," said Mallory. "Let *her* pay for it."

"C'mere, cat-thing," said the goblin, pulling a bottle out of his overcoat. "Let me give you a free sample. Stand back, everyone. This will drive her mad with lust."

Felina approached him, and he directed a spray at her. There was no reaction.

"Do you have something in Very Dead Tuna?" she asked.

"How dead does it have to be?" replied the goblin.

"Why?" interjected Mallory.

"My wife's pet tuna is in a tank on the next block," explained the goblin. "I could pop over there, slaughter the ugly beast, chop it into small unappetizing pieces, put them under a tanning lamp to rot and start to stink, and get back in, oh, say five hours." He turned to Felina. "Will you wait?"

"She will not," said Mallory.

"Ten percent off," said the goblin.

"Go away."

"Tell you what—I'll throw in his leash as well."

"Your tuna has a leash?" said Mallory.

"Well, my dog Spot did," answered the goblin. "He's in bottle one-fifty-four now: Essence of Rin Tin Tin."

"Why not Essence of Spot?" asked Dawkins.

Mallory stared at him. "Even *I* think that's a dumb question."

"Oh, of course!" said Dawkins with an embarrassed smile. "Sprays are just one color. You could never prove it was Spot."

Mallory fought back an urge to apologize to the goblin for his companions. Finally he just began walking again.

"Hey, fella, capitalism is a two-way street!" yelled the goblin. "You're not keeping up your end of it."

Mallory kept walking, joined by Dugan, Dawkins, and Felina.

"Damn!" said the goblin just before they were out of earshot. "Two MBA degrees and five years apprenticing, and this is what it gets me! I should have taken that offer to star in *The Sylvester Stallone Story*. But no, not me—I'm a people kind of guy. I live for interaction with my peers." He stopped and sniffed the air. "What smells?" He frowned. "Could it be me? But I bathed just last July! Nah, it must be my imagination."

They reached the Vampire State Building in another five minutes.

"Yo, Mallory!" called the guard, who was hanging by his heels from the top of the doorway. "How's it going?"

"Hi, Boris," said Mallory, waving to him.

"You *know* him?" asked Dawkins, obviously impressed.

"I had a case that took me here last Halloween," said Mallory.

"Is it true what they say about lady vampires?" continued Dawkins.

"I suppose it all depends what they say."

"I'm too embarrassed to repeat it out loud."

"Then it's probably true," replied Mallory. "How long now?"

"That's a very personal question, Mr. Mallory," said Dawkins in outraged tones.

"How long until we get to Horrid Hubert's?"

"Oh," said Dawkins, blushing. "I thought since we were talking about sexy lady vampires . . ."

"Only one of us was," said Mallory.

"No, I was too," said Dawkins.

"Are you going to answer my question?"

"It's four more blocks."

They passed a religious-goods store that specialized in crosses (life size, with or without hammer and nails), a barer bond shop ("Our leather bonds are nakeder than anyone else's!"), a bar catering exclusively to vampires (guaranteeing the most authentic Blood Marys in town—while Mary lasted), a block-long department store that advertised departments of all shapes and sizes, a pair of palm readers (who were studying a novel that had been carved into the trunk of a potted palm tree), and a restaurant catering to Vegan vegetarians (whose manager had just thrown a well-dressed young man out onto the sidewalk, snarling "Can't you read? If you're not from Vega, you're not welcome here!").

"I just remembered," said Dugan as they neared their destination. "It's in the cabinet just to the left of the refrigerator."

"What is?" asked Mallory.

Dugan frowned. "I don't know."

"What do you usually keep next to the refrigerator?"

"I don't have a refrigerator."

Mallory looked from Dugan to Dawkins and back again, then sighed and shook his head. "And Harry lets you both live. Amazing."

"Dugan isn't technically alive," noted Dawkins.

"Thanks for that correction," said Mallory. "Now I want both of you to shut up until we get there."

"Get where?" asked Dugan.

"I'll let you know," said Mallory. He turned to Felina. "You too. And if you say 'No, me Felina,' what's left of you will be stringing a tennis racket."

The cat-girl giggled. "You're funny, John Justin."

Mallory decided he might explode if he counted all the way to ten, so he stopped at five and began walking again. He slowed down when he saw a line of morbidly obese men, women, and children entering a nondescript shop a few yards up ahead. The red bricks had seen better days, the dirt on the small windows was so thick it actually hid a couple of cracks, and the door had Happy Hubert's emblazoned on it in tarnished gold letters.

"That's it?" he asked Dawkins.

"That's the place."

"*Happy* Hubert's?" said Mallory.

"Well, I suppose *he's* happy."

Mallory stared at each of his companions in turn. "Dugan, you come with me. You other two, stay outside."

"Why?" asked Dawkins.

"Because you're drooling already, and Felina will grab anything that isn't nailed down."

"Or glued," said the cat-girl helpfully. "You forgot glued down, John Justin."

"I lost my head," said Mallory. "Or glued down. Happy now?"

"Yes, John Justin," she said, rubbing against him. "Skritch my back."

"Later."

"Why?" she asked.

"Because we're on a case."

"Oh," said Felina. A brief pause. "Is it later yet?"

"I'll let you know," said Mallory.

"Thank you, John Justin. You're a very nice man . . ."

"You're welcome."

". . . for a fiend who won't skritch my back."

"Dawkins," said Mallory as they reached the Arkham Spell and Curse Shoppe, "make yourself useful and skritch her back. Come on, Dugan."

As they were entering the store, Mallory heard Felina hiss and say, "You're *scratching*! I want you to *skritch*!"

Then they were inside. There were display cases and shelves filled with newt's eyes, lizard's tongues, raven's claws, the teeth of some lizard that Mallory hoped he'd never encounter, and hundreds of dusty, moldering grimoires and spell books. There was also a large candy counter filled with millions of calories in incredibly tempting forms, and it was here that almost all the people were lined up.

Behind it sat the strangest man Mallory had ever seen. Plump was an understatement. So was fat. So was obese. There was simply no word that properly described him. Mallory guessed that he topped out at eight hundred pounds, possibly more.

His head was round, and totally hairless. It sat on his body like a basketball on a beachball. His eyes were barely visible behind his pudgy, bloated cheeks. His mouth seemed twice the normal size, and his teeth practically glistened in their whiteness. The sides of his head were so flabby that his ears almost disappeared from view. His body had some protrusions, and it took

Mallory a minute to realize they were his arms and legs. A colorful macaw sat on his left shoulder, which convinced Mallory he'd been right to leave Felina outside.

The detective stood in line, nudging Dugan, whose mind was clearly elsewhere if at all, every time they had to move forward, and after ten minutes he found himself facing Horrid Hubert.

"I don't recognize you," said Hubert in a voice that was smoother than oil. He smiled, and Mallory could see that his teeth had been filed.

"This is my first trip here," said the detective.

"Ah! Fresh flab!" said Hubert enthusiastically.

"Fresh blood," the macaw corrected him.

Hubert tried to stand up to greet Mallory. He grunted, but nothing happened except that he turned a bright red. He tried again, and began gasping for air.

"Maybe I'll just stay seated," he said at last.

"You'd better," agreed Mallory. "I think you were in danger of passing out."

Hubert shrugged, which sent ripples down to his toes. "I really need to get to the gym more often," he said. "Once they reinforce the floors." A smile that was meant to be ingratiating spread across the fullness of his face. "Which of my goodies can I sell you—or are you here for a spell?"

"I'm here for some information," replied Mallory.

"We sell that too," said the macaw.

"You heard him," said Hubert.

"Have you sold any elephant-shaped chocolate marshmallow cookies today?"

"Ah!" said Hubert. "You must be Mallory! He warned me that you might show up here."

"Brody?"

"Who else?"

"Did he have a dragon with him?" asked Mallory.

"No," said the macaw.

"That one's on the house," added Hubert. "The next one is going to cost you."

"Where was he taking the cookies?" asked Mallory.

"Five thousand dollars," said the macaw.

"Are you open to a counteroffer?" said Mallory.

"Certainly," said Hubert. "What is it?"

"Tell me what I want to know, and my friend here"—he patted Dugan on the shoulder—"won't tear your shop apart."

"No," said Hubert thoughtfully. "I'd rather have the five grand."

"You have ten seconds to change your mind," said Mallory. "Then I turn him loose."

"In a spell and curse shop?" said Hubert with a laugh. "You have delusions of grandeur. *Abra cadabra!*"

Dugan froze. He hadn't been moving before, but suddenly Mallory knew at a gut level that the zombie was now incapable of motion.

"Now, Mr. Mallory, how about that five thousand dollars?"

"I haven't got it."

"Then you are destined to leave without what you came here for," said Hubert.

Mallory decided to play his one trump card. "Okay," he said. "The Grundy can get his own damned information."

A look of terror crossed Hubert's face for a moment, and then he suddenly smiled. "Nice try, Mr. Mallory, but the Grundy doesn't need to hire a detective."

You'd better be watching, thought Mallory. Aloud he said, "Grundy, you want to set him straight?"

"I have commissioned John Justin Mallory to find a missing dragon," said the Grundy's voice.

Now I owe you one, thought the detective.

"Omygod!" said the macaw, starting to tremble. "Omygod! Omygod!"

"Hey, Mr. Grundy, sir, we were just kidding around!" yelled Hubert. He turned back to Mallory. "I don't know where he's holed up, but I know he was going to the Cut-Rate Elixir Shop when he left here. He was looking for something to calm his nerves."

"I'll bet he was," said Mallory. "He probably figured out who really wants that dragon found." Suddenly a strange odor came to his nostrils. "What the hell is *that*?"

"What?" asked Hubert, looking around.

"That smell."

"Oh, that's just the furnace next door."

"But I smell it *here*."

"The two stores are connected," said Hubert.

Mallory frowned, his nostrils smarting. "What's it burning?"

"It's rendering lard," answered Hubert. "We supply it for the whole city."

"'We'?" repeated Mallory.

"I own both stores."

"Okay," said Mallory. "Take the spell off the zombie and we'll be on our way."

"Anything for a friend of the Grundy's," said Hubert earnestly. *"Presto!"*

Mallory stared at Dugan. "I don't notice any difference."

"Tell him to move."

"Dugan, lift your hand," said Mallory.

"Which of them?" responded Dugan, who had clearly lost count of how many he had.

"Okay, he's functional again," said Mallory. "So to speak." He began walking toward the door. "Come on, Dugan," he said, resisting the urge to add *"Heel!"*

He noticed that the shop was almost empty now. When he and Dugan reached the street, he walked up to Dawkins. "Have you been watching the store?"

"Yes."

"How many people have come out since I entered?"

"Ten or eleven."

"There were maybe forty in the place when I walked in," said Mallory. "There can't be a dozen left."

Dawkins struggled with the math for a moment. "What does it all mean?" he asked.

Mallory looked at the smoke rising from the lard shop's furnace.

"It means I know why they call him Horrid Hubert," said the detective.

CHAPTER 22

5:16 AM–5:55 AM

They'd gone three blocks through a forest of skyscrapers which seemed unlikely venues for elixir shops when Dawkins came to a stop.

"What's the matter?" asked Mallory.

"I'm trying to remember exactly where the place is," explained Dawkins. "I stopped going when they stopped serving chocolate sodas."

"I never knew chocolate sodas were elixirs," remarked Mallory.

"Oh, sure," said Dawkins. "Sodas, phosphates, and also extra-thick double-chocolate malts."

"You make it sound more like an ice cream parlor."

"No," said Dawkins. "They have an elixir for whatever ails you: gout, lumbago, even an unfaithful spouse."

"What ails *you*?" asked Mallory.

"Hunger, usually."

"Well?"

"Well what?" asked Dawkins.

"Do you remember which way to go?"

"No, but there's a flawless method for deciding what course to follow," explained Dawkins. He spat on his left hand, held it palm up, and then slapped it with his right hand. A small particle of spittle flew into Dugan's left eye.

"I hope you're not going to tell me that the store is in Dugan's eye," said Mallory.

Dawkins frowned. "You know, as many times as I've tried that, it never works."

"And that surprises you, does it?"

"Not anymore," admitted Dawkins. "But it still disappoints me."

Mallory pulled Belle out of his pocket. "Wake up," he said.

"Hi, Lover," she replied. "I was dozing, and I had this dream that you were running your hands all over my naked, pulsating body—and here you are, doing just that."

"Has your naked, pulsating body ever worn clothes?"

"Don't ask such intimate questions in front of strangers."

Mallory surveyed his companions. "They *are* a little stranger than most," he acknowledged.

"Less talking and more petting," said Belle.

"Less romance and more work," replied Mallory. "Find the number of the Cut-Rate Elixir Shop, buzz them, and get their address."

"Only if you say 'I lust for you with a passion that knows no bounds.'"

"Felina," said Mallory, "see if you can hunt up a phone booth."

"All right, all right," said Belle. "I'll do your bidding—but I warn you, my tears may short me out at any second."

"I don't see any tears."

"That's because I'm laughing on the outside."

"The very best place for it. Now, the address?"

"In a minute," answered Belle. "Not everyone's as cruel and unfeeling as you are. Some of them are polite and caring. Some of them try to put a girl at her ease."

"Some of them aren't working on a deadline," said Mallory. "Get me the damned address."

There was a sudden earsplitting shriek.

"What was *that?*" asked Mallory.

"You cursed at me," said Belle. "You humiliated me in front of all these people—and after all we've been to each other."

"We haven't been anything to each other," said Mallory. "And 'all these people' consists of a walking appetite, a cat-girl, and a zombie."

"Details," sniffed Belle.

"He's taking my job!" said Felina suddenly, pointing an accusing claw at Dawkins. "You always say that *I'm* a walking appetite."

Mallory sighed deeply. "I wonder if the Grundy could use a security chief?" he muttered.

"Oh, all right," said Belle petulantly. "The corner of Forty-eighth and Seventh."

"Forty-eighth Street and Seventh Avenue," said Mallory. "Got it."

"No," she replied. "Forty-eighth Avenue and Seventh Street."

"It doesn't exist," said Mallory.

"It does, if you know how to get there," said Dawkins.

"But you don't," noted Mallory.

"But I know you *can*, because I've been there. That's a start, isn't it?"

"*I* know where it is," said Felina with a triumphant smile.

"Why do I sense a negotiation in the offing?" said Mallory wryly.

"I'm happy to take you there, John Justin," said the cat-girl.

"Good. Let's go."

"For a canary, two ravens, four bald eagles, and a rhinopotamus."

"No."

"Okay," she said. "Three bald eagles instead of four."

"Forget it."

"Forget what?" asked Felina.

"Never mind," said Mallory, walking off toward the west.

"Where are you going?"

"Forty-eighth Avenue."

"You'll never get there if you go that way," said Felina with a catlike grin.

"Enlighten me."

"You go left for a block, then turn left for a block, then turn left for a block, and then turn left for a block."

"We'll wind up right back here."

"Okay," said Felina, turning her back and assiduously licking a forearm. "Do it your own way, and be sure to bring your swimsuit."

Mallory stared at her for a long minute, then turned to Harry the Book's two henchmen. "I don't suppose either of you knows how to get to Forty-eighth Avenue?"

"I'd go to Forty-ninth Avenue and then backtrack a block," offered Dawkins.

"Belle?"

"I don't go to elixir shops," said the cell phone. "Love is my elixir. You want to sneak off and cuddle for a few minutes?"

Mallory sighed deeply. "All right, Felina—lead the way."

"Three bald eagles," said the cat-girl.

"No."

"Three hairy eagles?"

Mallory just stared at her, and finally she sighed and began walking. They went south for a block, then east, then north, and then west . . . but Mallory noticed that the buildings he passed on the final block weren't the ones he'd seen before, and when Felina came to a stop he looked at the street sign.

"Forty-eighth Avenue," he read. "Well, I'll be damned."

"Let's sneak off and be damned together," said Belle.

"And we're at Ninth Street," he said, ignoring her. "So the elixir shop should be two blocks to my left." He turned to Felina. "Right?"

"Not right—left," she said, and giggled.

He began walking past a row of taverns. One catered to goblins, one to leprechauns, one to trolls, and one to things he thought existed only in his nightmares.

"Stay close," he said to Dugan, "just in case we run into one of those creatures."

"I'm not happy, John Justin," announced Felina as they came to Eighth Street.

"I'm crestfallen," said Mallory. "What's destroying your happiness this time?"

"We keep passing stores and none of them are selling the earrings you promised me."

"Earrings?" repeated Mallory, puzzled.

"That the woman was wearing in the wrong places."

"We're busy now. I'll get them tomorrow or the next day."

She shook her head sadly. "You probably won't live that long."

"I may disappoint you and live until I'm ninety," said Mallory.

"Then you'd better stop walking," said Felina.

Mallory was about to ask why when he heard a roar that made the question redundant.

Approaching them down the middle of Eighth Street was a dragon which looked exactly like the photos of Fluffy except that it was twenty feet in height and seventy feet in length. Flames shot out of its mouth, twin bursts of smoke came from its nostrils, and it flapped its wings noisily.

"Stop him!" yelled a voice from half a block away.

"How?" asked Mallory. "I left my bazooka in my other suit."

"Good God, don't hurt him!" said the voice as the dragon melted a mailbox and a parked car. "He's just being playful."

"He's got an interesting notion of play," said Mallory.

"Just step in front of him and tell him to stop!"

"You're kidding, right?"

"There's ten bucks in it for you if you'll do it," said the voice.

"Ten bucks won't pay for my casket, let alone my funeral."

"Please! I beg of you!"

"*I'll* stop him," offered Felina.

"Bless you!" said the voice.

"For two halibut, a dolphin, and a camel."

"I can see you now. You're a cat-girl, aren't you? Stop him and I'll give you twenty dollars to spend at the fish market on Sixth Street."

Felina reached over and pulled Mallory's handkerchief from his pocket, then stepped out into the street right in front of the dragon. She waved the handkerchief at him, and he practically skidded to a stop and stood there trembling.

A small man with thick glasses and a shopworn tuxedo raced up to them, gasping for breath. "Thank you, thank you!" he burbled. "I was afraid he might do some damage."

Mallory gestured to the car and the mailbox, two molten blobs on the pavement. "You don't call that damage?"

"No one was in the car," said the man.

"No one was in the mailbox either," said Dawkins.

The man reached into a pocket, pulled out a twenty-dollar bill, and handed it to Felina. "Thank you, cat-girl," he said. "I can't have poor Fido tiring himself out before Eastminster."

"He's a show dragon?" asked Mallory.

The man drew himself up to his full, if minimal, height. "Can't you tell?" he said coldly.

"I thought they were smaller," said Mallory.

"They come in all sizes," said the man. "By the way," he added, extending a hand, "my name is Alexander Hamilton."

"Really?" asked Mallory, taking his hand.

"Actually, it's Philbert Potts, but people pay attention when I say I'm Hamilton."

"Well, I'm glad we could help you, Philbert."

"It wouldn't have mattered yesterday," said Potts, "but the word on the grapevine is that Champion Fluffy is missing, so that means we have a chance. All we have to do is beat"—he gulped—"the Grundy's entry."

"Good luck."

"Why don't you come by and cheer for us?" suggested Potts.

Before Mallory could answer, Fido melted a fire hydrant, water gushed out, and Potts explained to the dragon in very gentle tones why that was unacceptable social behavior.

"Why not just smack him on the nose?" asked Mallory.

"We have a show tomorrow," explained Potts. "It wouldn't do to break his spirit." He unwound a lasso from around his waist, twirled it over his head a few times, and hurled the noose over Fido's head. "I'm sorry we can't stay and visit," he said, leading the dragon back down Eighth Street, "but we need our rest before the show."

"He'd better feed that beast an elephant or two, or it might decide to eat the judge," remarked Mallory when Potts and Fido were out of earshot.

"That was a dragon, wasn't it?" said Dugan, looking after it.

"I'm glad to see you're as quick on the uptake as ever," said Mallory, crossing the street and heading toward the next corner. Suddenly he stopped

"What the hell is *that*?" he said.

"What is *what*?" asked Belle.

"It looks exactly like a gingerbread house out of a fairy tale," said Mallory.

"That's the place," said Dawkins.

Mallory approached it and saw a sign spelled out on the frosted door in licorice letters: *Ye Olde Cut-Rate Elixir Shop.*

Mallory entered, followed by his companions. The interior—walls, counters, shelves, everything—seemed to be made exclusively of cake and candy. A row of bottles, in rocky candy containers, was prominently displayed. A small, wiry, gray-haired woman wearing a print dress, with a knitted shawl wrapped around her shoulders, came out from a back room to greet them.

"Welcome, welcome, welcome," she said, putting her knitting and needles into a pocket of her apron. She studied Mallory. "You've come to the right place. She'll never give you a second look until you drink Aunt Granny's Elixir of Sublime Attraction."

"That may well be, but I came here for—"

"I know," interrupted the old woman. "Your boss puts you down, insults you in front of your workmates, makes you feel inferior. Aunt Granny's Elixir of Righteous Revenge will fix that in no time."

"You're Aunt Granny?"

"The one and only," she replied proudly.

"I don't suppose you'd like to let me get a whole sentence out before interrupting?" said Mallory.

"Feeling oppressed and inferior?" said Aunt Granny. "You need my Elixir of Dynamic Compensation."

Mallory simply stared at her, unwilling to keep being interrupted all night.

"Cat got your tongue?" suggested Aunt Granny.

"Why would I want his tongue?" asked Felina curiously.

"Sorry, cat-thing," said the old lady. "Nothing personal."

"I need some information," said Mallory.

"You also need a better suit, a shave, breath mints, and a haircut," noted Aunt Granny. "I'm saying this for your own good, you know."

"That sounds like an Aunt Granny, all right," said Mallory.

"No backtalk from you," said Aunt Granny, "or I'll drink my Elixir of Sensual Perfection and become the most desirable and most unattainable creature you ever saw. You'll go crazy with lust, and kill yourself when you can't have me."

"And I'll kill him if he can," said Belle.

"Your chest has a mind of its own," observed Aunt Granny. "Does it often contradict you?"

"We have a deep and ongoing romance," said Belle.

Aunt Granny took a step back. "Your chest doesn't need an elixir so much as a tranquilizer."

"Can we get back to the subject?" said Mallory.

"Which subject was that—your chest or your appearance?"

"My information."

"Okay, I'm listening," said Aunt Granny.

"I'm not offering it, I'm asking for it," said Mallory, starting to grow annoyed.

"Fine. I'll give you the best information I have," she replied. "Buy low, sell high. Never bet on claimers who are moving up in class. Stay out of commodities."

"Are you through?" said Mallory.

"My goodness, how much information do you want?"

"You had a client tonight, big fellow with horns growing out of his head."

"Ah, yes, Mr. Earp."

"Wyatt?"

"How did you know?" she asked.

"A shot in the dark," said Mallory. "What did he buy?"

"Aunt Granny's Elixir of Magnesia."

"What the hell is that?"

"It calms the stomach. He seemed very nervous."

"Not without cause," said the detective. "Did you notice if he happened to have a small dragon with him?"

"No," she replied. "All he had was a small suitcase with ventilation holes at each end."

"Did he say where he was going next?"

Aunt Granny shook her head. "No."

Mallory frowned. "He can't leave town, because he has to be here to collect his bets. So he's hiding somewhere in Manhattan."

"That narrows it down to maybe four million apartments, condos, and hotel rooms," said the old lady. "Maybe you should consider buying a bottle of Aunt Granny's Elixir of Unexcelled Cerebration."

"I'll take a rain check," said Mallory.

"Your loss," said Aunt Granny. "Is there anything else I can help you with?"

"Not unless you can tell me where he's hiding."

"What have you done to make him so afraid of you?"

"Nothing compared to what a consortium of bookies is going to do to him if he stays hidden until dinnertime tomorrow . . . I mean today."

"Have you had any sleep, young man?" asked Aunt Granny.

"No, and no."

"I only asked you one question."

"No, I haven't had any sleep, and no, I'm not a young man."

"I'll tell you what," she said, reaching behind a counter and pulling out a small bottle. "I'm going to give you a gift."

"What is it?" asked Mallory, staring at the bottle.

"Aunt Granny's Elixir of Singular Concentration. It will keep you alert."

"So would a cup of coffee," said Mallory.

"But my elixir doesn't require cream, sugar, or a cheese Danish," she replied. "It's all the rage in Bohemian coffeehouses down in the Village."

"Thanks," he said, resisting the urge to ask her which Village, and starting to put it in a pocket.

"*Now!*" she said severely.

He held the bottle up to the light. "What's in it, really?" he asked dubiously.

"Dreams, hope, thoughts, conclusions, deductions, and a hell of a lot of caffeine," answered Aunt Granny. "Now drink it up."

Mallory stared at the bottle.

"Don't force me to become severe with you, young man."

He sighed, opened the bottle, brought it up to his mouth, and drained it.

"Well?" she said expectantly.

"It's not Dom Perignon," replied Mallory. "If truth be known, it's now even Old Peculiar."

"But is it working?" she persisted. "Are you thinking more clearly."

"Of course not," he said. "It's probably just unsweetened coffee." He made a face. "It's really pretty awful. Tastes kind of like—" Suddenly he froze.

"Are you okay, Mr. Mallory?" asked Dawkins.

"His heart is beating," announced Belle.

Suddenly Mallory blinked his eyes rapidly. "Son of a bitch!" he exclaimed.

"What is it?" asked Dawkins.

"I know where Brody's hiding!"

As they passed a crowded delicatessen, Felina pressed her face up against the window, staring at the lox on a diner's plate.

"Looks pretty good, doesn't it?" said Dawkins, moving next to her. "But I prefer the matzo ball soup, and maybe some chopped liver."

"I want *those*!" she said, pointing a claw toward a pile of sardines on another plate.

"I wonder how they'd go with a knish or two?" mused Dawkins.

"Uh . . . I hate to be a killjoy," said Mallory, walking back to them when he noticed they had stopped, "but we're about to apprehend the villain and rescue the princess."

"What princess?" asked Dawkins.

"Well, she's a princess among eleven-inch dragons," said Mallory. "Do you suppose you two could drag yourselves away from the deli's window, or do I have to order Dugan to drag you?"

"But we're hungry!" protested Felina.

"When are you ever not?" said the detective.

"A month ago last Blisterday, at fifteen o'clock in the twilight," she replied.

"If Brody's hiding, he probably isn't about to go anywhere," said Dawkins, stepping aside as a pair of trolls in yarmulkes entered the deli. "So perhaps we have time for some blintzes, and maybe a corned beef sandwich."

"Now," said Mallory.

"How about a bagel and cream cheese?"

"See those sauerkraut balls?" said Mallory, pointing to a plate on another table. "You come with me now, or yours will end up on the same plate."

"Okay, I'm coming, I'm coming," whined Dawkins, his hands covering his groin.

"Felina?"

"I'm not afraid of you *or* Dead End Dugan," announced the cat-girl.

"Are you afraid of never being fed again?" asked Mallory.

Felina bounded past him. "Stop loafing, John Justin!" she said. "We're closing in on the Bad Guy!"

"I'm sorry to be slowing you down," said Mallory dryly.

"Where are we going?" asked Dawkins.

"The one place he knew I'd never think of looking."

"A men's clothing store?" asked Dawkins.

"The shower?" chimed in Felina.

"It wouldn't have to be security," muttered Mallory to himself. "I'm adaptable. Maybe the Grundy needs a butler or a gardener."

"I'm glad to hear that," said Belle. "I love a man who's adaptable."

"He can't quit," said Felina. "Who would skritch my back?"

"Or my front?" added Belle.

"I don't want to hear this," said Mallory wearily. He looked ahead. "Turn right at the corner."

They walked in silence for a few blocks. Skyscrapers were replaced by apartment buildings, fine restaurants by sandwich shops, elegant groceries with Noodnik's Emporium and other of its ilk. Then Felina stopped and turned to the detective.

"This is wrong, John Justin."

"Oh?"

She nodded. "If we keep walking this way, we'll be at your office in another block."

"That's right."

"But that's the last place we want to be," said the cat-girl.

"And that's what Brody's counting on."

"You want to explain that, Hot Lips?" said Belle.

"It was when we were talking to Aunt Granny," said Mallory. "She mentioned Bohemian coffeehouses, and everything fell into place."

"You work in a Bohemian coffeehouse?" asked Belle, confused. "I thought you were a shamus."

Mallory shook his head, then realized that she couldn't see him from inside his pocket. "No," he said. "But it was the word. I'm a detective. One of the great detective stories was *A Scandal in Bohemia*, where Irene Adler hides the letters Sherlock Holmes wants by leaving them in plain sight."

"But if Brody's in your office, he's *not* in plain sight," Dawkins chimed in.

"It's the principle that counts," said Mallory. "You hide something valuable in an easily accessible place, and whoever's searching for it walks past it a dozen times, looking for clever hiding places." He paused and stared at three confused faces, one human, one nonhuman, and one no longer human. "Look," he said, "he knows Winnifred or I could go to the office any time we want. We have the keys, so he can't lock us out. But he hasn't had to. We *left* the office to find him. We've been all over the city looking for him. The one place we'd never consider searching is our own office. Remember, he's not hiding out for days or weeks; he just has to stay hidden another nine or ten hours. Where better to do it than the office of the two people who are searching the city for you and your dragon?"

"The Bronx?" guessed Dugan.

"Borneo?" suggested Dawkins.

"The moon," said Felina with absolute certainty.

"That was a rhetorical question," said Mallory disgustedly.

"I *like* redheaded questions," announced Felina.

Mallory was about to correct her, thought better of it, and just resumed walking. He reached his building at 7 Mystic Place in five minutes, opened the door, and walked down the corridor. His office was actually a converted apartment that he'd appropriated from a magician when he'd first arrived, and the landlord was constantly taking down the *Mallory & Carruthers Investigations* sign he had on the door.

He stood before the door and turned to Felina. "Well?"

The cat-girl inhaled deeply. "People smoke too much in the hallways," she announced. "Mr. Miller has a girlfriend. Miss Pringle has two . . . no, three . . . boyfriends." She grinned. "One of them's *really* strange."

"What about Brody and Fluffy?"

"Oh, they were here," said Felina. "Didn't I tell you that?"

"*Were* here?" said Mallory sharply.

"In the hallway. I won't know if they're in the office until you open it."

Mallory inserted his key in the door, and turned to Dugan. "You first," he said as he opened the door.

The zombie walked into the office. "I almost remember that I liked those kind of pictures back when I was alive," he said, staring at the Playmates on the wall behind Mallory's desk. He pointed a mottled forefinger at the under-garments Winnifred had meticulously drawn on the models with a magic marker. "I don't remember *those* though."

"Sometimes my partner can't keep her artistic sensitivities in check," said Mallory, standing by Winnifred's meticulously arranged desk. "Felina, are they here?"

The cat-girl shook her head. "No, John Justin."

"How long ago did they leave?"

Felina walked around the office, sniffing the air. "Maybe twenty minutes."

"You're sure?" persisted Mallory.

"Of course I'm sure," she said with dignity. "I'm a cat-person." A pause. "I have a question, John Justin."

"Yeah?"

"How long is a minute?" said Fellina. "Is it longer than a mile?"

"If you don't know how long a minute is, how do you know they've been gone for twenty of them?"

"Okay, thirty, then," she said agreeably.

"Shit!" said Mallory. "I'm better call Winnifred and tell her they're still at large."

He pulled Belle out of his pocket, and an instant later the room rever-berated to an earsplitting shriek.

"What the hell was *that?*" demanded Mallory.

"Naked women on the wall!" she screamed. "And after all we've meant to each other! How *could* you?"

"They're not naked anymore," Dawkins put in helpfully.

"But they were once!" moaned Belle.

"Most people were once," said Mallory. "Now, are you going to call Win-nifred for me, or do I use my desk phone?"

"That's right!" cried Belle. "First humiliate me, and then abandon me!"

"It'd be hard to do it the other way around," said Mallory, unimpressed.

"I've fallen for a sadist!"

"You've got ten seconds to call Winnifred."

"All right," she sniffed. "But my heart is absolutely shattered. It may affect your reception."

Mallory held the phone to his ear.

"Hold me as if it was for the last time," breathed Belle.

"Just call her, or it *will* be the last time."

"Squeeze me a little. Run your fingers over my numbers. Give me something to remember you by."

"One more word and I'll give you more than you bargained for to remember me by," growled Mallory.

"Hello?" said Winnifred's voice.

"Hi. Just checking in."

"Any progress, John Justin?"

"Not so's you'd notice it. You might as well leave Harry's and join up with us. Brody's not going to be at any of those addresses until after the show."

"You're sure?"

"Yeah. He's also not in our office, though Felina tells me he was here recently."

"How recently?"

Mallory stared at the cat-girl. "That's a point of some debate."

"So what's next?"

"I'm stuck for ideas," he answered. "Come on back to the office and we'll put our heads together."

"On my way," said Winnifred, hanging up.

"You'll put your head together with the fat broad but not with me?" said Belle, on the verge of tears again.

"Strictly speaking, she didn't leave Harry's," added Dawkins helpfully. "She left Joey Chicago's."

Mallory turned to the zombie. "Talk to me, Dugan."

Dugan blinked and looked mildly confused. "What should I say?"

"Whatever comes into your head."

"Nothing's coming into my head," replied Dugan. He frowned. "*Why* am I talking to you?"

"Because everyone else in this office is driving me crazy."

"Oh," said Dugan. He stared silently at the detective.

"Well?" said Mallory.

"I'm thinking. Nothing's coming."

"You know," Mallory mused aloud, "until tonight I actually envied Harry the Book. He sits there in his booth at the bar, he sends you guys out to collect his money, he has his own personal mage." Mallory sighed deeply. "I had no idea what the poor son of a bitch puts up with."

"True, true," said Dawkins. "It's a tension-ridden, time-consuming, economically unstable job."

"That too," agreed Mallory, as Winnifred entered the office. "That was fast," he said to her.

"I caught an express bus."

"The kind with wheels, or the kind with a trunk and tusks?"

"With wheels," she replied. "They're getting rarer and rarer these days."

"So are Brody and Fluffy," Felina chimed in with a cherubic smile.

"Imagine the nerve of that man!" said Winnifred in outraged tones. "Paying us to hunt all over the city for his dragon, while all the time he was hiding her here in our office!" She hung up her coat, unbuttoned her cuffs, and rolled up her sleeves. "Well, let's get to work."

"I thought that's what we've been doing," said Dawkins.

"And now we're going to work some more, this time at finding some clue to tell us where he might have gone," said Winnifred, starting to go over the papers that were neatly stacked on her desk.

"Dawkins, check the kitchen," said Mallory. When he saw the huge smile on Dawkins's face, he held up a hand. "On second thought, *I'd* better check it. Start going through wastebaskets, shelves, anything." Suddenly he froze. "Oh, hell—I keep forgetting: We've got a witness." He walked over to the magic mirror. "Hey, Periwinkle—wake up!"

A face formed in the mirror. The eyes blinked. The mouth yawned. "Can't a guy get a few winks of sleep every now and then?" complained Periwinkle.

"I need your help."

"How thoughtful. You want me to choose between showing you Fifi von Climax or Bubbles La Tour."

"You couldn't have slept the whole time Brody and his dragon were here."

"Ugly beast," remarked Periwinkle.

"We're being paid to find that ugly beast, and Brody took it on the lam before I could confront him here," said Mallory.

"I was referring to Brody."

"Do you have any idea where they went?"

"Has he got a girlfriend?" asked the mirror.

"How the hell do I know?"

"Well, he kept saying that he'd stayed here as long as he felt he could, and they were going over to Gracie's. So find a girl named Gracie who knows him, and the case is solved."

"Just Gracie?" said Winnifred. "No last name?"

"It was garbled," replied Periwinkle. "Manfried, Manly, something like that."

"There's no sense going through the phone book, not with eight million people in Manhattan," said Winnifred unhappily.

"Just a minute," said Mallory. He turned to Periwinkle. "Think carefully now. Instead of Manfried or Manly, could he have said Mansion?"

"It's possible," said Periwinkle. "Silly name for a girl, though."

"Yes, it is," agreed Mallory. "But not for the mayor's residence."

"I don't know, John Justin," said Winnifred dubiously. "He's a stranger in town. How would he have access to Gracie Mansion?"

"Maybe a relative works there," said Mallory; "or maybe a dragon breeder who's entered tomorrow and is only too happy to help him hide the favorite. Who knows?"

"But the mayor's house?" persisted Winnifred. "That would be making him complicit in a crime."

"I don't know if it *is* a crime to pull your entry," said Mallory. "Besides, if the mayor doesn't know what's going on, how can he be complicit?" He paused. "I supposed we'd better be off. East End and Eighty-eighth Street, right?"

"No," said Periwinkle. "The name was garbled, but I heard the address plain and clear: 666 Dybbuk Place."

"All right, let's go," said Winnifred, holding the door open for Dawkins, Dugan, and Felina. "You have the strangest expression on your face, John Justin."

"I don't think we're in Kansas anymore," said Mallory. "Or on the way to the mayor's house, either," he added grimly.

"So where is this Dybbuk Place, anyway?" asked Mallory as they proceeded down obscure side streets he never knew existed.

"Just off Bleak Street, as I recall," replied Winnifred.

"Figures," muttered Mallory, stepping around a drunk who was snoring noisily in the middle of the sidewalk.

"We must be getting close," said Winnifred. "We're passing one moldering Victorian monstrosity after another."

"Those aren't Victrola monsters," said Felina. "They're just houses."

"Big, dark, foreboding houses," added Gently Gently Dawkins nervously.

A banshee swooped down toward them. *"Beware!"* it intoned, flying off just before Felina could leap up and catch it.

"I don't like this area," said Dawkins. "I especially don't like banshees that say 'Beware.'"

"You'd prefer 'Nevermore'?" asked Mallory.

"I'd prefer to be back in my favorite restaurant, or in bed, hiding under the covers," replied Dawkins.

As he spoke, a cloud of bats flew down the length of Bleak Street. One by one they landed, each in front of a different decaying mansion, morphed into black-clad men and women, and entered the houses.

"What was *that* all about?" asked Dawkins in a quavering voice.

"Just a bunch of vampires beating the sunrise after a night on the town," said Mallory. "Nothing unusual." Suddenly he chuckled.

"What's so funny, John Justin?" asked Winnifred.

"I was just amused by how quickly I've adjusted to this Manhattan," said Mallory. "Suddenly it makes perfect sense that I'm walking down Bleak Street in the middle of the city, looking for Dybbuk Place and watching a bunch of vampires returning from dinner."

Suddenly Dead End Dugan stopped walking and looked right and left with a puzzled expression on his face.

"What's the matter?" asked Mallory.

"I think this is the very spot where I was killed," said Dugan. "The first time," he added.

"How many times *have* you been killed?"

Dugan frowned. "Four, I think."

"You don't know?" asked Mallory, surprised.

"Maybe five. I lost count."

"Probably it was the bullet to the head the second time," suggested Dawkins.

"You think you can bring yourself to join us and start walking again?" said Mallory.

"I think so," said Dugan, not moving.

"What now?" said the detective.

"He'll start walking in a minute," said Dawkins. "He's like the dinosaurs. It takes a long time for a thought to travel from his brain to his legs."

Sure enough, Dugan fell into step a few seconds later. Felina led the way, leaping over every square that displayed the builder's insignia.

"Dybbuk Place," announced Winnifred as they came to a narrow street that was very little more than an alley.

The Victorian houses were replaced by more ancient buildings, each sporting a score of gargoyles. Mallory stared at them for a moment, then tensed.

"One of them just moved," he announced.

"Are you sure?" asked Winnifred.

He nodded without ever taking his eyes off the gargoyle.

"I could go back for my .550 Nitro Express," said Winnifred.

"Let's not give Brody a chance to run again," said Mallory.

"Well, I do have *this*," she said, pulling a large handgun out of her purse.

"A .72 caliber Magnum," said Mallory, impressed. "That thing shoots through steam engines."

"Well, a girl can't be too careful on the streets of New York," explained Winnifred.

"You use that against muggers?" said Mallory. "Fire it and there won't be enough of your attacker to bury, or even identify."

"That's an occupational hazard you have if you decide to become a mugger," she said.

"It stopped moving," noted Dawkins, indicating the gargoyle Mallory had been watching.

"But two others are moving now," noted Felina. She waved to them. "They're cute."

"They're even cuter when they're standing still," said Mallory. "Stop attracting their attention."

"You never let me have any fun," pouted the cat-girl.

"You think it's fun to wrestle with a three-ton gargoyle?" asked Mallory.

"I thought *you* could wrestle and I could cheer," said Felina.

Mallory decided not to ask which side she would cheer for.

"I think that's it up ahead, John Justin," said Winnifred, indicating a moldering black building halfway down the block.

"Why that one?" asked Mallory. "They all look equally foreboding."

"See those empty ledges? I think even the gargoyles were frightened of what lies within, and they all flew off."

"I was afraid you were going to say something like that," replied the detective.

"Well," said Winnifred, taking a deep breath, "we've come this far. We might as well go the rest of the way."

"All right," said Mallory, starting forward. "But keep that gun handy."

"I don't think it works against stone gargoyles, John Justin."

"I'm more concerned with whether it'll work against whatever scared the gargoyles away," said Mallory.

The little party cautiously approached the old black building. When they stood in front of it, they could see the tarnished numerals "666" above the door.

"Well, if *he* got in, *we* should be able to get in," said Mallory.

"And if he didn't?" asked Dawkins.

"We'll know that pretty damned quick."

Mallory began advancing cautiously up the front stairs and walked across the stoop to the door, which opened as if it sensed his approach. An ancient corpse, its nose rotted away, one eye hanging down its cheek, suddenly stood in the doorway.

"What is your business here?" it demanded in an accent Mallory couldn't identify.

"We're looking for a dragon," said the detective. "We have reason to believe it's here."

"We do not welcome strangers here," said the corpse.

"My name's John Justin Mallory. Now we're not strangers anymore."

The corpse positioned itself in the middle of the doorway. "I will not permit you to pass."

"I'm sorry, but we're coming in."

"Have you no fear of the dead?" demanded the corpse.

Mallory turned to Dugan. "Are you afraid of dead things?"

Dugan stepped forward. "No."

The corpse pointed a bony finger at Dugan. "Begone, turncoat!" it intoned.

Dugan slapped at the finger, and the corpse's entire hand came away.

The corpse stared at the end of its wrist, then at Dugan, then back at its wrist. "Now what did you want to do *that* for?" it whined. "How am I going to shuffle a deck of cards now?"

"Doesn't sound quite the same, does he?" said Winnifred to Mallory.

"And that was the hand I write with," continued the corpse. "What if someone wants an autograph?"

"Learn to write with your other hand," said Mallory.

"You keep quiet!" snapped the corpse, pointing at Mallory with the forefinger of its remaining hand.

"Are you sure you want to do that?" asked the detective.

Suddenly the corpse pulled its hand back. "This isn't supposed to be happening," it whined. "Just sound terrifying and mysterious, that's what they told me, and everyone will cower and run away. I'm filing an official complaint with the union steward."

"Don't let us stop you," said Mallory.

"I may be back to take your affidavits," said the corpse, walking out of the building and heading down the stairs toward the street. Suddenly it stopped and turned to Dugan. "I don't hold it against you, fella. You're just doing what they pay you to do."

"Pay?" repeated Dugan, blinking his eyes in confusion.

The corpse reached into a fold in its ragged garment and pulled out a card. "My agent," it said, handing it to Dugan. "Give him a call when you get a chance."

Then it was walking down the street, and one by one Mallory's party entered the ominous black building.

Felina wrinkled her nose. "There are things here."

"What kind of things?" asked Winnifred.

"Almost-dead things," replied the cat-girl.

"How about the dragon?" asked Mallory. "Can you smell it?"

Felina shook her head. "There are too many ghouls and monsters."

"How comforting," said Mallory as an inhuman howl came to their ears.

Dawkins turned around and raced to the door. "I gotta go to the bathroom!" he yelled over his shoulder. "I'll catch up with you later."

Mallory and Winnifred exchanged looks.

"You didn't really expect him to be any use here, did you?" she said.

"He'd have been another distraction," said Mallory. "Another target."

"Do you like spiders?" asked Felina suddenly.

"Not especially," said Mallory.

"That's too bad, John Justin," said the cat-girl. "It's really a shame. Maybe you could try to like them just a little."

"Why?" he asked apprehensively.

She smiled and pointed to a doorway. He looked where she'd indicated, and found himself confronting a spider the size of a buffalo.

"Winnifred, you got your gun out?" asked Mallory, never taking his eyes off the spider.

"I think shooting it will just make it mad," she said, but she pulled the Magnum out of her purse anyway.

"It looks hungry to me," said Mallory as the spider slowly began approaching them. "Mad would be better."

Winnifred aimed a shot between the spider's eyes. The bullet careened off and buried itself into a wall.

"What a dumb way to die!" muttered Mallory.

Winnifred fired off two more shots, with no effect.

"Damn!" said Mallory. "Hasn't anyone in this Manhattan ever heard of the square-cube law?"

"Oh, shit!" said the spider, echoing Mallory expletive. "You *had* to say that, didn't you?"

Its body slowly sank to the floor as its spindly legs were suddenly unable to support its enormous weight.

"I was fine until you reminded me!" moaned the spider.

"Have you ever heard a spider speak English before?" asked Winnifred.

"I don't suppose it's any stranger than a spider weighing two thousand pounds," replied Mallory. He took a tentative step toward the spider. "Where's the dragon?"

"Oh, God!" said the spider. "Don't tell me there's a spider-eating dragon sneaking up on me!"

"I'm looking for one this size," said Mallory, demonstrating with his hands.

"Why should I help you?"

"Because we're not leaving until we find it, and the sooner we leave, the sooner you can forget the square-cube law and lift your weight on those puny legs again."

"There's a twisted but compelling logic in that," admitted the spider. "Why do you want the dragon?"

"She's due in the ring at Eastminster this afternoon," said Mallory.

"I'll have to think about it."

"Think about this," said Mallory. "If you don't tell me, I'll have her big brother help search the building." A pause. "Her *very* big brother." Another pause. "He *likes* spiders."

"All right," said the spider. "You win. The dragon and the man with the horns are here. I let them in—for a consideration, of course."

"What room?"

"I have no idea," said the spider. "I was too busy eating the consideration."

"Chocolate marshmallow cookie, shaped like an elephant?" suggested Mallory.

"How did you know?"

"I'm a trained detective." He gestured to Winnifred and the others. "Okay, let's go."

"Watch out for the gorgon," said the spider.

"We will."

"And the gryphon, and the five-legged snake, and the sea serpent."

"Sea serpent?" repeated Winnifred. "*Here?*"

"In the bathtub," said the spider. "Now go away so I can start forgetting."

"Forgetting is easy," offered Dugan. "It's remembering that's hard."

They found the main staircase and climbed up to the second floor. Mallory could hear something breathing, something *big*, in the first room they came to. He couldn't tell what it was, but he was very glad the door was closed.

"Felina, can you catch a scent yet?" asked the detective.

"I can smell all kinds of things, John Justin," replied the cat-girl. "Big things, little things, dead things, almost-dead things, hungry things . . ."

"How about a dragon?"

"Thank you, John Justin," she said. "I'll have one on toast."

"Do you smell one?"

"Yes, John Justin."

"Is Brody with it?"

She sniffed the air. "Yes."

"Then we've got them!"

"No, John Justin."

"Of course we do," said Mallory. "We're on the second floor. Her wings are vestigial, and Brody must weigh three hundred pounds. He can't jump out the window and she can't fly out."

"It doesn't matter, John Justin," said Felina.

"Why not?"

She smiled a very feline smile and pointed to the shadows just beyond him.

"It was very nice knowing you, John Justin," she said. "I think it's probably time to desert you now."

CHAPTER 25

7:53 AM–9:02 AM

A very strange figure slowly emerged from the shadows. Mallory could hear its harsh breathing before he could see its outline. Gradually it took shape, as if its disparate parts were just coming together at that moment. It stood almost nine feet tall and had four long, sinewy arms sprouting out of each side of its torso. Its legs bent, but they were not jointed like those of any human or animal Mallory had ever seen.

The head was a large oval, with a single, piercing blue eye, a five-inch prehensile nose not unlike an elephant's trunk, and a red slit for a mouth. It seemed androgynous, but Mallory thought of it as a male, simply because of its height. There were two snakes and a trio of rats in the corridor; the instant they saw the new arrival they raced for the staircase.

Winnifred aimed her pistol at the creature's chest. Dugan seemed unimpressed, but then, nothing impressed Dugan. Felina began assiduously licking a forearm.

"Why have you intruded upon my privacy?" demanded the creature, his mouth barely able to form the words, his voice almost a growl.

"Is this your house?" said Mallory, trying to keep his voice from shaking.

"It is—and you are uninvited."

"We're detectives, and we're looking for someone else who is uninvited."

"What is that to me?" said the creature.

"You don't seem to want visitors," said Mallory. "We'll remove them from your premises."

"Why shouldn't I just kill you now, and then find the other intruders and do the same to them?"

"Because there are twenty-seven building violations that I've spotted so far," said Belle suddenly, "and I am connected to the courthouse even as we speak. If you lift a finger against the gorgeous hunk who's been talking to

215

you, I'll have the judge issue an order to demolish this pile of bricks before sundown."

The creature stared at Mallory. "Your left lung is speaking to me," it noted.

"I'd believe it if I were you," replied Mallory.

"I think it's bluffing," said the creature, taking another step forward. Winnifred kept her gun trained on it.

"Have you got a place to spend the night if it's not bluffing?" said Mallory.

"I have not left this house in two centuries."

"Then why take the chance?" said Mallory. "Let us look for the man we're after. If we find him, we'll remove him from the premises; if not, we'll leave without him. Either way, we'll be gone and your house will still be standing."

The creature stared at him for a full minute, then nodded his head once. "You may look."

"Thank you," said Mallory.

"In fact, I will help you. It is a very large house, and some of the rooms are not in this dimension."

"Thanks, again."

"Have you a name?"

"Mallory. And this is Colonel Carruthers, Dead End Dugan, and Felina."

"And I am Fernando Grazi."

"That's a very human name," noted Mallory.

"Why shouldn't it be?"

"Have you looked in a mirror lately?"

"Do you judge everyone you meet by their appearance?" asked Grazi.

"Pretty much," admitted Mallory.

"That's strange," said Grazi. "You do not strike me as a fool."

"You *did* threaten to kill us," said Mallory.

"He *can't* kill me," said Dugan helpfully.

"Most of us," Mallory amended.

"And does no man ever defend his property against armed intruders?" asked Grazi.

"You've got a point," admitted Mallory. He paused, then asked: "Why have you stayed inside for two centuries?"

"Because you are not the only man who distrusts or fears what is unfamiliar to him. This house became my refuge shortly after General Washington drove the British out of Manhattan Island. I thought the country was at peace, but for the past few years I keep hearing the sound of gunfire in the night. Have the British returned?"

"No," said Mallory. "They've never come back. Well, not since 1812, anyway."

"Then who is our new enemy?"

"We are."

"Revolution?" asked Grazi.

"Crime," said Mallory.

"You are not encouraging me to leave my house."

"You're safer here," agree Mallory.

A door creaked open and an inhuman head glared out at them, growled something unintelligible, and vanished back into the recesses of its darkened room.

"*Possibly* you're safer," amended Mallory.

"Let us begin our search," said Grazi. "Who are we looking for?"

"The main thing we want is a dragon, eleven inches at the shoulder. There'll be a man with him, a big burly guy with a couple of horns growing out of his head."

"I notice you have no difficulty calling *him* a man," noted Grazi.

"You have a point," admitted Mallory.

"Can we begin?" asked Winnifred.

"Yes," said Grazi.

"Just a minute," said Mallory. He turned to Dugan. "Go back down the stairs and wait by the front door. Nobody leaves until I say so. Got it?"

"Yes."

"Okay, get going."

"Follow me," said Grazi as Dugan headed for the staircase. He walked down the corridor with surprising grace, given his structure, then stopped before a door. "My library," he announced, opening the door and leading them into the room, which was filled with old, musty volumes.

"A lot of Shakespeare," noted Mallory.

"And Chaucer," said Winnifred. "Given your taste for British writers, I'm surprised you don't have any Dickens."

"Who was he?" asked Grazi.

"You truly don't know?" she said, surprised.

"If he wrote after 1800, I have no way of knowing about him," replied Grazi.

"If we find the dragon here, I'll send you a set to thank you for your help," said Winnifred.

"I'd appreciate that," said Grazi. "These are all fine writers, but one can get tired of even the same fine writers after more than two hundred years."

He then led them to a bedroom where the furniture floated a foot above the ground, the mirror showed an endless array of animals that had never existed on Earth, and the window looked out onto a brilliant yellow sky filled with exploding blue stars.

"Ninth dimension," he explained.

"It's very disorienting," remarked Winnifred.

"The fourteenth is worse," said Grazi.

"How?" asked Mallory dubiously.

"Cause follows effect, you smell colors and see music, and the Galactic Court repealed the law of gravity by a vote of eight to three."

They spent the next three-quarters of an hour going through every room in the mansion, checking closets, armoires, trunks, every place that could possibly accommodate Brody and Fluffy, but they came up empty.

"I guess we had some false information," said Mallory as they came back to the head of the stairs. "I'm sorry to have bothered you."

"It's been so many decades since I had any company," said Grazi. "I wonder . . ."

"Yes?"

"When your case is over, would you and the Colonel like to come by one evening for a game of whist?"

"We'd be honored," said Winnifred.

"And you won't forget to bring something by this newcomer—this Dickens?"

"I won't forget."

"I hate to rush off, but we still have a dragon to track down," said Mallory.

"Good luck," said Grazi.

"We're going to need it. We're running short on time."

Mallory, Winnifred, and Felina went down the stairs and walked to the front door.

"Nothing's come or gone through here, right?" said Mallory as they approached Dugan.

"Right," said Dugan. "I obeyed your orders, and sent them out the back way."

"Explain!" snapped Mallory.

"You said nothing could leave through the front door, so when they tried, I stopped them and told them they had to use the servants' door in the kitchen."

"Told *who?*"

"The man with the dragon," answered Dugan.

"I don't suppose the man told you where he was going?"

"Yes, he did," said the zombie.

"Where?" demanded Mallory.

"Out," replied Dugan.

Mallory glared at him for a long moment. "You don't know how lucky you are that you're already dead," he said at last.

CHAPTER 26

9:02 AM–9:23 AM

Mallory walked out the front of the Grazi mansion, but couldn't see any sign of Brody and the dragon. He buttoned his coat against the frigid morning wind. Then, on a hunch, he walked to the alley behind the house, followed by the rest of his team.

"What's that down there?" asked Winnifred, pointing at a spot half a block away.

"Your eyes are sharper than mine," said Mallory. "All I see is a big lump, like a bundle that fell off a truck."

"I think it's moving," said Winnifred.

"He's trying to sit up," said Felina with an amused giggle. "But he's too fat."

Mallory broke into a run, Felina at his side, and they reached Gently Gently Dawkins a moment later. He took one arm, Felina the other, and they pulled the man to his feet.

"What the hell happened?" demanded the detective, as Winnifred and Dugan caught up with him.

"Thank goodness you came!" said Dawkins. "I was afraid I was going to have to lay there all day. Fortunately, I had some candy in my pocket so I didn't starve to death."

"You didn't answer my question."

"It was the strangest thing," said Dawkins. "I left the mansion, and went up to the corner, and bought a doughnut and a few cheese Danishes and a foot-long hot dog with relish, mustard, onions, ketchup, and cheese to comfort myself and calm my nerves, and I figured if I came back the same way I left I wouldn't finish eating by the time I arrived, so I went the long way, through the alley." He paused, frowning. "There I was, minding my own business, gnawing on my last Danish and not bothering anyone, and this strange-looking man came racing up the alley carrying something under his

221

arm. I figured he'd run around me, but he was so busy looking behind him that I don't think he even saw me until we collided."

"Strange-looking in what way?" demanded Mallory.

"Believe it or not, he had horns growing out of his head," said Dawkins. "Isn't that the weirdest thing?"

"And what was he carrying under his arm?"

Dawkins shrugged. "I don't know. Something green."

"Do you remember which way he went?" asked Mallory.

"Which way am I facing?"

"South."

"He went north," said Dawkins.

"Did he say anything?" asked Winnifred.

"I think he said *'Oof!'*"

"And you have no idea who it was, have you?" asked Mallory disgustedly.

"Just that he was a funny-looking man in a hurry."

"Joe En-lai is looking better and better."

"You're not thinking this through, Studmuffin," said Belle.

"Another quarter heard from," muttered Mallory. "All right—enlighten me."

"He knows you're after him," said Belle. "He barely got out of your office ahead of you, and he was still in the mansion when you arrived, so it's clear you're gaining on him—and he can't know that Dawkins wouldn't be bright enough to recognize him . . ."

"Recognize *who?*" asked Dawkins.

"He needs a place to hole up, and he needs it fast. For all he knows, you're less than a minute behind him, and you're not encumbered by a dragon."

"You know, she makes sense," said Winnifred.

"Go on," said Mallory.

"I'd check every hotel in the next block, and see which ones allow pets. When you find one that does, see who's registered in the last five minutes, and there you have it."

"Not bad," said Mallory.

"I can call ahead and eliminate the ones that won't allow dragons. Maybe I can even find a hotel that just accepted one."

"Sounds good to me."

"It's stuffy in here."

Mallory pulled the phone out of his pocket. "Better?"

"Now touch my buttons."

"Just make the calls."

"Fair is fair," said Belle. "First the buttons."

Mallory quickly hit each button in sequence and tried to ignore the ear-splitting squeal after each one.

"Oh my God!" breathed Belle. "I never knew it could be like this!"

"The calls?"

"Right, Honey," she said as Mallory and his party began walking north through the alley.

By the time they reached the next street, Belle had eliminated the three nearest hotels. As they were crossing it and a light snow began falling, she announced that the closest hotel that accepted pets was the Dunn Inn, half a block away.

"Has anyone arrived in the last five minutes?" asked Mallory.

"Three guests."

"You'd think people would be checking out at nine in the morning, not checking in."

"Life is full of surprises," said Belle. "After all, look at us."

"I'm trying not to," said Mallory, replacing the phone in his breast pocket.

"Our hearts are beating in unison!" announced Belle.

"You don't have a heart," said Mallory.

"Certainly I do, despite your callous attempts to break it."

"I see it up ahead, John Justin," said Winnifred, pointing to a ramshackle hotel that had seen better decades.

They headed toward it, passing three other hotels—those that didn't accept pets—along the way. As they entered, Mallory surveyed his surroundings: a threadbare carpet, a few wooden chairs that any antiques dealer would label "distressed," one leather couch with cracks in the leather, and an unimposing front desk with a bored-looking middle-aged clerk behind the counter.

The detective turned to Dawkins. "Can you recognize the guy who knocked you down if you see him again?"

"Yes."

"Even without his dragon?"

"What dragon?" asked Dawkins.

"Never mind. If you see him, point him out to Dugan." Mallory paused. "Dugan, once Dawkins identifies him, your job is to make sure he doesn't leave the hotel. Got it?"

"Yes," said the zombie.

"Can this wait a minute?" asked Dawkins.

"This is a hell of a time to go to the bathroom," said Mallory.

"Not the bathroom," Dawkins corrected him. "The candy counter in the gift shop."

"One minute, no more," said Mallory. He approached the hotel desk. "Excuse me, but has someone name Brody checked in recently?"

The clerk checked the registration book. "Nope. Got an N. Feratu from Transylvania. Came with a big wooden suitcase."

"No, that's not the one."

The clerk continued checking the book. "Igor and the Graverobbers just took out their usual suite."

"Igor and the Graverobbers?" repeated Winnifred, frowning.

"A rock band," explained the clerk. "They get a little raucous after a concert. Just silly childish pranks like setting fire to the draperies, throwing the furniture out the window, and playing host to ten or twelve underaged girls. They usually get thrown out of the Plaza by four in the morning, the Waldorf by six, and the Leamington by eight. I guess they weren't as noisy and destructive as usual; the Leamington let them stay until a quarter to nine."

"And the third room?" asked Mallory.

"A Mr. Earp."

"Wyatt?"

The clerk nodded an affirmative. "Yes, sir."

"What's his room number?"

"I can't reveal that information, sir."

Mallory pulled out a twenty-dollar bill. "Even for a consideration?"

The clerk shook his head. "Regulations are regulations."

"Felina?" said Mallory, and the cat-girl approached the desk. "Say hello to the nice man."

Felina held up a hand. Suddenly, one after the other, each finger sprouted a two-inch claw.

"I'm afraid I can't reveal our address to the hospital after she removes your face," said Mallory. "But regulations are regulations."

"Room 751, sir," said the clerk hastily.

"Thanks."

"And the consideration, sir?"

Mallory shrugged. "What the hell," he said, laying it on the counter.

"Thank you, sir. And may I offer a word of advice?"

"I'm all ears."

"I am certain that your business with Mr. Earp is totally legitimate and aboveboard, but if it can in any way be subject to misinterpretation and you and your party have to leave in haste, there's a service elevator at the far end of the building. It will let you off near an entrance that's reserved for deliveries—laundry, food for the coffee shop, and of course the Gravediggers' young friends."

"That's very thoughtful of you, young man," said Winnifred.

"And if anyone should happen by and ask who paid Mr. Earp a visit, what shall I tell them?" asked the clerk.

The trace of a smile played across Mallory's mouth. "Tell them it was the Clanton Gang," he said. "And we're really pissed off because of the O.K. Corral."

The clerk wrote it down on a piece of note paper. "All right, Mr. Gang. And good luck."

"Thanks," said Mallory, heading off toward an elevator. "We could use a little."

CHAPTER 27

9:23 AM–10:09 AM

The elevator had a poster for Madam Rochefort's All-Night Tarot-Reading Service. Another announced that this was your last week to catch Igor and the Graverobbers before they went on the road, to be replaced by Vlad and the Impalers, and there was also a scrawled message on notebook paper offering fifteen dollars for the return of a magic wand that answered to the name of Cedric.

Mallory and his crew took the elevator to the seventh floor. They emerged into a corridor with a carpet that had seen better days, tried to ignore the musty odor that assailed their nostrils, and began walking toward room 751.

"Dugan," whispered Mallory, "go to the service elevator"—he pointed to it—"and if the guy you saw at Grazi's place makes a break for it carrying a dragon under his arm, don't let him pass. Do you understand?"

"Yes," said Dugan, heading off to the service elevator.

"Felina, go to the main bank of elevators with Dawkins. If Brody tries to escape, stop him."

"For a parakeet, three angelfish, and a dry buffalo."

"A dry buffalo?" Mallory repeated.

"I don't like water buffaloes."

"We'll negotiate later. Just make sure you don't let the dragon get by you." She gave him a huge feline smile. "And don't hurt it."

"You never let me have any fun."

"We all have a function in life," answered Mallory dryly. "Mine is to never let you have any fun."

"What's mine?" asked Felina.

"To do exactly what I tell you."

"Oh," replied Felina, evidently satisfied with his answer. She and Dawkins walked back to the elevators, and Mallory turned to Winnifred. "You ready?"

"Absolutely," she said. "Seven floors is too high to jump, and I checked: The fire escape is on the far side of the building. So he's going to have to let us in."

"When I nod," said Mallory, "I want you to giggle."

"Giggle?" repeated Winnifred.

"Right," said Mallory. "High-pitched and feminine."

"I don't giggle," said Winnifred.

"*I* do," Belle cooed.

"Good," said Winnifred. "I haven't giggled since I was a child."

"I'll take care of the giggling," said Belle. "You shoot anyone who threatens Cuddles, here."

"It's a deal," said Winnifred.

"Are we satisfied with the division of labor now?" whispered Mallory with a sardonic grimace. "Can I get this show on the road?"

Winnifred nodded, and Belle whispered, "Ready when you are, Sweetie."

Mallory knocked on the door.

"Who's there?" said Brody's voice.

"Room service."

"I didn't order anything from room service."

"Gift from the management," said Mallory. "I think you'll like it."

"Now," he whispered, and Belle began giggling.

"Blonde, redhead, or brunette?" asked Brody.

"That's for you to discover, sir."

The door slowly cracked open, and as it did so, Mallory and Winnifred threw their entire weight against it. Brody grunted in surprise and fell across the room as Mallory and Winnifred stumbled through the doorway.

"Shut the door," said Mallory. "We don't want Fluffy running off."

Winnifred closed the door while Mallory looked around the room for the dragon. There was a bed with a sagging mattress and a patched bedspread, a scarred nightstand with a cheap lamp, a beat-up desk and chair, and a black-and-white television with a twelve-inch screen.

"All right," said the detective at last. "Where have you stashed her?"

"I don't know what you're talking about," said Brody. "You're supposed to be searching for my dragon, not harassing me."

Mallory walked over to a dresser, opened the top drawer, then the second, and finally found what he wanted.

"Here, Fluffy!" he said, taking an elephant-shaped chocolate marshmallow cookie out of the drawer and tossing it on the floor in the middle of the room. A small green dragon shot out from beneath the bed and greedily gobbled it up, then began backing up toward the bed again.

"Why, she's adorable!" said Winnifred, staring at the little dragon.

"I guess she wasn't as lost as you thought," said Mallory to Brody.

"What's the price for you to go away and forget this?" asked Brody.

"Oh, twice what you're going to make from all your bets on Carmelita ought to do it," said Mallory.

"*What!*" demanded Brody.

"Of course, we'll want a little more than that not to tell Harry the Book and Hot Horse Hennigan and other select members of their profession where you're hiding."

"Out of the question!" snapped Brody.

"I thought it might be," said Mallory. "I guess we'll just have to fulfill our contract and deliver Fluffy to Eastminster by ring time."

"Look," said Brody desperately, "there's a *lot* of money involved, more than I think you can imagine. I'll give you and your partner half of my winnings if you'll just let me and Fluffy hide here until tonight."

"I'm afraid not," said Mallory. "The Grundy's already paying us double what you offered."

Brody frowned. "To keep Fluffy out of the ring?"

"To deliver her," said Mallory. "He's a sportsman. Or a sportsdemon, if you prefer."

"And now, Mr. Brody," said Winnifred, "you can come peacefully, or you can come forcibly, but you *are* coming, and so is your dragon."

"All right, all right," said Brody with a sigh. "Let me get her leash."

He walked to the closet, reached in, and suddenly he had a wicked-looking gun in his hand.

"I'm sorry, Fluffy," he said, aiming it at the dragon. "But I can't let you get into the ring."

A shot rang out. Mallory expected the dragon to keel over, but instead Brody's gun flew against the wall and he yelped in pain and surprise.

"That was foolish, Mr. Brody," said Winnifred, her Magnum in her hand. "Please don't try anything like that again."

"You shot me!" he said accusingly.

"You're remarkably observant," she said with a sweet smile.

"I can't believe it!" he said, pulling out a handkerchief and wrapping it around his hand, where a trickle of blood was beginning to appear. "You actually shot me!"

"I shot your gun," said Winnifred.

"You shot *me*! I'm bleeding!" He glared furiously at her. "I'm a *person*! I was only going to shoot a dragon."

"A dragon that's worth considerably more than you are," she said.

"I love that dragon!" he said. "It was a business decision."

"And it was a business decision on my part to keep the dragon alive," replied Winnifred.

"Mr. Mallory," said Brody, "you have a bloodthirsty fiend for a partner."

"But an honest bloodthirsty fiend," said Mallory.

"What are you complaining about?" demanded Brody. "You were well paid."

"You *used* us as a cover for your scam," said Mallory, "and we resent it."

"I gave you five thousand dollars for less than twenty-four hours of your time."

"You gave us *one* thousand dollars with the rest due when we found and delivered Fluffy," said Mallory. "The way I see it, you owe us the other four thousand right now."

"I haven't got it," said Brody. He held up his right hand. "I give you my word of honor as a gentleman." Mallory could hear Belle chuckle at that. "All my money is in the hands of the bookies."

"Then I guess we'll keep Fluffy until you come up with the cash. I suppose we might as well take her to the Garden while we're waiting."

"But if you take her there, everyone will know what I tried to pull," whined Brody, starting to pace nervously back and forth. "My life won't be worth a plugged nickel."

"Do they still make plugged nickels?" asked Mallory pleasantly.

"Damn it, you know what I mean!" said Brody. He pulled a cigar out of his pocket, felt around for a lighter, couldn't find it, and hurled the cigar against the far wall.

"You're not thinking this through," said Mallory. "If she wins the show, the bookies will pocket your bets and let bygones be bygones. It's if she *doesn't* show up and word gets out about what you pulled that you're a walking dead man . . . and not like the one I have guarding your escape route."

"Then don't tell them, and I'll make it worth your while!" urged Brody desperately.

"Too late," said Mallory. "Harry the Book and Hot Horse Hennigan already know, and I'm sure they're not keeping it a secret."

"It's all your fault!" said Brody. "You've ruined me!"

"I'm sure glad to see you know where to place the blame," said Mallory.

"I thought society encouraged entrepreneurs," said Brody bitterly. "Whatever happened to innovation and creativity?"

"Innovation and Creativity sounds like a bad rock band," said Mallory.

"There aren't any good ones," said Winnifred.

"I've got every bookie in town after my scalp, and you're talking about rock bands," moaned Brody. "What's going to become of me?"

"Well, if you'd broken any laws, I'd say a hotshot lawyer would have you back out on the street before the cops finished filling out their paperwork," said Mallory. "But bookies aren't courts and judges. If I were you, I'd take Fluffy into the ring, try my damnedest to win the show, and write the losses off."

"I can't!" yelled Brody. "I mortgaged everything I own and borrowed from all my friends to make those bets!"

"I'd say you've got yourself a hell of a problem, Mr. Brody," replied Mallory. He tossed Fluffy another cookie. "Where's her leash?"

"You go to hell!" said Brody.

"I may, eventually," answered Mallory. "But I'm going to Eastminster first."

Winnifred scouted around in the closet for a few seconds and withdrew a leash and a collar.

"Asbestos," she remarked. "Makes sense."

"Put it on her and let's be on our way," said Mallory. "Somehow, I don't feel confident letting Mr. Brody hold on to the other end of the leash."

Winnifred knelt down and called to Fluffy. The little dragon approached her, and stood still while she attached both the collar and the leash.

"Such a friendly animal!" enthused Winnifred. "She hardly acts like the winningest dragon in the country."

"She probably doesn't know she is," said Mallory. He tossed another cookie on the floor, and Fluffy emitted a happy little screech and pounced on it.

"I think I'd better take the rest of these," said Mallory, pulling a dozen cookies out of the drawer and setting them atop the dresser. "Who the hell knows if we can find more before the show?"

"Let me check the bathroom and see if I can find something to put them in," said Winnifred. "I know it's cold out, but once we're inside Madison Round Garden they'll probably melt if you have them in your pocket."

"So what?" said Mallory. "They'll taste the same."

"If she won't eat a chocolate marshmallow cookie shaped like a rhino or a hippo, she won't eat one that's totally lost its structural integrity," replied Winnifred.

"Okay, that makes sense," agreed Mallory.

"Here," she said, handing him the leash. "I'll go look."

As she disappeared into the bathroom, Brody made a break for the door, opened it, and slammed it shut behind him. Winnifred raced out the bathroom, a plastic bag in her hand.

"What happened, John Justin?" she asked.

"Brody flew the coop," answered Mallory. "I didn't want to choke the dragon to death chasing after him, and I didn't want to let go of the leash and maybe have her escape while I was after him."

"But he'll get away!" said Winnifred.

"I don't think so," replied Mallory. "We've posted our people at both elevators, remember."

"I hope Harry's men are dependable," she said. Winnifred quickly put the cookies into the plastic bag, and placed it in her purse. "Well, let's go see which of them caught him."

They went out into the corridor. Mallory took a step toward the main elevator bank. "Felina!" he called. "Did he come your way?"

The cat-girl shook her head, grinned, and pointed toward the service elevator.

Mallory picked Fluffy up, tucked her under an arm, and walked toward Dugan, followed by Winnifred.

"Well?" he said when he arrived.

"Well what?" asked Dugan.

"Where is he?"

The zombie shrugged. "I don't know."

"I know he came this way. Tell me you didn't let him get on the elevator."

"I didn't let him get on the elevator," said Dugan.

"Good. Where is he?"

"On the elevator."

"But you just said he didn't get on it."

"You told me to say that," replied Dugan reasonably.

"I also told you not to let the guy you saw at Grazi's pass!" snapped Mallory.

"No you didn't," answered Dugan. "You told me if he came running out of the room with a dragon under his arm, not to let him pass. He didn't have a dragon." Dugan's eyes fell on Fluffy, who was still tucked under Mallory's arm. "Should I let *you* pass?"

Mallory growled an obscenity, turned, and walked toward the main elevator bank.

"I'm starting to loathe zombies," he said to Winnifred.

"You have to adjust to his limitations," she replied.

"That's like telling the dinosaurs they had to adjust to a comet hitting the Earth," said Mallory. He took a deep breath, let it out slowly, and turned back to Dugan. "All right—come on."

When the five of them were assembled, they summoned an elevator, went down to the main floor, walked out through the lobby, and were soon on the sidewalk.

"What now?" asked Winnifred.

"What time is it?"

She checked her wristwatch. "Ten oh seven."

"Well, she's not due in the ring for a few hours," noted Mallory, "but as long as we've got her, we might as well take her over to the Garden."

They began walking toward Madison Avenue. When they were still half a block away two shots rang out.

"Was that a car backfiring?" asked Dawkins.

"Those were gunshots," said Winnifred with absolute certainty. "Are you all right, John Justin?"

"Yeah. How about you?"

"I'm fine," she replied. "Mr. Dawkins?"

"I'm okay."

"Mr. Dugan?"

"I feel a draft," replied Dugan.

Mallory turned to the zombie, and saw two fresh holes in his chest.

Another shot, and the store window behind them blew apart.

"What *is* it, John Justin?" said Winnifred, crouching down behind a car and pulling her gun out of her purse.

"I have a feeling that finding Fluffy was the easy half of this job," said Mallory, ducking behind a van and trying to spot the shooter. "Getting to the Garden without being killed is going to be the hard part."

As if for emphasis, a bullet thudded home into the wall an inch above his head.

Two more shots rang out.

"Can you see anyone?" asked Winnifred.

"No," said Mallory. "They seem to be coming from the left of that pet shop across the street, but I can't be sure."

"I can't see anyone either," said Belle from inside Mallory's pocket. "Or anything. It's dark in here."

"You're safer there," said Mallory.

"How's Fluffy?" asked Winnifred.

He looked at the little dragon that was still tucked under his arm. "I guess she's okay. How do you tell?"

He looked around. Dawkins was kneeling behind a parked van, eating one candy bar after another for comfort. Felina, who was right next to Mallory, had found an anthill between cracks in the street, and was enjoying herself torturing the ants. Dugan was standing, oblivious of the danger and the snow that was starting to fall, watching a trio of banshees circling high above them.

Mallory dared another look across the street, saw the flash of a gun, heard the thunderous report, and ducked back behind a 12-cylinder Dusenburg.

"Grundy," he said softly, "I hate to be a pest, but if you want me to get this dragon to the ring, I think we're going to need your help."

"Are you talking to me, John Justin?" asked Winnifred. "I can't quite hear you."

"He's talking to the Grundy," said Felina helpfully.

"As if we didn't have enough trouble already," moaned Dawkins.

"Don't worry," replied Felina. "The Grundy's not answering."

Mallory tried to spot the shooter again. All he got for his trouble was a bullet hole through the brim of his hat.

"Grundy!" he said, louder this time. "How about it?"

"I'm busy grooming Carmelita," said the Grundy's disembodied voice.

"Can't you see what's going on here?"

"Of course I can," replied the demon. "What do you want?"

"You're kidding, right?" snapped Mallory. "Get us out of this jam!"

"You have the wherewithal to extricate yourself with no risk to you or the dragon."

"What the hell are you talking about?" demanded Mallory.

"You're a bright man," said the Grundy. "You'll figure it out. Now please stop bothering me. I have a show to prepare for."

"You want to give me a hint, at least?" said Mallory.

There was no answer.

"What was that all about, John Justin?" asked Winnifred.

"I'm not sure," said Mallory, frowning. "I have to think." Suddenly a huge smile spread across his face. "I'm an idiot!" he exclaimed.

"I always knew it, John Justin," said Felina.

"Don't you dare say that to the man of my dreams!" retorted Belle.

"Shut up, both of you," said Mallory. "Dugan?"

The zombie looked down to where the detective was crouching behind the van. "What?"

"Brody's across the street, shooting at us."

"I *thought* I heard some noise," said Dugan.

"Go take his gun away and bring him to me," said Mallory.

"Take his gun away and bring him to you," said Dugan. "Got it." A pause. "When?"

"Now would be nice," said Mallory.

Dugan walked across the street, undeterred by the hail of bullets that tore into him. Suddenly the zombie's voice called out: "It's not Brody."

"Disarm him anyway, and bring him here!" yelled Mallory.

Mallory heard a scream, and a moment later Dugan came back, dragging a man by the foot. He handed the man's gun to the detective, who in turn put Fluffy on the ground and gave her leash to Winnifred.

"Was he the only one?" asked Mallory.

"The only one of what?" asked Dugan.

"The only one shooting at us?"

"Yes," said Dugan. "Probably."

Mallory stared at the zombie. "You've been pretty well ventilated," he observed. "This can't be the first time. How do they patch you up?"

Gently Gently Dawkins climbed laboriously to his feet and walked over. He reached into his mouth and pulled out some freshly chewed bubble gum, which he dabbed onto the bullet holes. "This will do until we can stop for morticians' putty at Creepy Conrad's All-Night Mortuary. That's where Harry sends me or Benny Fifth Street to pick it up whenever Dugan comes back from what Harry calls a difficult collection."

"I take it this isn't a new problem?" remarked Mallory.

"Yes it is," said Dugan. "This guy has never shot me before."

"I stand corrected," said Mallory dryly.

"Do you suppose he has any more henchmen waiting along the way?" asked Winnifred.

"Who knows?" replied Mallory. "I didn't think he had *this* one." He paused. "Theoretically he's dead broke and in hock up to his ears, but I suppose he could have paid for some firepower in advance."

"How could he know we'd figure out his scam?"

"He couldn't. This was just insurance. We're not the main targets anyway."

"We're not?" said Dawkins, surprised.

"It's Fluffy," answered Mallory. "He can't afford to let her reach the ring. *She's* what this guy was after. Dugan, put him on his feet and let's find out what he knows."

The zombie picked up the gunman and set him upright, none too gently.

"Hi," said Mallory with a smile. "I get the distinct impression that you want to talk to us."

"You go to hell," said the gunman as Dugan held him motionless.

"My mistake," said Mallory easily. "I guess you'd rather play with my cat."

"Your cat?"

"Felina," said Mallory, "say hello to the nice man."

Felina approached him with a toothy smile, the morning sun glinting off her claws.

"Call her off!" said the man, trying to back away but unable to free himself from the zombie's viselike grip.

"She doesn't answer to 'Off,'" said Mallory. "Are you *sure* you wouldn't rather talk to me than play with her?"

"You win!" said the man in panicky tones. "I'll talk!"

"My God, you're so masterful!" exclaimed Belle.

"That'll be all for now, Felina," said Mallory, ignoring the cell phone. The cat-girl made a face and hissed at him. "But stick around, in case he decides he doesn't want to talk after all." He turned to the man. "You got a name?"

"Bullseye."

Mallory looked amused. "You miss ten shots from right across the street and you're Bullseye?"

"If you were a bull you'd be dead," Bullseye assured him. "People's eyes are smaller and harder to hit."

"I'll take your word for it," said Mallory. "How long have you been working for Brody?"

"Brody?" repeated Bullseye. "Is that who I'm working for?"

"You don't know?" said Winnifred incredulously.

"Hey, I'm temping for Gunsels R Us—just until I catch up on my Christmas bills, you understand. I guess this Brody made a down payment a couple of months ago." He tried unsuccessfully to shrug free of Dugan's grasp. "My supervisor tells me to tail the guy with the horns, and if anyone takes the dragon away, get it back or kill it."

"Did Brody hire just one of you?"

"They tell me he put money down on two more, but they're not from my organization. They're real specialists."

"Any idea who they are?"

"The scuttlebutt around the office is that they're Marius the Mage and Percy Picayune."

"Percy?" said Belle suddenly. "Watch out for him!"

"More dangerous than the magician?" asked Mallory.

"Infinitely," said Belle. "He used to be an IRS auditor. He is absolutely without mercy."

Mallory turned back to Bullseye. "Is there anything else you can tell us?"

"No."

"You're sure?" said Mallory.

"Well, I can tell you that the track's coming up muddy at Jamaica, and never buy commodities on margin, and beware of aggressive redheads named Thelma."

"But nothing about Brody?"

"No."

"All right," said Mallory. "Get out of here, and don't let me see you again."

"You weren't supposed to see me the first time," said Bullseye bitterly. He paused awkwardly. "Can I have my gun back?"

"Hell, no," said Mallory.

"How about if I say 'please'?"

"You just tried to kill us with it."

"That was *business*," said Bullseye. "We're all friends now—except maybe for the cat-thing."

"Go away before I turn you over to her."

"But that's not fair!" complained Bullseye. "I'm a freelance assassin. How am I going to make ends meet if you keep the tool of my trade?"

"That's the risk you take when you don't kill your target," said Mallory.

"What the hell," said Bullseye with a shrug. "Maybe I can borrow my mom's. I just hate to walk that far with the snow starting to get worse."

"We all have to live with life's little inconveniences," said Mallory.

"All right," said Bullseye. "But promise you won't tell any of the guys. This is the third kill I've blown this month, and I hate all their teasing. It's good-natured, I know that, but it's still humiliating."

"My lips are sealed."

"Well, good-bye, then," said Bullseye, shaking his hand. "And good luck making it to the Garden. You haven't got a chance, what with Marius and Percy waiting for you, but I hope you at least give them a run for their money."

And with that, he turned and began walking down the increasingly slippery street, sidestepping the occasional skidding car.

"Does anyone know anything about this Marius the Mage?" asked Mallory, turning back to his team.

Nobody answered.

"What about Percy Picayune?"

"Just what I told you," said Belle.

"It would be nice to know what they looked like, at least," said Mallory.

"Is Percy twice as big as a dinosaur, with blue skin and huge claws and beady eyes and each of his teeth as long as a grown man?" asked Felina, looking just over the detective's shoulder.

"An IRS auditor?" said Mallory. "I sure as hell doubt it. Why?"

"Then that must be Marius the Mage walking down the street toward us," said the cat-girl.

CHAPTER 29

10:21 AM–11:49 AM

Mallory looked up the street, which was fast becoming covered with snow. He'd seen a lot of strange sights in this Manhattan, but none of them had quite the effect of the enormous blue monster strolling down the middle of the street, some forty feet at the shoulder and four times that long.

But it was nothing compared to the effect when it faced him directly and hissed "John Justin Mallory, turn over that dragon or face the consequences!"

"No!" screamed Belle. "Not now that I've finally found him!"

"Shut your pocket up!" hissed the creature.

"You can't!" cried Belle. "I mean, we haven't even—"

The creature roared. Gently Gently Dawkins fainted dead away. Dead End Dugan displayed no fear whatsoever (nor did he display courage, or interest, or animation). Winnifred pulled out her Magnum and tried to figure out where the creature's most vital spot might be. Felina yawned, turned her back, and began assiduously licking a forearm.

"Anyone got any suggestions?" asked Mallory of his companions.

"We're not giving Fluffy up without a fight," said Winnifred. "I faced creatures this big when I was a white hunter."

"With a handgun?" asked Mallory.

"The bigger they are, the harder they fall," said Winnifred.

"If he falls, he could collapse the subway for a whole block."

"Are you convinced there's no escape?" demanded the huge blue creature.

"Grundy?" said Mallory.

There was no answer.

"Winnifred?"

"Let him *try* to take Fluffy away," she said, never lowering her Magnum. "I'm ready for him."

"Put that silly toy away!" thundered the creature. "My skin is three inches thick and armor-plated. You couldn't pierce it with a rocket. Just hand over the dragon and I might let you live."

An arm suddenly sprouted out of its neck and continued growing to enormous length as it reached for Fluffy. The little dragon jumped back in terror, yanking on the leash and spinning Winnifred halfway around. As she tried to turn back the gun went off.

There was an inhuman howl of anguish—and standing there on the street, where the blue creature had been, was a skinny, undersized man in a monk's robe. He was barefoot, and blood was spurting out of the big toe on his left foot, turning the snow around him a bright red.

"What the hell happened?" asked Mallory.

"Is he gone?" asked Belle.

"Kind of," said Mallory, frowning.

"Good!" she said. "Now I don't have to die an almost-virgin."

"Amazing!" said Winnifred. "I never saw anything like that before!"

"Where did he go?" said Dawkins, who was awake again and cowering behind Dugan. "One second he was blotting out the sun, and now he's gone and I'm being snowed on again."

Even Felina appeared interested in the skinny man.

"What did you want to go and do that for?" he whined, kneeling down and wrapping a handkerchief around the toe. "What did I ever do to you?"

"You were about to kill us," said Mallory.

"Hey, did I touch you?" said the man.

"You threatened to."

"They were just words. That's no reason to blow a man's foot off."

"Stop sniveling!" said Winnifred. "It's only a toenail. It'll grow back."

"Put your damned gun away," said the man. "Who the hell knows where you'll aim it next?"

"May I assume that your name is Marius?" asked Mallory.

"Of course it's Marius!" said the man angrily. "You don't suppose that Spellsinger Sol or Big-Hearted Milton could turn into a creature half as impressive as that?" He got to his feet with all the dignity he could muster. "I am the greatest magician in Manhattan. Hell, in all five boroughs. Maybe even in the whole state."

"So why is the greatest magician working for a small-time crook?" asked Mallory. "Why aren't you delving into all the secrets of the universe?"

Marius looked up and down the street to make sure no one could overhear him. "You promise you won't tell anyone?" he said. He paused as if considering how to proceed. "The one secret of the universe I could never solve was claimers who were moving up in class on a muddy track. It seems to be an eternal verity that they win when I bet against them and lose when I bet *on* them."

"So you're in hock to your bookie?"

Marius nodded unhappily. "Eight thousand dollars," he admitted. "Brody sent a retainer to my management firm a month or two back and said that if he needed my services—it would just be for a few hours, tops—he'd cover my debt." He shrugged. "He got word to me this morning that I should keep an eye on the dragon."

"Brody's broke," said Mallory. "He can't cover his own bets, let alone yours."

"What am I going to do?" said Marius. "I can't let word get out that I couldn't even magic Gallant Gertie out of that traffic jam on the far turn!"

"Who's your bookie?"

"Hot Horse Hennigan."

"Tell you what," said Mallory. "You ride shotgun for us until we get to the Garden, and I think I can convince Hennigan to cancel your debt."

"Can you really do that?" asked Marius hopefully.

"If the dragon doesn't get there, he stands to drop a hell of a lot more than eight grand."

"It's a deal!" said Marius enthusiastically.

Mallory turned to Dugan. "Put Dawkins on his feet."

"He's awake," said Dugan.

"Do it anyway."

"My God, you're so forceful!" cooed Belle.

Dugan grabbed Dawkins's arms and jerked, and the rotund man almost flew to his feet.

"You want a little mustard with that?" Mallory asked Felina, who had begun assiduously licking her other forearm.

She smiled at him. "Yes, John Justin."

"Next mustard farm we pass," he said. "All right, let's get going."

They began walking, made it to Madison Avenue, and turned right. They passed a few blocks of run-down stores and shops in the process of being refurbished, then came to a movie theater that advertised a triple feature of *The Man Who Would Be King*.

"How can there be a triple feature of one film?" asked Winnifred.

"Easy," answered Marius. "The first one is the film John Huston tried to make in the 1940s, with Humphrey Bogart and Clark Gable. Warner Brothers, which owned Bogart, and MGM, which owned Gable, couldn't come to an agreement, and Huston put it on the back burner for almost two decades. The second film on the bill, with Marlon Brando and Richard Burton, fell apart when he couldn't get the financing. And then there's the one he actually made, with Sean Connery and Michael Caine."

"That's the most fascinating triple feature I ever heard of," said Winnifred.

"I prefer *The Wizard of Oz* triple feature myself," replied Marius. "There's the version with Judy Garland as Dorothy and Frank Morgan as the Wizard, and there's the one MGM wanted to make, with Shirley Temple and W. C. Fields."

"And the third one?"

"That's the one with Bette Davis as Dorothy and Groucho Marx as the Wizard."

"*Bette Davis?*" said Winnifred in surprise.

"It was a stretch," admitted Marius.

Suddenly a pair of thugs burst out of an alley, their guns trained on Mallory and Winnifred.

"Freeze!" commanded the first one.

"Except for the fat broad," said the second. "I want you to bring the dragon over."

"What did you call me?" said Winnifred ominously.

"Do something quick!" Mallory whispered to Marius.

"Don't worry," said the mage. "They probably won't hurt her."

"I'm not worrying about *her*," said Mallory. "I've seen that look in her eye before. Do something before *she* kills *them*!"

"Really?" said Marius, his face alight with interest. "I'd pay to see that." Suddenly the interest vanished. "If I had any money."

He pointed toward the two thugs. "Abra cadaver!" he intoned.

Suddenly instead of wicked-looking guns, the two thugs found themselves holding wicked-looking rats, which immediately began gnawing on their hands. They screamed and threw the rats to the ground, then pulled out knives.

"Presto!" cried Marius, and the knives changed into two pieces of spaghetti. The spaghetti instantly morphed from pasta to steel and wrapped itself around their wrists, handcuffing them. The thugs looked at their wrists, then the rats, then Marius, and suddenly bolted back into the alley.

"Not bad," said Mallory.

"Not bad?" repeated Marius. "It was goddamned brilliant!"

"You go ahead to the show," said Felina, stealthily tiptoeing through the snow toward the rats. "I'll make sure the poor things aren't in any pain."

"For long," said Mallory dryly.

"Cute little furry little plump little things!" purred Felina.

"You're all heart," said Mallory.

"I'll catch up with you in a few minutes," she said as one of the rats bolted for the alley and she blocked his line of retreat.

"Let's go," said Mallory to his party. "It's too cold to stand and wait for her. Besides, she likes to play with her dinner. You really don't want to watch."

They kept walking. The area was in transition, with elegant seventy-year-old buildings and ugly twenty-year-old buildings being torn down and replaced by characterless twenty-week-old buildings, though the same grifters and panhandlers—some human, some reptilian, some defying all description—had made their adjustments and were plying their trade.

Mallory's party ran the gamut of entrepreneurial goblins selling everything from Everglades real estate to thick tomes of philosophy by Descartes and Schopenhauer (but filled with full-page pornographic illustrations to liven up the text) to flea circuses complete with tightropes and trapeze. By the time they were within a block of Madison Round Garden, uniformed police—some human, some with scaly green tails—had dispersed the goblins, and Felina rejoined them as they began their final approach to the stadium.

"I hope you enjoyed yourself," asked Mallory.

"They make great playmates," replied Felina happily, stifling a ladylike burp.

"What's that up ahead?" asked Dawkins, pointing to where a crowd had gathered just outside the Garden.

"I don't know," said Mallory. "They're not in one of the ticket lines."

"I smell smoke," said Belle.

Mallory frowned. "Something's on fire."

"Not yet," said Marius, staring ahead. "Something's hanging, and they're trying to set it on fire."

"Oh, that's probably Heartless Herman," said Dawkins knowingly.

"The coach of the Manhattan Misfits?" asked Mallory.

"Well, he *is* three-and-forty-nine for the season," said Dawkins.

"So they're hanging him in effigy," said Mallory with a shrug. "You have to expect it with a record like that."

"They're not hanging a dummy, John Justin," said Winnifred suddenly as she peered ahead. "They're hanging *him*!"

Mallory stared intently for a few seconds. "Son of a bitch!" he said. "That *is* him!"

"It's snowing," observed Felina. "Maybe the fire will warm him up."

"Stand back," said Winnifred, stepping forward.

A single shot rang out. The bullet severed the rope that was holding Herman up, and he fell to the ground just before they could set him afire. Winnifred kept her handgun out in plain sight and pushed her way through the crowd.

"Aren't you ashamed of yourselves?" she demanded.

"You betcha!" said one man disgustedly. "I'm ashamed I ever bought season tickets once they announced Heartless Herman was going to be the coach."

"I'm ashamed we didn't think of this sooner," added a woman.

"I want you to break this up and go about your business," said Winnifred.

"Don't be silly!" said another woman. "Hanging Herman *is* our business."

Winnifred fired a shot in the air. "You heard me!"

"The fat broad's got some moxie," whispered Belle. "I'll give her that."

"Yes, she does," said Mallory admiringly.

"She's a lot of woman," agreed Marius.

"I wouldn't word it quite that way," said Mallory. "She's a little sensitive about some things."

"Of course, if you ever touch her," added Belle, "I'll scratch your eyes out."

Mallory resisted the urge to ask what she'd scratch his eyes out *with*, and watched as the crowd, ugly and grumbling, slowly dispersed.

When they'd all gone, Winnifred walked over to the fallen coach. "You can get up now," she said.

Herman got to his feet, brushed himself off, and turned to her. "You saved my life," he said. "I owe you a—" He broke off and stared at her, his mouth hanging open.

"What is it?" she asked.

"Winnifred?" he said slowly. "Winnifred Carruthers?"

"That's right."

"It must be Fate!" exclaimed Herman. "I had a crush on you when we were in grammar school together."

"Herman Bouillabaisse?" she said, staring at him.

"Yes!" he said happily. "It's me!"

She reached over and slapped his face.

"What was that for?" demanded Herman.

"For what you tried to do that afternoon near our lockers."

"What the hell did I do?"

She slapped him again. "That's for not remembering."

"You always had a lot of spunk," he said ruefully, rubbing his jaw.

"You're one very lucky man," said Winnifred.

"That you showed up?"

"That you're three-and-forty-nine. If you were two-and-fifty, I'd probably have lit the fire myself." She looked around. "If I were you, I'd leave before they came back."

"You're right," he said. He trudged off a couple of steps, then turned back to her. "You know something? You're still very special. I was right to have fallen for you all those years ago."

Mallory watched her turn her head and wipe a tear away, while all other eyes were on Herman, who scuttled off without another word and soon disappeared between buildings across the street from the Garden.

"Well, so much for that," Winnifred said to Mallory with forced nonchalance. "Shall we proceed?"

"Might as well," said Mallory. He turned to Marius. "You kept your end of the bargain. I'll speak to Hennigan."

"Thanks," said Marius. He checked the hourglass suspended from his neck. "If I hurry, I can make it out to Jamaica in time to dope out the Daily Double."

He spun around three times and vanished in a puff of smoke, which startled Mallory, Winnifred, Dugan, and Dawkins, but elicited nothing more than another burp from Felina.

"Okay," said Mallory, heading toward the exhibitors' entrance. "Let's go."

A uniformed man was standing just in front of the door. "Good afternoon, sir," he said. "May I help direct you?"

"Why not?" said Mallory agreeably.

"Are you here for the dragon show, the snake-charming seminar, the basketball game, the Steel Cage Tunisian Death Match between Wilbur the Slug and Mad Dog Marvin, or perhaps the Travel Patagonia slide show?"

"The dragon show," said Mallory.

The guard studied the little group. "Excuse me, sir, but would your name happen to be John Justin Mallory?"

"Yes."

"Fine," said the guard with a smile. "Will you and your party come this way, please? One of our directors, Percy Picayune, is waiting to personally process you."

CHAPTER 30

11:49 AM–1:15 PM

"I don't like the feel of this, John Justin," said Winnifred softly.

"Neither do I," said Mallory. "But we can't get to the ring if we don't enter the building."

They fell into step behind the guard and were ushered down a narrow corridor to a small office. Seated behind a long wooden desk was a balding, slightly plump man with exceptionally thick glasses. He wore an expensive blue sharkskin suit, and a number of rings glinted on the fingers of both hands.

"John Justin Mallory?" he said as the guard left the office and shut the door behind him.

"You know it is," answered Mallory.

"Allow me to introduce myself. I am Percival Picayune."

"I know who you are."

"I must admit I am surprised that you got this far," said Picayune. "I was under the impression that Marius the Mage was hired to stop you."

"He failed," said Mallory. "So did the gunmen. You might consider that before you go too far out on a limb."

"Gunmen?" repeated Picayune, arching an eyebrow. "I strongly disapprove of such methodology. I am an enforcer of the law; I have never broken it, and I don't intend to break it today." He stared at Mallory. "Are you aware that you don't exist?"

"You wouldn't say that if you'd been as intimate with him as I have!" snapped Belle.

"There is no record of your birth," continued Picayune, ignoring the cell phone. "There is no record of you attending school. You don't have a Social Security number. You do not have a driver's license. You are legally a nonperson. I think we may have to arrest you for impersonating a human being."

"Try to keep me away from the show and they may have to arrest you for impersonating a human being with a split lip, a bloody nose, and a black eye," said Mallory angrily.

"Others have tried," said Picayune confidently.

"I'm not others," said Mallory. "Dugan, open the door and let's get to the ring."

Dugan grabbed the knob and turned it. "It's locked," he announced.

"Put the damned thing off its hinges," ordered Mallory. "Put your back into it."

The big zombie pulled. Nothing happened.

"There's a magical force field around it," Picayune informed them, "and only I know the words that will open it. Now let's all sit here calmly and quietly, and I'll end the spell when our discussion is over. It shouldn't take more than another six or seven hours."

Suddenly Winnifred's Magnum was in her hand, pointing at Picayune. "I think you'll do it now," she said.

"I don't yield to threats," he said calmly.

"John Justin?" said Winnifred.

"Shoot him in the wrist," said Mallory. "He'll still have one hand left to vote for corrupt politicians."

Winnifred aimed the gun and squeezed off a shot. The bullet bounced off Picayune's wrist and careened around the room, finally burying itself in a sedate portrait of Bubbles La Tour with her clothes almost on.

"What the hell's going on?" muttered Mallory.

"I am armored in my righteousness," answered Picayune.

"Dugan, you want to take a whack at him?"

The zombie took a step forward, then stopped with a puzzled expression on his face.

"What's wrong?" asked Mallory.

"My hand's stuck to the doorknob," replied Dugan.

They remained in the room for almost an hour. Every few minutes Mallory would shoot at Picayune with Winnifred's gun, or throw something at him, but to no avail.

"We'd better think of something soon," said Winnifred. "It's after one o'clock."

"I'm open to suggestions," said Mallory.

"If you'll tell me you lust for my ripe young body, I'll tell you how to get out of here," said Belle.

"This is no time for jokes," said Mallory.

"Who's joking?"

"If you know how to get out, why didn't you say so an hour ago?"

"You weren't desperate enough an hour ago," answered Belle. "Just tell me you lust for me, and I'll tell you what to do."

"Tell me now."

"This office needs new wallpaper," she said.

"Damn it, Belle!"

"And the ceiling needs a paint job."

"All right," said Mallory. "I lust for you. Now tell me."

"You've got to say it with sincerity," replied Belle.

"Why don't you ask for a million dollars while you're at it?" said Mallory.

"I'm never speaking to you again," said Belle, stifling a sob.

Mallory held the phone to his lips. "I lust for your hot young body," he whispered.

"Louder."

Mallory looked uncomfortably around the room. Finally he sighed, took a deep breath, and yelled: "I lust for your hot young body!"

"Much better," said Belle.

"Okay, I kept my end of the bargain. How do we get out of here."

"Percy Picayune is keeping you here because none of you own Fluffy, so you're trying to enter under false pretenses, and he's armored in his righteousness, right?"

"Right," said Mallory impatiently.

"Well, there's someone in the room who has even more right on her side," said Belle. "She's been kidnapped, she's legally entered in the show, and Percy has no right to keep *her* out."

"You know," said Winnifred, "it makes a twisted kind of sense."

"It's ridiculous!" said Picayune uneasily.

"Sounds pretty good to me," said Mallory, taking Fluffy from Winnifred and holding her up. "What do I do now, Belle?"

"Point her at a wall," said Belle.

Mallory did as he was told.

"Now I'm going to hit M over high Q," announced Belle. Instantly the room was filled with a high-pitched whistle that was intensely painful. Winnifred winced and moaned, Mallory thought his fillings were going to fall out, Dawkins applied his favorite defense mechanism by fainting dead away for the third time in six hours, Picayune clasped his hands to his ears—and Fluffy, startled, opened her mouth and spewed forth a sheet of flame. Only Dugan seemed unmoved.

"Now point her at Percy," said Belle.

Mallory held the little dragon up a foot from Picayune's face.

"Now, Percy," continued Belle, "do you still feel armored in your righteousness, or are you going to let us go to the ring?"

Picayune's face and body sagged in defeat. He turned to the door. "Open, Sesame," he intoned, and the door swung inward.

"'Open, Sesame'?" repeated Mallory. "What's so magical about that? I could have said it any time."

"But you didn't," replied Picayune. He walked over to where Dugan was helping Dawkins to his feet for the third time that morning. "Is your boss going to be here?"

"Absolutely," answered Dawkins. "There's a lot of money riding on this one."

"Good," said Picayune. "I'll walk you to ringside."

"Why?"

"Conditions have changed," replied Picayune, "and I've got some bets to lay down."

The first problem was to get past the seemingly endless line of middle-aged and elderly ladies waiting to get into the wrestling arena, each with a shining hatpin in her hat or her hand. The beer vendors were selling an occasional glass to the occasional male customer, while some entrepreneur had set up a stand that sold sherry and brandy to the hatpinned ladies and was doing a land-office business.

They had just made it past the worst of the crowd when they bumped into a burly, bald, bearded man wearing dark glasses and an overcoat with its large collar turned up. His glasses began slipping, and he quickly grabbed them, turned his back to the entrance to the wrestling area, and put them back on.

"Don't give me away, I beg of you!" he whispered.

"To whom?" asked Winnifred, looking around for a potential enemy.

He gestured toward all the women who were waiting to purchase their tickets. "*Them!*"

"Why would they be interested in you?" she persisted.

He briefly lifted the sunglasses. "*Now* do you know?"

She looked mystified. "No."

"What kind of rasslin' fan are you?" he demanded.

"I'm not any kind," she replied. "We're on our way to the Eastminster show."

"*I* know him," said Picayune. "You're the Belgrade Butcher, aren't you?"

"I used to be," replied the man. "But the political situation keeps changing. I've been the Belgrade Butcher, the Borneo Butcher, the Beijing Butcher, the Brazilian Butcher . . . you name it, I've been it."

"So why are you hiding?" asked Mallory.

"I haven't read a newspaper in years," said the man. "How was I to know that anyone called the Baghdad Butcher was supposed to be a good guy these days? I climbed into the ring two weeks ago, and I gouged out one of Handsome Henry's eyes—his glass one; we're friends, and I wouldn't want to hurt him—and I chewed on his ear, and I threw a metal chair at his grandmother who was sitting at ringside, just the normal stuff, you know? But the Commissioner came to the dressing room later and told me that if I was going to be the Baghdad Butcher I couldn't do any more gouging and biting and kicking because Baghdad is our friend these days. So last week I fought fair against the Mongolian Monster—and I thought my own fan club would kill me. You never saw so many bloodthirsty little old ladies in your life!"

Two elderly women in print dresses began yelling and threatening each other with hatpins, one declaring her loyalty to the Crazed Czech while the other kept screaming that he didn't belong in the same ring with Lovable Luke.

"Let me see if I've got this straight," said Winnifred, trying to ignore them. "Your fans are mad because you didn't break any rules?"

"Or any heads," said the Butcher. "They don't understand that it's all an act, that no more than two or three rasslers actually die in the ring during any given week. Well, okay, Halloween got a little out of hand, and we all thought Drooling David's axe was a phony at Thanksgiving, but we're not out there to kill each other—well, most of us aren't—and my fan club just won't accept it."

"Still, you're a huge well-muscled guy—so why are you hiding from a bunch of little old ladies?"

"*You* stand up to seventy enraged women brandishing hatpins and see how *you* like it!" said the Butcher bitterly. "Besides, now they want all their Christmas presents back—the M-16, the rack, the AK-47, the switchblade, the vial of acid, all of the things they wanted me to use in the ring—and the fact of the matter is that I hocked them to buy more volumes of poetry. They'd kill me if they found out." He dared a glance at the box office, where some women were eyeing him curiously. "Don't give me away, please!"

"We won't," said Mallory. "But what are you doing here if you're not wrestling?"

"Picking up my paycheck for last week's match," said the Butcher. "Then it's off to a nice, secluded island with Keats, Shelley, Frost, and Milton. I'll give them a year or two to forget, and then I'll come back as the Vehement Venezuelan . . . or is that too literate?"

"Just a bit," said Mallory.

"How about the Terror of Tehran?"

"Watch a newscast or two just before you come back to see who we're mad at," said Mallory. "You'll come up with the right moniker."

"They don't even have electricity where I'm going."

"It sounds idyllic," remarked Winnifred. "Why even come back?"

"I miss the glory."

"There's glory in being a bad guy?" asked Mallory.

"When I've got Straight Arrow Slim on the mat, and ten thousand little old ladies are screaming 'Defenestrate him!' . . . well, there's nothing quite like it."

"No, I don't suppose there is," said Winnifred distastefully.

Just then a little old lady walked by. She passed a note to the Butcher and kept going to the box office. He opened it, and a smile came to his face.

"What's that?" asked Mallory.

"One of my fans. She recognized me despite the coat and shades, and gave me a recipe for kidney pie."

"That was very thoughtful of her," said Winnifred.

"It's for Heroic Henry's kidneys," said the Butcher. He looked around. "You know, if *she* could spot me, so can others. I'd better leave before they do."

And with that, he made his way to the exit.

"How much worse can a dragon show be?" said Winnifred.

A huge gorgon passed by, led by a small green elf, as if to remind them that a lot more than dragons were competing.

"Let's follow the elf," said Mallory. "He seems to know where he's going.

They ran the gamut of goblins selling everything from hot dogs and beer to Waterford crystal and secondhand pulp magazines, passed the basketball venue (he could tell by the chorus of boos that Heartless Herman and the Manhattan Misfits were off to their usual horrendous start), the pornographic movie theater, a sparsely attended meeting of the DAR (Daughters of the Armenian Revolution), and finally came to the huge arena that had been set aside for the Eastminster show.

They got in line behind a gorgon, a chimera, and a gryphon, and gradually made their way to the entrance.

"Got your admission passes?" asked a bored man in a candy-striped jacket and straw hat, both of which seemed totally incongruous on a snowy February day.

"This is Mr. Brody's entry, Fluffy," replied Mallory, indicating the dragon. "We're just delivering her."

"Nobody gets in without a pass, Mac," said the man. "Am I gonna have to call Security?"

Percy Picayune stepped forward. "Let me handle this."

"You can argue all you want," said the man, "but no one gets in without—"

"I'm not here for the show," said Picayune, flashing his outdated IRS credentials. "We've been meaning to speak to you about your charitable deductions."

The man suddenly looked very nervous. "It's my wife's fault," he said. "I told her and told her that Saks and Bloomingdale's aren't charities."

"Let's talk about your medical expenses," said Picayune.

"If I don't lose seven hundred bucks to my doctor on the golf course, he might misdiagnose me on purpose."

Picayune just stared at him without saying a word.

"Okay, okay, so it was fifty bucks," said the man, suddenly drenched in sweat. "But the principle is the same. I just wrote down the wrong number."

"And what about your entertainment deduction?"

"My God, how did you find out about her?" said the man.

"It's my business to find out."

"Don't tell my wife or she'll kill me!"

"We'd better talk about this down at the main office," said Picayune.

"Isn't there any way we can just forget about all this? If I promise never to do it again?"

Picayune frowned. "All right," he said. "You have us at a disadvantage. We're in a hurry. Let us pass, and I will ignore your little fiduciary indiscretions—*this* time."

"Thank you, sir," said the man.

He was still thanking Picayune when Mallory's party was fifty feet inside the arena, walking past grooming tables, portable pens, hitching posts for the larger entries, even a huge barred aviary for banshees and harpies. The place smelled of grooming lotions, and the occasional chattering of the toy and miniature animals was drowned out by the occasional roar of the giant ones.

"How did you know?" asked Winnifred when Picayune had caught up with them.

"Know what?" replied Picayune.

"That he cheated on his charitable and business deductions?"

"Doesn't everyone?"

"I hate to interrupt," said Mallory, "but we seem to be surrounded by gorgons—and more than one of them has a lean and hungry look."

Winnifred pointed to a sign that said *Grooming Area*.

"It's an all-breed show," Belle spoke up. "Even I know that. You just have to find out where the dragons are."

"Dugan, you're taller than the rest of us," said Mallory. "Do you see them?"

"See what?" asked Dugan.

"Sorry I asked," said Mallory with a sigh. He walked over to a middle-aged woman who was trimming a huge gorgon's whiskers. "Excuse me, ma'am," he said, "but can you direct me to the dragons?"

She turned to him. "You don't want dragons, young man," she said firmly. "Not when you could have a gorgon, by Champion Monstro out of Champion Behemoth. We're expecting a hatching next week, and only eleven are already spoken for."

"I appreciate your offer," said Mallory, "but I really need to find the dragons."

"You haven't thought it through," she said. "Dragons and gorgons don't get along. If you have a dragon, what are you going to do with your gorgon?"

"I don't have a gorgon."

"I just told you we're expecting a hatching. Five hundred dollars takes twelfth choice away."

Mallory decided he was never going to get his answer. "Thank you, ma'am," he said, starting to walk off.

"Wait!" said the gorgon exhibitor.

"You've decided to tell me where the dragons are?"

"I need your address so I know where to deliver your gorgon," she said. "Would you prefer to pay with cash, check, or a credit card?"

"I don't want a gorgon."

"Are you ill?" she said incredulously. "Of course you want one."

"No, thank you."

"But I have three hundred and eighteen eggs due to hatch in six days!" she said. "What am I going to do with them all? Do you know how much a baby gorgon eats?"

"I think I'd rather remain in blissful ignorance," said Mallory, walking away again.

This time she didn't try to stop him, and a moment later he and his party came upon the chimera grooming area. All but one of the exhibitors had crowded into a tiny area, leaving the bulk of the grooming space to the remaining exhibitor, who was meticulously trimming his chimera's nails while she stood patiently on a grooming table.

"Hello, Grundy," said Mallory, stepping forward while his entourage kept their distance from the demon.

"You made it," said the Grundy. "But then, I knew you would." He reached into the air and magically produced ten thousand-dollar bills. "I am a demon of my word," he said, handing the money to Mallory. "I will see you in the ring later this afternoon."

"How does it work?" asked Mallory. "You have a chimera, I have a dragon. Do you sneak into the dragon ring, or do I sneak into the chimera ring? And either way, won't someone notice?"

"You've never been to a show before, have you?" said the demon.

"No."

"The competition is divided into breeds. Then the various Best of Breed winners compete for—"

"Best in Show?" suggested Mallory.

"Eventually. But to narrow the competition still further, the breed winners compete for Best in Group, and the Group winners compete for Best in Show."

"Group of *what?*" asked Mallory.

"There is the Winged Group, the Fire-Breathing Group, the Clawed Group, and so forth."

"So which group is Fluffy in? She's got wings, she's got claws, and she breathes fire."

"The Fire-Breathing Group," answered the Grundy. "The wings don't work very well, and the claws are not used in battle."

"How do you know all this stuff?" asked Mallory.

"I am a sportsman," replied the Grundy with dignity.

"You're also Evil Incarnate."

"That too," acknowledged the demon.

"So where do we find the dragon area?" said Mallory, reaching out to pet Carmelita's head and pulling his hand back just before she could bite it off.

"She's very high-strung," explained the Grundy. He pointed to a spot about ninety feet away. "I assume you are going to handle her yourself."

"I'll hire someone, now that I've been paid," said Mallory. "I don't even know the rules. I sure as hell don't know how to handle Fluffy in a ring."

The Grundy smiled. "Then you had better learn fast."

"Why?" said Mallory. "I just told you—"

"No professional handler will take your money, John Justin Mallory."

"Why the hell not?" said Mallory, pulling out his wallet. "You didn't pay me with bogus bills, did you?"

"No."

"Then what's the problem?"

"The problem is that Fluffy is the favorite," answered the Grundy.

"So?" said Mallory.

"So no one wants to be the handler who defeats me," said the Grundy. "I have been known to become . . . *irritable* on such occasions." He paused. "The last time it happened, there were *six* New York boroughs."

"What do I know about handling a dragon in the show ring?"

"You have two hours to learn," said the Grundy. "I suggest you get busy."

"I think I liked you better when we were mortal enemies," said Mallory.

"We still are," replied the Grundy. "This is a temporary truce, but I shall win in the end."

"We'll see about that."

"Death always wins in the end."

"Well, you may win in the end," said Mallory, "but I'll be damned if you're going to win today."

"Indeed you will be," said the Grundy. "Now please go away. I still have work to do with Carmelita."

Mallory turned and rejoined his group.

"Are you crazy?" whispered Dawkins. "He kills people just for looking at him."

"Not my cavalier," said Belle. "He's not only gorgeous, but he fears absolutely nothing."

"Both of you shut up," said Mallory. "I've got to learn what's involved in handling Fluffy in the ring."

"I think I'll take my leave of you," said Picayune. "I just saw Harry the Book and Big-Hearted Milton enter the arena and head off toward their seats, and I've got some bets to make."

He began walking off.

"Wait!" said Dawkins. "I'll join you." He turned to Mallory. "I've saved your life and found your dragon. You don't need me anymore, do you?"

"No, you deserve a rest after all that heroism," said Mallory. He turned to Dugan. "*You* stick around."

"Surely you don't expect another attack, John Justin," said Winnifred.

"Why not? Brody's still on the loose, and he's got two hours to stop us before we're due in the show ring."

"I guess you have a point," she admitted.

"Fear not," said Belle. "I'll never desert you."

"I can't tell you how comforting that is," said Mallory wryly.

"*I'll* desert you," said Felina brightly.

"I thought you were going to desert me a couple of hours ago," said Mallory.

"I keep forgetting," she explained apologetically.

They passed the sea serpents, the gryphons, the hydras, the banshees, the unicorns, the six-legged basilisks, the tree-dwelling watersnakes, and all the rest, until they came to a crowded area that seemed to be reserved for dragons of all sizes. Mallory gave the elephantine ones a wide berth and wandered over to a section that was clearly set aside for miniature and toy dragons.

"She's gorgeous," said a nattily dressed young man, who spotted Fluffy from a distance and wound his way through the grooming tables to get a closer look at her. "Good luck—though she's so feminine I can't imagine she'll have any trouble winning."

"She'll have more trouble than you think," said Mallory. "I've never even seen a show before, let alone been in the ring. I have no idea what I'm supposed to do."

"Then perhaps you'll let me help you."

A number of nearby exhibitors looked daggers at him, but no one said a word, and the young man ignored them.

"I assume we're competitors," said Mallory. "Why would you want to help me?"

"You're John Justin Mallory, aren't you?"

"Yes."

"My father embezzled money to pay for my mother's hospital bills. You could have turned him over to the cops. Instead you got him a night job with the Prince of Whales so he could pay off the money and go free. My whole family owes you for that."

"How can you throw a guy in jail for paying his wife's medical bills?" said Mallory with a shrug.

"There are plenty who would have done just that," said the man. "By the way, my name's Murray." He walked over to where Winnifred was standing with Fluffy, gently took the leash from her, and led the little dragon over to his own rubber-topped grooming table. "Now," he said, lifting her up and setting her on the table, "let's get to work."

"Where's your own dragon?" asked Mallory.

"Right there," said the man, pointing to a fireproof cage beneath the table. "Easiest way to keep her clean, now that she's been groomed."

"I was wondering about all the crates and cages we're been walking past," remarked Mallory.

Murray rummaged through a box filled with grooming equipment, picked out what he needed, and laid it at the front of the table.

"First we'll trim her whiskers and eyebrows," he announced, picking up a scissors and going to work. "Next," he said when he had finished, "the nails." He quickly and expertly clipped all of Fluffy's toenails.

"Her feet are filthy," Murray observed. "In fact, her whole body looks like she's been out on the street during a snowstorm."

"Well, a light snow," said Mallory.

"*Any* snow turns black in mere minutes in Manhattan," replied Murray. He lifted a bottle. "This is a dry shampoo; we don't have time to properly soak her. You can help me rub it in."

"Will she mind it?"

"I never yet saw a dragon that didn't love a massage, and that's what this will feel like."

They finished, and then Murray set Fluffy down on the floor and handed the leash to Mallory.

"Okay, she's presentable," said the detective. "What do I do with her in the ring?"

"At various times the judge will ask you to pose her, to gait her, and to fly her."

"Fly her?" repeated Mallory.

"You'll walk around the ring and she'll fly at shoulder height. He'll judge her on grace and strength. When he gaits her, she'll trot on your left side. If she gets too full of herself she'll break into a run; then restrain her and get her back to trotting. That helps him judge her body structure."

"Is there a practice ring?" asked Mallory.

"No, but you can practice right here in the grooming area."

"Now, what about posing her?"

"Just get her to stand four-square and look alert. If you have any of her favorite food, bait her with it, which is to say: Hold it up when you want her attention. The judge will study her overall outline, and the sweetness of her expression."

"Sweetness?" said Mallory with an expression of disbelief. "She's a dragon."

"But a beautiful, feminine dragon," said Murray. "Now, at some point the judge's assistant is going to let something loose—you won't know in advance if it's a bat, an insect, a rat, or even a mechanical toy—and she'll be judged on how quickly and accurately her flame shoots out at it." He paused. "And finally, the judge will ask you to place her on a table so he can examine her structure with his hands, and check to make sure you haven't added any illegal fuels to her flame."

"Okay. Then what?"

"Then the judge announces his choice, and you go on to the next level or you go home."

"Seems simple enough."

"Oh, it is," agreed Murray. "Most exhibitors get pretty good at it after ten or twelve years. But most exhibitors aren't walking into the ring with Fluffy."

"So you know," said Mallory.

"She's entered today, and there can't be two dragons that look like this." He lowered his voice confidentially. "That's why no one else offered to help, when you so clearly needed it. They all think they might have a chance to win if you're handling her." He paused and looked admiringly at the little dragon. "She's so good she'll win in spite of you."

"Thank you, I think," said Mallory. "I appreciate your help, especially considering we're competitors."

"Not immediately. Fluffy's a toy, my Minnerva is a miniature. We won't meet until the Group, and if we do meet then it means each of us has already won Best of Breed."

"Okay," said Mallory. "I'll practice right here. Where's the ring?"

"Each ring has a number," replied Murray. "Toys are in Ring 4."

Mallory thanked him again, then went to work with Fluffy. He managed the trotting easily enough, but it took him almost fifteen minutes to figure out how to make her fly alongside him. He then went to a food stand and picked up a chocolate chip cookie, a hot dog, and some candy, but none of it interested the little dragon.

"Dugan," he said, "we haven't got time for you to leave the building, but check the vendors and see if you can find some elephant-shaped chocolate marsh-mallow cookies. I've only got half a dozen, and I have no idea how many I need in the ring. I think we have maybe twenty minutes, tops, before ring time."

"Are you sure?"

"That I want the cookies? Hell yes."

"I mean, are you sure you want me to leave?"

"Yes."

Dugan shrugged. "You're the boss."

He walked past Mallory on his way to an exit, and as he did so a shot rang out. People screamed, dragons hissed, gorgons roared, and Mallory scanned the crowd looking for the source of the shot. Winnifred pulled out her Magnum and tried to spot the shooter.

"Is it okay if I get some more morticians' putty too?" asked Dugan.

"You're not going anywhere!" said Mallory. "Help me spot the gunman."

"Be careful!" breathed Belle.

"It's the guy with the horns," announced Dugan.

"Get him!"

The zombie walked forward, and the crowd parted before him like the Red Sea until he was face-to-face with Brody. He slapped the gun out of Brody's grasp, and placed a massive hand around his neck.

"What now?" asked Dugan.

"Bring him over."

Dugan dragged Brody across the floor until they stood before Mallory.

"Where did the bullet hit you?" the detective asked the zombie.

"My calf," replied Dugan.

"You weren't trying to kill *me*," said Mallory to Brody. "You were aiming at *her*."

"It went off by accident," said Brody.

"And you're going to jail by accident," replied the detective.

"No!" protested Brody.

"You should be grateful," said Mallory. "Given who you owe money to, I wouldn't want to be in your shoes when they finally release you."

A pair of the Garden's security team fought their way through the crowd and soon arrived at Mallory's side.

"This the guy with the gun?" asked one of them.

"Yeah," said Mallory. "Take him away for safekeeping. I'll file charges tonight or tomorrow." As they were cuffing Brody, Mallory held up a hand. "Just a second."

They looked at him curiously, as he reached a hand into Brody's pocket and came away with half a dozen elephant-shaped chocolate marshmallow cookies, which he transferred to his suit pocket. "Okay, he's all yours."

"You were magnificent!" said Belle. "I get all hot and bothered whenever you're forceful."

"Dragons at ringside, please!" came a voice over a loudspeaker. "Toy dragons in Ring 4, miniature dragons in Ring 5, full-sized dragons in Ring 6. Judging will commence in three minutes."

Mallory began making his way to the ring when an irate exhibitor walked up to him.

"Are you the guy who came here with a cat-thing?"

"What about it?" replied the detective.

"Come get her. She's eating all the fish we bait the serpents with."

"Winnifred?" said Mallory, turning to her.

"I'll take care of it, John Justin," she answered, heading off toward the sea serpents' grooming area. "You just concentrate on the show."

"Thanks."

"Now, I don't want you to be nervous at all," said Belle as he reached ringside. "Don't even think of the fact that you have no idea what's going on and are a total innocent in the ring. Don't worry that this is second nature to most of the handlers. Forget that Fluffy doesn't even know who you are and can't possibly feel comfortable with you. The judge probably speaks English, though I know one of the more popular dragon judges speaks only Sanskrit."

"Shut up," said Mallory.

"What a thing to say!" responded Belle. "I was just trying to calm your nerves."

"They didn't need calming until you started talking."

"Go ahead, hurt my feelings," said Belle. "Just because I love you and want nothing but the best for you. Just say any heartless thing you want. See if I care."

"Ring call," said a voice over the speaker system. "All toy dragons in the ring, please."

The ring steward checked each entry off against the program book. As Mallory walked by, the steward stopped him. "Excuse me, sir," he said, "but did you know that your chest is sobbing?"

"It gets emotional at shows," replied Mallory.

"It should get together with my rheumatiz," said the steward. "The two of them probably have a lot to talk about."

Then Mallory received an armband with a number from the ring steward and entered the ring. As he walked Fluffy around the perimeter he passed Harry the Book, who was sitting in the first row, flanked by Big-Hearted Milton and Gently Gently Dawkins.

"Glad to see that you made it," said Harry. "For a time there I am afraid Brody is going to cost me half a million dollars, give or take. But now you are here and Fluffy is here and everything is copasetic."

As Mallory glanced across the ring at exhibitors and dragons who looked like they'd been doing this all their lives, a single thought raced through his mind: *What the hell do I do now?*

CHAPTER 32

4:01 PM–5:07 PM

The judge, a short man dressed in a tux and tails, stood in the center of the ring, and was eventually surrounded by eleven toy dragons standing on the mat that formed the outer boundary of the ring.

"Gait them twice around the ring, please," he said. The other handlers, most of them human, but also including an elf and a troll, began trotting with their dragons, and Mallory and Fluffy fell into step behind them. Mallory didn't know one dragon from another, but even he could tell that Fluffy was moving so smoothly and gracefully that her feet barely touched the ground.

"Okay, pose them," ordered the judge.

Mallory glanced at the nearest handler, who got down on her knees and began setting her dragon's feet exactly where she wanted them. He was about to follow suit, but when he checked Fluffy's feet they were in precisely the position the handler had set *her* dragon's feet.

Other handlers were getting their dragons' attentions with various types of bait: dead mice, boiled liver, bonbons, whatever most interested their particular charge. Mallory looked down at Fluffy: she seemed incapable of standing wrong or running awkwardly, but showed no interest whatsoever in the proceedings or her surroundings. He took an elephant-shaped chocolate marshmallow cookie out of his pocket and tossed it to her. She emitted a very refined, ladylike little roar and gobbled it up, then looked alertly at him, ready for another. He noticed that the judge was walking from one dragon to he next, studying each in turn. He waited until the judge was approaching Fluffy, then pulled another cookie out of his pocket. She practically trembled with excitement just as the judge reached them.

Mallory waited until the judge walked over to the next dragon in line. Then, acutely aware that he had only five cookies left and that she ate nothing else, he put the cookie back in his pocket.

The judge summoned a dragon and its handler to one end of the ring. "Gate down, fly back" were his instructions.

The handler set off at a trot, the dragon trotted alongside him, and when they reached the far end of the ring he turned, said "Up!," and the dragon flew back just off his left shoulder until they were once again in front of the judge.

"Next!" said the judge.

Mallory was fourth in line. When all eyes were on the dragon being gaited and flown, he whispered "Up!" to Fluffy, who merely stared at him. He tried "Fly!" with an equal lack of success. He'd run through half a dozen more words when the judge summoned him over.

"Down and back, same as the others" were his instructions.

Mallory trotted slowly across the ring with Fluffy gaiting alongside him. He hoped that this was such an ingrained routine that she'd automatically start flying when he reached the far end and began running back, but she didn't.

In desperation, he pulled out another cookie and held it straight out at shoulder height. Fluffy flew up, grabbed it out of his hand, and flew the rest of the way.

Then came the individual examinations on the table, and the test of the strength and accuracy of the dragons' flames, and finally the judge stood back, surveyed the field thoughtfully, and pointed to Fluffy.

"Best of Breed!" he announced.

This was followed by thunderous applause, which seemed not to bother the little dragon at all, and then the judge presented Mallory with a trophy.

"I don't know what happened to her regular handler, that little gremlin," said the judge softly, "but you'd better improve damned fast if you want to win the Group."

"Don't you belittle my Lover Boy!" said Belle heatedly.

Mallory gave the judge an apologetic smile and led Fluffy back to the grooming area, where he turned the dragon over to Winnifred and set the trophy down on Murray's table.

"Good job, Mallory," said Harry the Book, who had wandered over from his ringside seat. "Now do it two more times."

"Don't get your hopes up," cautioned Mallory. "She won in spite of me. I didn't know what I was doing in there."

"This did not exactly escape my notice," replied Harry.

"I see you have your mage with you," said Mallory. "I hope you don't think he can hinder the Grundy in any way whatsoever."

"Big-Hearted Milton?" said Harry. "He knows better than to go up against the Grundy, or indeed to annoy him in any way whatsoever."

"Then what's he here for? Surely he's not a fan of dragon shows."

"He is here because Brody was still on the loose until a few minutes ago, and somehow I did not believe that the Grundy would lift a finger to hinder him should he come looking for a little revenge. I am not an oddsmaker for nothing, and I decide that if he has a grudge against anyone in the world, you are a one-to-five favorite."

"Incidentally, I returned your two flunkies," said Mallory. "So where's my samurai goblin?"

"He's guarding Jeeves back at Joey Chicago's," answered Harry. "His assignment ends when the show ends, and then he will be free to seek his fortune wherever he wants, and indeed I myself am considering offering him employment."

Murray and his miniature dragon returned to the grooming area just then, carrying a trophy that looked identical to Mallory's.

"Well, I will leave you to prepare for the wars," said Harry, starting to head back to his seat. "By the way, watch out for the banshee. I hear on the grapevine that they have hired a most effective handler." He didn't wait for a reply, but just kept walking.

"Congratulations to you and Minnerva on your win," said Mallory.

"Congratulations on yours," replied Murray, gesturing toward Mallory's trophy.

"What happens now?"

"They have a few more breeds to finish judging, and then the Group judging begins," said Murray. "I've seen the competition. You should waltz right through it."

"I just wish I knew what the hell I was doing," said Mallory.

"You won, didn't you?"

"I could ride Man o' War to a win in a cheap claming race, too," said Mallory. "But winning the Belmont Stakes is different." He paused. "I don't know a thing about dragons, but I know every eye was drawn to Fluffy, and she seemed to do everything right in spite of my ignorance and inexperience. But now she's got to beat a bunch of Best of Breed winners; we're moving up in class from claimers to the Belmont." He looked around. "Where the hell did she go?"

"The fat broad is exercising her," said Felina, pointing across the arena to where Winnifred was walking Fluffy.

"We don't need either of them," chimed in Belle. "We've got each other. Nothing else matters."

"Girl problems?" suggested Murray with a smile.

"Not like anyone else's," said Mallory with a grimace.

The speaker system came to life. "Group judging in five minutes. The Fire-Breathing Group will be judged first."

"Might as well get over to ringside," said Murray, giving a tug on Minnerva's leash.

"I'll join you," said Mallory. "Felina, tell Winnifred to bring Fluffy to the ring."

"Maybe," she replied.

"Let me rephrase that: Felina, tell Winnifred to bring Fluffy to the ring or I'll never feed you again."

"I'm on my way!" said Felina, racing off.

"You just have to know what motivates her," Mallory explained as he began walking to ringside with Murray.

Winnifred met them there and turned Fluffy over to Mallory, then leaned over and whispered to him: "I discovered the word."

He stared at her uncomprehendingly. "To get her to fly," continued Winnifred, "just say 'Sky.'"

"Thanks," said Mallory, taking the leash from her. He turned to Murray. "Good luck."

"Luck won't be enough," said Murray. "Fluffy's that much better than the rest."

They entered the ring, Mallory felt a little more comfortable this time, and fifteen minutes and two cookies later Fluffy had won the Fire-Breathing Group. As Mallory was walking out of the ring, carrying an even bigger trophy than before, he passed the Grundy, who was entering the ring with Carmelita for the Clawed Group judging.

"I'll see you soon," the demon promised him.

CHAPTER 33

5:07 PM–5:41 PM

"How many animals compete for Best in Show?" Mallory asked Murray, when they'd returned to the grooming area, which had emptied out considerably as most of the losing animals and their handlers had left the premises.

"At the beginning of the day, perhaps two thousand," answered Murray. "By the time the Group winners meet, five: Winged, Clawed, Fire-Breathing, Water-Breathing, and Miscellaneous."

Mallory resisted the urge to ask how a legless water-breathing sea serpent could trot across the ring.

Winnifred decided to exercise Fluffy again, which Mallory concluded was far more for Winnifred's benefit than the dragon's. Murray began packing his equipment, though like most of the beaten exhibitors he planned to remain for the Best in Show judging, and Mallory wandered over to a nearby kiosk and ordered an Old Peculiar. He nursed it while the other Groups were judged, and by the time he'd finished it the announcement came over the public address system that the five Group winners were due in the ring for the Best in Show judging.

Winnifred was waiting at ringside with Fluffy, and Mallory studied his competition. The Grundy was approaching with Carmelita. The Water-Breathing Group winner was a serpent that resembled nothing more than a six-foot-long version of the Loch Ness Beast; it wore a water-filled transparent helmet and undulated to the ring at the end of a leash that looked remarkably like a piece of seaweed. The Miscellaneous winner was a ten-legged spiky monstrosity that seemed almost puppyish in its love for everybody. Finally the winner of the Winged Group appeared, and a collective gasp arose from the crowd.

The gasp was not for the banshee that had won the group, but for the handler at the other end of the rope that kept the banshee from flying up to the rafters. It was Bubbles La Tour, star of stage, screen, centerfold, and numerous indecency trials, and most of the males at ringside just stared, unblinking, mouths open.

"You wouldn't think she could fall out of her clothes in so many directions at once," remarked the Grundy to Mallory.

Even the judge was staring, transfixed by her.

"This is going to be even harder than I thought," muttered Mallory.

"What has that hussy got that I haven't got?" complained Belle.

"You want me to enumerate?"

"Go ahead, insult me!" said Belle. "Break my heart! See if I care!"

"Be quiet," said Mallory. "It's hard enough to concentrate as it is."

"Fine! I hope you and Miss 44 Double-D will be very happy together!"

"Enter the ring, please," said the steward, suddenly coming to his senses.

The five Group winners walked into the ring. The crowd and the judge ignored four of them.

"Trot them once around the ring, please," said the judge.

The five winners and handlers trotted around the ring. No one looked at the animals or four of the handlers.

The judge wiped some drool from his chin and approached Bubbles La Tour. "Will you trot around the ring once more, please?" he said. "I'll hold your banshee so she doesn't get in the way."

"Just a minute!" complained the serpent's female handler.

"Be quiet!" said the judge.

"This isn't fair!"

"You're disqualified," snapped the judge immediately.

"*What?*"

"You heard me," said the judge. "Get out of my ring."

The woman turned on her heel and led the serpent out. "You'll be hearing from my lawyer in the morning!" she promised.

"Damned nuisance!" muttered the judge.

Mallory looked around ringside and saw Harry the Book whisper something to Big-Hearted Milton.

You'd better think of something before it's too late, thought the detective. *He's going to give her Best in Show as soon as she takes about two more deep breaths.*

Big-Hearted Milton began muttering something, and made a mystic sign in the air—and suddenly Bubbles La Tour was no longer wearing a low-cut blouse and a high-cut miniskirt, but was covered, neck to ankle, with a shapeless Mother Hubbard.

"Saved me the trouble," said the Grundy.

"Why didn't you do it sooner?" asked Mallory, who was lined up next to him.

"I don't want it said that I used magic to win," replied the demon.

"You cut it awfully close."

The Grundy shook his head. "I'd have stricken him mute before he could declare her the winner. This is between you and me, John Justin Mallory."

"You mean between Fluffy and Carmelita," the detective corrected him.

The Grundy shrugged. "Same thing."

The judge showed no further interest in Bubbles or her banshee, and it was clear that he couldn't decide whether the Miscellaneous winner should be more horrific or more cuddly, but he clearly felt it lacked some intangible *something*. It soon boiled down to Fluffy and Carmelita, as everyone had known it would. They were gaited, they were posed, they were examined, they were put through every pace they had, and finally the judge stood them side by side and stepped back to study them.

It was obvious that he was about to make his decision, and Mallory reached into his pocket to withdraw another chocolate marshmallow elephant cookie and get one last vibrant pose out of Fluffy—and discovered that he had used the last of them to get her to leap up and fly around the ring. He desperately dug into his other pockets, but came up empty.

Carmelita was on her toes, baiting for a small, wriggling snake that the Grundy dangled just in front of her, and Mallory realized that he was going to lose.

Then a familiar voice yelled, "Mallory—*catch!*"

He looked up and saw Gently Gently Dawkins hurling something at him. He caught it, and found it was a chocolate marshmallow elephant cookie.

"I forgot I had it," said Dawkins with a guilty smile.

Mallory held it out, and Fluffy's response was electrifying: she stared at it with famished interest, her whole body tense and alert. The judge took one last look, and then pointed to Mallory and the dragon. "Best in Show!" he announced.

The Grundy walked up to Mallory. "I'll beat you next year!" he said in a cold fury.

"I'm afraid not," said Mallory. "Fluffy and I are both retiring from the ring."

"You can't!" snapped the Grundy, his eyes blazing.

"Watch us," said Mallory, starting to walk back to the grooming area.

"John Justin Mallory!" yelled the Grundy as the crowd gasped. "As of this minute we are at hazard again!"

"Until the next time you need me," said Mallory without turning around or breaking step.

Evening, February 15

There was some confusion concerning what to do about Fluffy.

Dragons weren't allowed in jail, and besides, it was generally considered that Brody had lost all claim to her. Jeeves would soon be serving a minor sentence for collusion, and couldn't take her either. It was even suggested that she be given to the Grundy, who had the funds to continue showing her, but Mallory decided they couldn't trust the demon not to take his wrath out on her and vetoed it.

Winnifred decided that she and Mallory would take the little dragon back to the office until they could figure out how to dispose of her. Then Fluffy took matters into her own hands: she absolutely refused to leave her source of chocolate marshmallow cookies, and before dinnertime Gently Gently Dawkins had a pet.

Winnifred went home to her apartment to feed her songbird, Felina heard things scurrying in a nearby alley and decided to spend a few hours making and eating new friends, and after he grabbed a sandwich at a local greasy spoon, Mallory went back to the office.

"So this is where we live," said Belle when he closed the door behind them.

Mallory realized he'd forgotten that she was still in his pocket.

"Some of the time," he said, pulling her out and holding her up. "That's the kitchen, this is my desk, that's Winnifred's desk, this is our magic mirror Periwinkle, that's—"

"Forget all that," said Belle. "Where's the bedroom?"

APPENDIX 1
Stalking the Dragon
BY COL. WINNIFRED CARRUTHERS

(speech delivered before the Blood Sports Enthusiasts
of Lower South Manhattan)

Before I begin, I want to make it clear that the true sportsman not only gives his prey a fighting chance to escape but also gives him a chance to become the predator as well. Hence, my remarks are aimed only at those who hunt the humongous dragons that stand more than eight feet at the shoulder, produce a flame in excess of 300 degrees Fahrenheit, and cruise at an altitude of more than two thousand feet.

Now what (I hear you ask) is the best weapon to use on a dragon?

If you are a Christian saint, a charmed sword is more than sufficient. If, on the other hand, you are like the rest of us, the first thing you have to do is identify your prey so you will know how best to bait him.

For example, the tree-dwelling dragon of the Ituri Rain Forest lives almost exclusively on a diet of okapis and chimpanzees. The rugged Namibian dragon thrives on young pachyderms, especially the hippopotamus and the black rhinoceros.

Here in New York, the favorite prey of the wild dragon is the drunken sot, followed by the unleashed Great Dane. Either of these should attract your dragon in a matter of a very few minutes, especially in daylight.

Now, I have always preferred the stopping power of the .550 Nitro Express, especially if you are using soft-nosed bullets. The poisoned arrow usually works, but it simply isn't sporting and we won't mention it here. The Amulet of Kobassen will slow him down enough to deliver the death blow with a blade blessed by a Mage of the Fifth Circle or higher.

If you're going to meet him in close quarters, which where a dragon is concerned constitutes anything his flame can reach, you're going to want protection from the intense heat and fire. My suggestion is that you stop by Alastair Baffle's Emporium of Wonders and pick up a tube of the same ointment magicians, acrobats, and ecdysiasts use to protect their bare flesh from the fire they work with. Failing that, an asbestos bodysuit and helmet seems to be your best bet.

I've seen would-be daredevils try to douse the dragon's flame with water, totally overlooking the fact that the average six-ton dragon drinks thirty-five gallons of water a day and is not above bathing in it. Actually, the very best way to eradicate a dragon's flame is to toss him something to eat: they're especially fond of suckling pigs, cheese blintzes, and chocolate marshmallow cookies . . . and it is a little-known fact that dragons do *not* like their food to be well-done, or even medium well. Feed a hungry dragon and you won't have to worry about the flame until he digests his meal.

Once the kill has been made, it's time to enjoy the spoils of conquest. I've never been partial to dragon steaks, but there's a cut of meat along the base of the tail, especially on young dragons, that is almost indistinguishable from veal, and this is the part of the dragon you should reserve for yourself, while doling out the rest to your trolls. Dragon whiskers—on those rare occasions that they haven't been burned away prior to your encounter—are prized religious artifacts, and you should always pluck them out and give them to your gunbearers (or swordbearers) and skinners.

And what if you spend a day tracking your dragon through Central Park, down the wilds of Ninth Avenue, through the caves of the Park Avenue subway, only to find out that he's a mere five feet at the shoulder, or that she is being followed by a brood of infant dragons?

That is why you should always carry a squirt gun filled with indelible and phosphorescent ink. Using the gun, squirt your initials onto the beast's left shoulder. This will tell all other members of the Lower South Manhattan Blood Sports Enthusiasts that you have claimed killing rights to this dragon, and are merely waiting for more sporting circumstances to end its life. Now, the police and the military probably will not honor this claim, especially if the dragon is attacking a lovely, terrified, half-naked woman, which seems to be the kind of human dragons prefer to attack, but under normal circumstances that dragon will be considered untouchable until you once again go a-hunting. (Indeed, an entire religious sect—The Cult of the Untouchable

Dragon—has grown up around this practice. In fact, so has the Cult of the Lovely, Terrified, Half-Naked Woman, but that needn't concern us here.)

Once you do slay your dragon, check to see if it is a female, and if so, assiduously seek out her nest, as a clutch of dragon eggs will usually bring a high enough price on the collectors' market to finance your next safari.

So get those weapons ready, assemble your team of trolls, make sure all your mystic protections have been thoroughly upgraded, pack your anti-burn medical kit, and good luck to you!

Official Standard of the Dragon,
AS CODIFIED BY THE DRAGON CLUB OF AMERICA

GENERAL CHARACTER: The Dragon is a gentle, loving creature except when enraged, which is altogether too often. He is loyal to a fault; his loyalties may shift on the spur of the moment, but he is always loyal to someone or something. He has a sly sense of humor, and enjoys pyrotechnics. The DCA (Dragon Club of America) has been in existence since 1873 and has yet to find anything that will frighten one of these courageous creatures, except a larger, meaner Dragon.

HEAD: The Dragon's head is bullet-shaped, with a prominent occipital bone, sharp teeth (all Dragons are carnivores, except for the ones that aren't), flaring nostrils that emit and occasionally aim streams of exceptionally hot smoke, and (usually) a slight overbite.

EYES: Set wide on the head, the eyes are round, and come in a variety of colors, including brown, green, puce, mauve, and magenta. Most Dragons possess a truly phenomenal range of vision, and can pick out a prey animal or an attractive member of the opposite sex (or sometimes the same sex, depending on the Dragon) at upward of a mile.

EARS: Yes. Two (2).

FLAME: The Dragon's flame runs upward of 300 degrees Fahrenheit (225 degrees for Toys; 250 degrees for Miniatures), shoots out one to two times the length of his body, and never needs refueling.

NECK: Approximately fifty percent (50%) of the body length, the best specimens have a noble arch to their necks. For the record, the head sits at one end and the body at the other.

BODY: The Dragon's body is covered with scales—the reptile kind, not the tell-your-weight kind. His musculature exudes a sense of raw power, except when he is morbidly obese (yes, even Dragons get morbid). His withers are somewhat higher than his hips, his tail tends to drag the ground when walking, and there is a slight ridge down the center of his back, which most riders find distinctly uncomfortable and a small handful find sexually stimulating.

WINGS: The Dragon's wings are approximately the length of his torso. On some—the West Coast Dragon, the Patagonian Dragon, and (especially) the Albanian Dragon—the wings are vestigial. On others—the Beverly Hills Dragon and the South Beach Dragon—a display of the wings attracts members of the opposite sex. (One is inclined to say the weaker sex, but there are no weaker sexes among the Dragon population.) The Dragon can fly long distances, but like any reasonable creature prefers to glide and be carried along by the wind.

LEGS: The preferred number is four. The claws are long and not retractable. Even a Toy Dragon can, when annoyed, rip your face off, if he chooses not to melt it, so always have his favorite snack in your pocket and his favorite toy within reach.

GATE (TROTTING): The Dragon double-tracks fore and aft, and gives the impression of absolute grace, unless he happens to trip on something.

GATE (FLYING): The Dragon is a graceful flyer. The smaller, lighter Dragons will ride the warm thermals, but the larger ones will flap their incredibly powerful wings, making enormous progress while disrupting the air currents for all insects, birds, and three-seat propeller planes.

TAIL: The Dragon uses his tail, which is broadest at the tip, as a rudder when flying, a balance when walking, and a weapon when attacked from behind.

COLOR: The most common color is green, but tan, gray, chocolate, and licorice are acceptable. Points are deducted for red, purple, or multicolored Dragons, and white Dragons, with or without halos, are disqualified.

SIZE: Dragons come in a variety of sizes. They include Toy (under 12 inches at the shoulder); Miniature (12 to 15 inches at the shoulder); Standard (15 to 60 inches at the shoulder); Large (5 to 8 feet at the shoulder); and Humongous (8 feet minimum at the shoulder).

Ode to JJM,
BY BELLE

My love is like a golden phone

How do I love thee? Let me count the ways.
1. Passionately
ABC2. Eternally
DEF3. Sexually
GHI4. Romantically
JKL5. Intellectually
MNO6. Physically
PRS7. Verbally
TUV8. Unreservedly
WXY9. Intensely
*. Wildly
OperO. Indefatigably
#. With bells on

Percy Picayune's Greatest Cases

1979: Finds Jimmy Hoffa. (1980: Loses Jimmy Hoffa.)

1983: Testifies before Congress, recommends an excise tax on exhaling.

1988: Issues a $1.07 rebate to Al Capone's estate for overpayment of 1928 income tax.

1992: As revenues drop, recommends amnesty for the tobacco industry, coupled with a tax on nonsmokers.

1998: Disallows Monica Lewinsky as a tax deduction on President Bill Clinton's return.

2001: Audits the books on *Star Wars*, *Titanic*, *Gone with the Wind*, and *Jurassic Park*, concludes that prior investigations were incorrect, Hollywood was right, and all four films are still in the red (though *Gone with the Wind* is nearing its break-even point).

2002: Based on his Hollywood findings, consortium of science fiction and fantasy publishers hire him away from the IRS to defend them against a suit brought by outraged writers.

2005: Initiates a class-action suit against the death tax on behalf of the Consolidated Cook County Cemeteries and Voters' League.

2009: Clears Illinois governor Rod Blagojevitch of all corruption charges.

2009: Hired as tax consultant for all members, current, future, and failed, of the Obama cabinet.

Recipe for Elephant-Shaped Chocolate Marshmallow Cookies

BY GENTLY GENTLY DAWKINS

1. Take an elephant. Preferably deceased.
2. Shrink it down to the size of a Ping-Pong ball. (That's a good old American Ping-Pong ball, not one of those square Tasmanian ones.) There are numerous ways to shrink an elephant.
   A. You might try to find a *very* large vice.
   B. You could wet the elephant down, then put it in a commercial dryer at a laundromat. I must confess that I have never tried it with an elephant, but it always shrinks my dress shirts and my pajamas.
   C. When all else fails, Big-Hearted Milton, Morris the Mage, Spellsinger Solly, and many other local mages will shrink an elephant for you. (Hint: don't pass any bogus bills when dealing with them. They shrink con men and debtors for free.)
3. Take a bag of marshmallows. Stick the elephant inside one of the marshmallows. Replace the others in the bag (or send them to me, Gently Gently Dawkins, in care of Joey Chicago's Three-Star Tavern).
4. Get some chocolate. Heat it in a small saucepan. If either cooking chocolate or the saucepan are unavailable, improvise. For example, you might hold a Hershey bar over a match.
5. Pour the chocolate over the marshmallow that is holding the elephant. Using a penknife, or a scalpel if no knife is available, hold the cookie (it *is* a cookie by now) under a light and cut away everything that doesn't look like an elephant.
6. Repeat the process as often as desired, or until you run out of elephants.

7. Eat.
8. Always keep an eye out for the elephant's friends and relations.

Or if you're in a real hurry, buy a bag of the commercial kind at Seymour Noodnik's Emporium. And if you have any left over, remember who suggested it.

The Deaths of Dead End Dugan

#1: Died from a batch of bad chili at Ming Toy Epstein's Five-Star Kosher Deli, November 2, 1992. Entombed in Hymen O'Banyon Five-Star Pizzeria and Mortuary, Bronx.

#2: Shot 24 times, 19 of them through the heart, by Genteel Giles Garabaldi, September 4, 1995. Buried in Our Lady of Shameful Passions Cemetery, Brooklyn.

#3: Pushed off Brooklyn Bridge by Shifty Malone, March 5, 1999. Body recovered by *The Mighty Modred*, a British passenger ship, in the English Channel, January 29, 2002. Given burial at sea with no military honors.

#4: Stabbed 43 times with a butcher's knife in a lover's quarrel with Fifi Schwartz, August 17, 2004. ("I must have been feeling . . . *irritable*," was her successful legal defense.) Buried behind the Chapel of Unexpected Manifestations on Staten Island.

#5: Shot 14 times, stabbed 11 times, bitten by poisonous snake, attacked by guard dog, run over by truck, burned, and poisoned by very annoyed person or persons unknown, July 19, 2006. Buried in Mosque of the Red Death Graveyard in Teaneck, New Jersey; Our Lady of Perpetual Frustration Cemetery in Queens; and Never Say Die Masoleum in Central Park.

About the Author

Locus, *the trade journal of science fiction, keeps a list of the winners of major science fiction awards on its Web page. Mike Resnick is currently fourth in the all-time standings, ahead of Isaac Asimov, Sir Arthur C. Clarke, Ray Bradbury, and Robert A. Heinlein. He is the leading award-winner among all authors, living and dead, for short science fiction.*

* * * * * *

Mike was born on March 5, 1942. He sold his first article in 1957, his first short story in 1959, and his first book in 1962.

He attended the University of Chicago from 1959 through 1961, won three letters on the fencing team, and met and married Carol. Their daughter, Laura, was born in 1962, and has since become a writer herself, winning two awards for her romance novels and the 1993 Campbell Award for Best New Science Fiction Writer.

Mike and Carol discovered science fiction fandom in 1962, attended their first Worldcon in 1963, and fifty science fiction books into his career, Mike still considers himself a fan and frequently contributes articles to fanzines. He and Carol appeared in five Worldcon masquerades in the 1970s in costumes that she created, and they won four of them.

Mike labored anonymously but profitably from 1964 through 1976, selling more than two hundred novels, three hundred short stories, and two thousand articles, almost all of them under pseudonyms, most of them in the "adult" field. He edited seven different tabloid newspapers and a trio of men's magazines, as well.

In 1968 Mike and Carol became serious breeders and exhibitors of collies, a pursuit they continued through 1981. During that time they bred and/or exhibited twenty-seven champion collies, and they were the country's leading breeders and exhibitors during various years along the way.

This led them to purchase the Briarwood Pet Motel in Cincinnati in 1976. It was the country's second-largest luxury boarding and grooming establishment, and they worked full-time at it for the next few years. By 1980 the kennel was being run by a staff of twenty-one, and Mike was free to return to his first love, science fiction, albeit at a far slower pace than his previous writing. They sold the kennel in 1993.

Mike's first novel in this "second career" was *The Soul Eater*, which was followed shortly by *Birthright: The Book of Man*, *Walpurgis III*, the four-book Tales of the Galactic Midway series, *The Branch*, the four-book Tales of the Velvet Comet series, and *Adventures*, all from Signet. His breakthrough novel was the international best seller *Santiago*, published by Tor in 1986. Tor has since published *Stalking the Unicorn*, *The Dark Lady*, *Ivory*, *Second Contact*, *Paradise*, *Purgatory*, *Inferno*, the Double *Bwana/Bully!*, and the collection *Will the Last Person to Leave the Planet Please Shut Off the Sun?* His most recent Tor releases were *A Miracle of Rare Design*, *A Hunger in the Soul*, *The Outpost*, and the *The Return of Santiago*.

Even at his reduced rate, Mike is too prolific for one publisher, and in the 1990s Ace published *Soothsayer*, *Oracle*, and *Prophet*; Questar published *Lucifer Jones*; Bantam brought out the *Locus* best-selling trilogy of *The Widowmaker*, *The Widowmaker Reborn*, and *The Widowmaker Unleashed*; and Del Rey published *Kirinyaga: A Fable of Utopia* and *Lara Croft, Tomb Raider: The Amulet of Power*. His current releases include *A Gathering of Widowmakers* for Meisha Merlin, *Dragon America* for Phobos, and *Lady with an Alien*, *A Club in Montmarte*, and *The World behind the Door* for Watson-Guptill.

Beginning with *Shaggy B.E.M. Stories* in 1988, Mike has also become an anthology editor (and was nominated for a Best Editor Hugo in 1994 and 1995). His list of anthologies in print and in press totals forty-eight, and includes *Alternate Presidents*, *Alternate Kennedys*, *Sherlock Holmes in Orbit*, *By Any Other Fame*, *Dinosaur Fantastic*, and *Christmas Ghosts*, plus the recent *Stars*, coedited with superstar singer Janis Ian.

Mike has always supported the "specialty press," and he has numerous books and collections out in limited editions from such diverse publishers as Phantasia Press, Axolotl Press, Misfit Press, Pulphouse Publishing, Wildside Press, Dark Regions Press, NESFA Press, WSFA Press, Obscura Press, Farthest Star, and others. He recently served a stint as the science fiction editor for BenBella Books, and in 2006 he became the executive editor of *Jim Baen's Universe*.

Mike was never interested in writing short stories early in his career, producing only seven between 1976 and 1986. Then something clicked, and he has written and sold more than 175 stories since 1986, and now spends more time on short fiction than on novels. The writing that has brought him the most acclaim thus far in his career is the Kirinyaga series, which, with sixty-seven major and minor awards and nominations to date, is the most honored series of stories in the history of science fiction.

He also began writing short nonfiction as well. He sold a four-part series, "Forgotten Treasures," to the *Magazine of Fantasy and Science Fiction*, was a regular columnist for *Speculations* ("Ask Bwana") for twelve years, currently appears in every issue of the *SFWA Bulletin* ("The Resnick/Malzberg Dialogues"), and wrote a biweekly column for the late, lamented GalaxyOnline.com.

Carol has always been Mike's uncredited collaborator on his science fiction, but in the past few years they have sold two movie scripts—*Santiago* and *The Widowmaker*, both based on Mike's books—and Carol *is* listed as his collaborator on those.

Readers of Mike's works are aware of his fascination with Africa, and the many uses to which he has put it in his science fiction. Mike and Carol have taken numerous safaris, visiting Kenya (four times), Tanzania, Malawi, Zimbabwe, Egypt, Botswana, and Uganda. Mike edited the Library of African Adventure series for St. Martin's Press, and is currently editing *The Resnick Library of African Adventure* and, with Carol as coeditor, *The Resnick Library of Worldwide Adventure*, for Alexander Books.

Since 1989, Mike has won five Hugo Awards (for "Kirinyaga," "The Manamouki," "Seven Views of Olduvai Gorge," "The 43 Antarean Dynasties," and "Travels with My Cats") and a Nebula Award (for "Seven Views of Olduvai Gorge"), and has been nominated for thirty Hugos, eleven Nebulas, a Clarke (British), and six Seiun-sho (Japanese). He has also won a Seiun-sho, a Prix Tour Eiffel (French), two Prix Ozones (French), ten HOMer Awards, an Alexander Award, a Golden Pagoda Award, a Hayakawa SF Award

(Japanese), a Locus Award, three Ignotus Awards (Spanish), a Xatafi-Cyber-dark Award (Spanish), a Futura Award (Croatia), an El Melocoton Mechanico (Spanish), two Sfinks Awards (Polish), and a Fantastyka Award (Polish), and has topped the Science Fiction Chronicle Poll six times, the Scifi Weekly Hugo Straw Poll three times, and the Asimov's Readers Poll five times. In 1993 he was awarded the Skylark Award for Lifetime Achievement in Science Fiction, and both in 2001 and in 2004 he was named Fictionwise.com's Author of the Year.

His work has been translated into French, Italian, German, Spanish, Japanese, Korean, Bulgarian, Hungarian, Hebrew, Russian, Latvian, Lithuanian, Polish, Czech, Dutch, Swedish, Romanian, Finnish, Danish, Chinese, and Croatian.

He was recently the subject of Fiona Kelleghan's massive *Mike Resnick: An Annotated Bibliography and Guide to His Work*. Adrienne Gormley is currently preparing a second edition.